COWBOYS
AND
INDIANS

WJ SPELLANE

PAGE PUBLISHING, INC.
Conneaut Lake, PA

First originally published by Page Publishing 2020

ISBN 978-1-64628-654-6 (pbk)
ISBN 978-1-64628-655-3 (digital)

Printed in the United States of America

I

His cowhide-covered chair creaked as Don Samuel Martinez rocked back and propped his pointed boots up on the corner of his desk. He was nursing his second shot of tequila and mulling over the disappointing loss of the last of his new bulls. He shifted his position so he could gaze out the window at the Rio Bravo below. His upstairs parlor offered the perfect vista of the wide river separating the ranch from Mexico. The rowels of his spurs gouged another notch into the mesquite desktop every time he repositioned his well-worn boots.

South Texas, once abundant with big but lean-bodied longhorn cattle, were now being replaced by red cattle with shorthorns, discovered by a close friend while on one of his many escapades to South America. His friend found that the red cattle adapted well to the ever-changing volatile weather extremes of the South Texas climate, and they produced much higher yields of beef.

The Palmitto Hill ranch, named for one of the few big hills on the coastal plains, bordered the banks of the Rio Bravo, twelve miles upriver from the Gulf of Mexico. The ranch was abundant with sacawesta grass and native saltweed, not ideal grazing for cattle, especially if they weren't indigenous to the South Texas flats. One section of the ranch had mesquite and ebony trees, with plenty of prickly pear and yucca cactus scattered evenly among the foliage. Don Simon's grandfather built the two-story hacienda atop the loma for two reasons: the thousands and thousands of acres of flat land was prone to flooding from storms that came in from the Gulf and from the Rio when it rained upstream. And Indians. In his grandfather's time, the Indians would lure ships to the shore and cannibalize the crew. The Indians rarely gave the ranch any trouble though, except for stealing a calf now and then. There was an unspoken tariff paid by the ranch, well worth the peace of mind to his grandfather. The site gave him the advantage of seeing anyone approach for miles from his hacienda on the hill.

Don Simon was in his midfifties and at a time in his life when he wanted to enjoy the rest of his days living out his years between the ranch and his palm-tree-studded estate on the outskirts of Fort Brown in Brownsville. He was growing tired of all the hustling and trading he had to do. It was wearing him down, and the fire inside him was fading.

He made most of his fortune selling beef to Fort Brown, an Army installation on the banks of the Rio Bravo in Brownsville. The cavalry soldiers would pass through the ranch often on their way to the Brazos Santiago Pass near the coast, stopping regularly to restock their jerky supply. He also sold beef to the steamships that navigated the river to Fort Ringold, almost one hundred fifty miles upriver. They, in turn, would mark the price up and sell it to the ports along the way. Don Simon was the major supplier of beef to every town for almost two hundred miles upriver. When he was in his prime, he enjoyed trading and hunting, and he traveled by ship to exotic ports in South America, Africa, and India. In fact, he was with his friend when he discovered the red cattle in Argentina. The Don was astute enough to realize that times were changing, and if he wanted to stay in the cattle business, he would have to change too. Longhorns were becoming a thing of the past. Cattle up north started dying during the drives to market in Kansas City, and everyone was blaming it on the Texas longhorn. He had no choice; he wasn't ready to give up the fight just yet. His only son, Gustavo, could do any trading that would take more than a week or two. He was in his midtwenties, still single, with nothing tying him down to the ranch. He was the only heir, and it was time he got involved in the business firsthand.

"Jovita!" Don Simon bellowed from the parlor. "Bring a me another bottle of tequila, por favor."

"Si, senor," the young lady replied and disappeared from the room. Jovita's family had worked for the Martinez family since she was a baby. Her mother did all the housework and cooking, and her father, Pepe, was the only vaquero for the ranch. At roundup time, Simon would hire day labor to help with the gathering of the herd. Local vaqueros would spend a couple of weeks at the ranch, bringing the herd to the corrals, branding and sorting the bulls from the heifers, slaughtering steers, pickling the meat, and drying some for jerky, all under Pepe's supervision.

Simon's wife died years earlier, when Gustavo was just sixteen. It was after a storm from the gulf flooded everything on the ranch except the hacienda on the hill. The water stood for weeks before it finally receded. The cattle found whatever high ground they could, which wasn't much. Even the sand dunes that separated the gulf from the ranch had disappeared from the driving winds and high surf. Three days after the storm passed, the mosquitoes were so thick that it was difficult to breathe without inhaling them. The cattle would run through the flooded flatland from one loma to another, desperately trying to evade the mosquitoes. Pepe gathered driftwood that washed up from the coast, reaching as far inland as the hacienda. Some of the trees were of a type he had never seen before and much larger than the mesquite or ebony he was accustomed to. He lit a fire on the south side of the loma, letting the prevailing breeze carry the smoke across the hill and into the house, quelling the mosquitoes, and making life a little more bearable for those inside.

Mosquitoes weren't the only adverse effect from the flooding. The high water flushed rattle snakes from the brush and burros of the lowlands, sending them searching for higher ground. Everyone had to be wary of every step they took. The snakes were everywhere around the high ground surrounding the hacienda.

Gustavo's mother was sitting in the kitchen sipping a cup of tea. She knelt down under the table to retrieve the slipper that flung off her foot. The snake never rattled his warning. It struck her in the throat, dropping her to the floor, where she lay gasping for air. Pepe could hear his wife's screams, all the way out to the bonfire at the bottom of the hill. By the time he burst through the door, Mrs. Martinez was dead. The snake was small comparatively, only about a foot and a half long, most were closer to eight feet, but it bit her right in the jugular vein. Death was instantaneous. The poison was injected directly into her bloodstream and traveled straight to her heart. This was a blessing in disguise for the family. By the time they would have traveled to Brownsville, she would have died in agony, suffering a slow and indescribable death.

Jovita appeared with a full bottle of tequila. She placed it on Simon's mesquite wood desk, popped the cork, and poured three fingers into his glass. She had stunning blue eyes, so blue and pure it was like looking directly into her soul. Don Simon loved looking at her. He had never seen such beautiful eyes in his life. Unheard of for a Mexican. Sometimes there are green eyes, inherited from Spanish conquistadores generations ago, but never steel blue. *She must be nineteen or twenty,* he realized. *She has gone from a child to a woman.* He always thought of her as a daughter, never noticed how she had matured. *Better watch Gustavo…and the tequila.*

Staring out over the Rio Bravo into Mexico, he was agonizing over what could have caused all his bulls to die, along with his hopes of a new herd. The water in the river had a little salty taste, but the longhorns and horses had no problem drinking it, but then, no choice either. The bulls came from one hundred miles north of here. He knew the grass and the water couldn't be that different. Then he wondered about the mosquitoes and the ticks. Surely they had the same problem at his friend's ranch.

He picked up his almost empty glass, shuffling his boots on the desk, notching another battle scar into the mesquite desktop, and gazed at the wall in the parlor. It was adorned with exotic trophy skins; some of the pelts were mementos from his faraway hunting expeditions. A rattle snake skin, longer than Simon was tall, he almost threw it away after his wife's death, out of spite for the snake and respect for his dead wife. But he made the decision to keep it, to remind him of the dangers that lay waiting to take a life when you least expect it.

The white-tailed deer, he shot with his pistol as it climbed out of the river crossing from Mexico.

The black panther skin, he trapped the cat using a sick calf for bait. Then shot him in the head just as he was about the finish gnawing his own leg off.

Hides of several coyotes that harassed the cattle as they gave birth.

The small spotted cat that looked like a leopard, but much too small, rarely seen in the daylight.

The lion he killed in Kenya on the Serengeti. It was during the drought before the rains. All the animals were loitering around the almost-dried-up water holes. The gazelles, the elephants, the jackals, and the hyenas. They all were driven by thirst over fear. He wanted to go to Africa to shoot a tiger, not knowing that tigers didn't live in Africa. They lived in Asia, in India.

The tiger...wait...the tiger!

He remembered his tiger hunting trip to India. It was during a severe drought, before the monsoons. A small village near the eastern coast was losing cattle to a tiger. The people that arranged the hunt decided they could make money on both ends. They charged the villagers for killing the tiger, and they charged Simon for the hunt. Cattle were everywhere as he remembered, white, black, red, all had horns of different lengths, and they all had big humps on their shoulders, similar to camels, but smaller. They all seemed docile as they roamed wherever they pleased. The bulls were magnificent and intimidating.

He remembered that they were taller at the hump than he was, and the ground seemed to shake as the beasts lumbered down the trail, slowly shifting the weight of their massive bodies from one limb to the other. There was almost no grass due to the drought, but the cattle all seemed to be in very good shape.

He was driven to the site of a calf kill in a rickshaw, pulled by a young man named Raj, a local who quickly became his friend. Raj was poor, as were the majority of Indians. It reminded him of his homeland in Mexico, where there were only rich people and very poor people. But Raj was a survivor. He had a wife and two teenage daughters, twin boys, and a baby on the way. He did what he had to feed his family.

"Why are all these cattle running loose?" Simon asked Raj.

"We are Hindu here in India," Raj explained. "We worship cattle, and it is not allowed to harm or kill them."

"With all these people starving, you can't slaughter a calf to feed your family?" Simon asked in disbelief.

"Our neighbor killed a weak cow that was going to die anyway, and he was executed in front of his family. He killed the cow by cutting her throat, so that is how he was killed. They tied him to a pole in the center of the town and cut his throat with a large dagger, the blood quickly devoured by the dry earth, accepted as payment for the man's sins. He was brave, he did not protest. He died like a man in front of his grieving family. He knew the punishment. You may not kill the cows—they are sacred."

At the kill site, the only thing left of the calf was the head and one front leg, still attached by a small strip of hide. The calf's mother was covered with blood. She had put up a good fight defending her calf against the tiger. The weapons nature armed her with to defend herself against her enemies were coated with the tiger's blood.

I need to send Gustavo to India to find Raj. Those are the cattle to save the Palmitto ranch. They will be much better than the red shorthorns. Don Simon was excited about his new revelation.

"Jovita!" he bellowed again. The tequila was setting in, and he was getting drunk. He never showed it, but he could feel it. "Jovita!" he yelled again. Simon was starting to show his age. He wasn't a tall man to begin with, but now his shoulders were starting to droop, and he was getting larger in the waist.

"Si, senor," Jovita replied loudly.

"Where's Gustavo?" Simon asked her excitedly.

"In Brownsville, senor yo creo, I think," she replied.

"When will he return? Tonight?" he asked.

"Yo creo que si, before dusk," the young girl answered.

"Tell him I want to see him first thing the morning, por favor."

"Si, senor," she said as she turned and left as quickly as she appeared.

When did she grow those breasts! They almost fall out of her dress. The dress that looked two years too small. Little Jovita is grown up. No more tequila! Better watch Gustavo!

Simon was a man who always commanded respect. His physical stature was shrinking, and his thinning hair and short cropped beard was now almost completely white. But when he spoke, people listened. No one ever questioned him. No one except Gustavo.

"Buenas dias, Papa," Gustavo said surprisingly cheerful. His eyes looked like two pee holes in the snow, and they were as red as the tips of the blood-covered horns on that mama cow in India. He sat down across from his father at the kitchen table and tried unsuccessfully to avoid direct eye contact.

Maria handed him a tincup steaming with fresh coffee. "Queres un café, senor?" she asked Simon.

"No, gracias," he replied to the housekeeper. He just had his fill of machacado and eggs on a flour tortilla, and if the truth were to be told, he was feeling the effects of last night's tequila. But he would never let on. If he was man enough last night, then he better act like a man today.

"Where have you been, mijo? You look as if you slept with the cattle last night."

"As a matter of fact, I did. There was a quinceañera in Matamoros last night, and before I realized, the night was gone. I was about halfway home and decided to take a short nap at the Gavito pens. I heard a loud scream, as if a woman screamed, my horse almost broke his stake rope. I couldn't get back to sleep, all my senses were alert, watching and listening, so I just decided to make my way home. I just arrived, and Jovita told me you wanted to see me right away. I think we have another cat. Better watch the baby calves, remember how many we lost to the last one." Gustavo was trying to distract his father. He anticipated that he was about to be chastised for staying out all night again.

"The colonel's daughter is only fifteen! That's quite young for a man of your age, wouldn't you agree, mijo? And she is white, does her father approve of her cavorting with an older Mexican?" Simon was almost scolding Gustavo, but he knew many fifteen-year-old girls were already married. His own wife was about that age when they wed. But the old man had an ulterior motive. He was about to send Gustavo away, and he didn't want anything to interfere, especially young love.

"Father," Gustavo said defiantly, "I don't think she even knows she's white. She has grown up here and speaks Española as well as she does English. Most of the time she speaks both in the same sentence!" Gustavo was about twenty-five and wanted a wife. He was beginning to feel like life was passing him by. And he was tired of always having to justify his actions to his father.

"Excuse me, Papa," Gustavo said, cutting the conversation short. He wasn't in the mood for a confrontation. "I have not slept, and I need to rest."

"Wait, wait, wait!" Simon said, trying not to raise his voice. Gustavo had been spoiled by Pepe's wife after his mother died, and Simon allowed it to happen, but if he could stay out all night and day, he should have to suffer the consequences. Pepe needed help. The ranch did not run itself. But Simon did not want a confrontation either. He had a more urgent matter at hand. He had to be calm and persuasive. After all, he knew Gustavo was ready to spread his wings and make his own mark in life. *Stay calm,* he had to keep reminding himself.

"Gustavo, you may not know, but Pepe found the last of the red bulls dead down by the horseshoe Resaca yesterday. All of the hopes I had for these bulls to improve the herd are now gone. I hope that at least some of the cows were bred, but I doubt it. These bulls were weak from the beginning, they never could adapt to the ranch. I have two choices. I can keep the longhorn herd and make a meager living, or I can try another breed of bull and improve the herd. The people want leaner beef, and the tanners want the solid-colored hides."

"What do you think killed them?" Gustavo was wishing this could be put off until the afternoon after a couple hours of sleep.

"I have given that a lot of thought. Have you ever noticed how much bigger the mesquites are in Brownsville than they are here and how much sweeter the water is, and it is only twenty miles away? This ranch along the coast is a hard place, and I can only guess that the red bulls could not adjust. Do you remember when I went to India to kill a tiger before your mother died?" he continued, speaking in a very calm but convincing tone. "Do you remember the big cattle with the camel hump on their neck? I told you about them."

"I remember that you told me that the people did not eat their cattle," Gustavo said, "and you were surprised at how big and gentle they were, like pet dogs, you said." Gustavo remembered.

"And there was a drought, and the cattle were fat, regardless of the weather conditions. And that cow that fought the tiger for her calf lived." Simon's voice was becoming excited now. The throbbing in his head was fading. The machacado and egg must have absorbed the tequila hangover. "Those cattle were near the coast, like here. I have decided that I would like to bring some of these bulls here, to our ranch. They would put the frame on these cattle that is needed to stay competitive." Simon paused for a moment, trying to gather his thoughts. He had to phrase his plan well enough to convince his son to realize the potential of the venture.

"I will put together a plan. My good friend is in the shipping business, and who knows, maybe he would like to purchase some bulls too!" Simon continued, "But, my son"—his voice was becoming more serious, and he was trying to be sympathetic to Gustavo, to his future—"I need you to make the journey for me. This ranch is not just mine, it is ours, and someday it will be yours alone, and you will be able to pass it to your son." Simon could be smooth talking when he had to be, and now he had to be. He needed to make Gustavo know that this was his ranch too.

"I hired a man named Raj when I was there, and he became a friend. He doesn't speak Spanish, but he speaks very good English, but with a heavy accent. I can put you in contact with him. However, he must not know in advance what you are there for. We'll set up a tiger hunt. After you arrive, you can explain what we need—bulls only. You must be most persuasive. It will be very risky for Raj, cattle are worshipped like a god by the Hindu people, so be sure to speak only to him. I got to know him well enough to know that he would do almost anything for money."

As he spoke, he was still developing a plan in his head. "Maybe buy a few cows also, but they must be pregnant, but not too far along. The journey will take a toll on them. There is an antelope there also, and its meat is delicious, much more so than venison. It is as big as a horse. The bulls are a gray, almost black, with horns like a chivo. The cows are red, almost the same color as the bulls that died. Try to get some of those also. That could be another reason for the trip. First speak of the antelope hunt, that will not draw much publicity, if it will not be possible, then you can pursue the tiger hunt."

Gustavo objected. He was trying to woo the colonel's daughter, and he had many other irons in the fire to be away too long. His father assured him that the venture should take no more than three months at the most, and if the colonel's daughter felt the same way, she would be here when he returned.

Gustavo conceded way too easy, he thought. It must have been his father's gift to persuade, a gift he hoped he had inherited. With the lack of sleep, his defenses were down. He should have waited before agreeing unconditionally to such a serious proposition.

Arrangements were made. The ship was arranged to set sail from Port Corpus Christi, around the horn of Africa, into the Indian Ocean. Contact was made for an antelope hunt with the same company that did the tiger hunt. A special request was made for Raj. The deal was sealed, and the wheels were turning.

The ship anchored off the sandy coast of India exactly thirty days from the day they set sail. Gustavo was met at the pier by Omar Habib, head guide for the hunting company. The antelope hunt was discussed and planned. Gustavo explained that his father wanted antelope bulls killed for their silver blue skins and horned skulls. He wanted four bulls and six females of breeding age to be captured alive to be transported back to South Texas.

Omar explained that the antelope were plentiful but very wary of humans and not docile like the cattle. "They could see you long before you could see them, and they avoided humans altogether. However, one thing that we know about them, and makes them easier to catch, is once they start running, they will run in a straight line and seldom changed course."

Unlike goats and sheep, that will zig-zag and leap like the white-tailed deer back home, Gustavo thought.

Omar knew of a range nearby that was abundant with the antelope. They were very territorial animals, so they would be easy to locate.

The plan was made to build a pen out of bamboo and cane and tree branches with a wing extending out forty-five degrees to one side. This would be built along the shore of a nearby river, thus using the water as a fence. The plan was that the antelope would be pushed by men on elephants from a distance but not pushed hard, just enough so the wing and the body of water would force them into the trap, where men will be waiting to close off a gate and block their escape. Since the antelope do not jump, the pen must be built strong enough, just in case they try to run through it or ram it. Cages large enough to hold the live animals will be built out of bamboo, and the animals will be blindfolded to keep them calm. One animal per cage. They will be transported by rickshaw to a barge and then transferred to the waiting ship anchored in the bay. It would take about two weeks to build the trap and cages, Mr. Habib informed Gustavo.

Perfect, Gustavo thought. This would give him plenty of time to approach Raj about the cattle and plan a way to transport them to the ship, all the while keeping it a secret.

Gustavo found Raj at a run-down back alley repairing a strap for the yolk of his rickshaw. He was weaving what appeared to be tree bark, sewing it together to make the strap. *Very resourceful,* Gustavo thought. *They are unable to use leather rawhide like we would in Texas or Mexico.*

The place was filthy! Shacks built on top of each other, sewage running freely in a permanent stream that emptied into the bay. Naked little kids running up and down the alley playing in the reeking green river.

How do these people live like this? In Mexico we have people every bit as poor as these, Gustavo thought, trying not to breathe through his nose. *But at least they were clean, at least compared to these people.* The Mexican kids had snotty noses and dirty faces, but they didn't live in filth like this. He could not get over the fact that this was real. The Mexican women kept their homes clean inside and out and were always sweeping something with their handmade straw broom. There was an excuse for being poor but not for being a pig, Gustavo surmised.

Gustavo made some small talk with Raj. *How is Don Simon— fine. How is your family—fine.* He talked fast, unable to concentrate. He was breathing through his mouth, trying not to inhale, but now he was tasting the filth, gagged, and almost puked right there on the rickshaw. No one probably would have cared anyway. Making an excuse to get out of there, he persuaded Raj to follow him to the edge of the slum to look at some tracks he had seen, possibly antelope.

What a relief! He was gagging all the way down the alley, and what luck, there was a herd of cattle right on the edge of the village. Two Indian women were milking a cow each into what looked like gourds. Unbelievable, the cows just stood there, no rope, no feed, no restraint of any kind, and no resistance from the cows. How do they do that? Gustavo thought.

"I thought cattle were sacred, how can you take the milk?" he asked Raj.

"The milk is considered a gift from the two cows," Raj replied. "As long as the two cows are not harmed, all is good. They have more milk than two calves can drink."

Made sense to Gustavo. He bet his father never even considered these cows' milk for production. Another plus!

"Raj, I am going to make a request, but I want you to think before you answer. My father, Don Simon, would like to purchase some of these cattle. He would like six or eight bulls, at least four ready to breed, and the same for the cows—young cows, and if they are pregnant, even better."

Raj couldn't believe what he was hearing. His first thought was that of his neighbor years ago who had his throat slit while his wailing wife and baby daughters looked on. He remembered how the wife and daughter had to turn to prostitution, servicing the fishermen down at the docks. It was the only way they could feed themselves. As much as he wanted to help them, he could barely feed his own family. His gut gurgled. The very idea scared him. He thought he would have to defecate right there!

"You must do this alone, or get someone you can trust to help you. The cattle belong to no one anyway. They wouldn't be missed as long as you don't take away any milk cows. The cattle will not be harmed, and they will live a peaceful life in South Texas with more grass than they could ever eat." Not quite a lie, Gustavo justified to himself. These cattle would be fine, but their offspring won't.

"I am prepared to offer you ten dollars per head." Gustavo baited him.

Ten dollars per head, Raj computed, was almost as much as he made in a year. His family had to get by on one dollar per month. But how could this be done in secret? Raj thought. How could ten or fifteen head of cattle be taken without anyone knowing? Raj was scared to death at the thought of getting caught, but he was also excited beyond belief at the thought of ten dollars per head. That and what he would make from the antelope capture is almost as much as he would make in a lifetime. No way! How could he possibly get away with it? Who would care for his wife and daughters if he got caught and was brutally executed in front of them? No way!

"I am sorry, Mr. Gustavo," Raj regrettably mumbled, "there won't be any way to remove that many cows and bulls without someone noticing."

"There is a way," Gustavo said, trying to be persuasive like his father. Thankfully he had inherited that gift. It worked on the young girls at home. Hopefully, it would work here on Raj. "We could build extra crates like the ones we will use for the antelope," Gustavo explained. "We will put together some cattle from different places as not to be missed. We will blindfold them and crate them before we trap the antelope, and we will move them altogether. No one will know the difference."

"How will they not know the difference?" Raj countered. "Everyone here knows the difference between cattle and antelope! They will know!"

"Not if we build the crates so that you couldn't see through them. You will tell them that it is for the safety of the antelope. You and some of the help you can trust will cage the cattle before the antelope roundup and explain that these are antelope caught the night before. No one will know the difference. If anyone gets too curious, make sure they stay with the antelope."

Raj was allowing himself to be convinced. The thought of all that money. He could start his own business. He could be hunting guide. He could do a lot of things with that kind of money, and why not? Could it possibly work?

"Raj, I came all this way because my father said that I would be able to rely on you. That you would be as trusted a friend to me as you are to him. He speaks very highly of you." Gustavo was working on his ego now, his sense of loyalty. Raj still looked apprehensive though.

"I tell you what, Raj, I will add two dollars per head. That's twelve dollars per cow. That plus the dollar a head for the antelopes is a lot of money."

The greed in Raj started to surface, and you could almost see dollar signs in his eyes.

"I will do it," Raj finally said. "We must be very careful. Allow me a couple of days to locate some cows and bulls. I am doing this for your father, Don Simon."

That makes two of us, Gustavo thought. He knew what they could do to Raj if he got caught. But what would they do to him? *Let's hope I never find out*, Gustavo thought.

II

The pickup turned off the farm to market road, and the driver shut off the headlights. They glided quietly onto the long driveway toward the secluded ranch house. The clouds had parted slightly, allowing the light from the full moon to peak through. The eerie shadows cast by the tall Coca Pamosa palm trees resembled huge spiders lying in wait to pounce and devour the vehicle as it quietly crept down the winding driveway.

The home looked more like a mansion than a house. The mustard-colored stucco walls contrasted perfectly with the red clay roof tiles. The tall flat roof was edged with a three-foot parapet that easily could have hidden gun turrets and be manned by armed security guards. The porch roof seemed to grow out of the walls at a slight pitch and was supported by several arched passages. The double-entry door was arched at the top, to match the porch, and adorned with ornate copper inlay and dark glass. The doorknobs were hand carved with the circle W brand in the middle of each one.

Julian La Hormiga tried the door handle, and wasn't surprised that it was unlocked. No one in his right mind would dare enter the remote ranch, much less the main house, without an invitation. He decided to kick the door open to make it look like a home invasion, like the ones occurring more and more frequently along the border. Julian had been in the house once before, when it was under construction and not yet lived in, so he knew the layout. He made it through the entry door with little effort. The hardware gave easily to the thrust of his boot and slammed against the foyer wall. Julian and one of his pistoleros went to the master bedroom to the left of the entry. The other two men went down the hallway to the right, to the children's and maid's quarters at the other end of the house, separated by the kitchen and a huge family room. It was 4:30 a.m., a little more than an hour before dawn, and Julian was counting on everyone being in a deep sleep.

"Chingau! Pinche perro!" the Mexican bodyguard yelled. The little black pug was barking hysterically. Its frantic alarm woke everyone up. The two pistoleros herded the terrified little girls into the maid's room and tried to get them under control and to quit screaming. The monster Halloween masks the two men were wearing weren't helping the task any. The little dog latched onto the calf of the masked pistolero and was shaking his leg back and forth like a great white shark ripping into the blubber of a harbor seal.

Mrs. Williams appeared at the entrance to the master bedroom brandishing a semi auto pistol. She managed to get off one shot before Julian easily disarmed her. She was less than three feet away from him and was amazed she missed at that distance. She was aiming at his head, and if she had aimed at his torso, she probably would have shot him.

"Callate cabrona!" Julian yelled at her.

Julian has seen the lady before, but at a distance, he knew that Mrs. Williams was beautiful, but he didn't realize how stunning she actually was. Her shoulder-length platinum-blond hair framed her dark face like the flaxen mane on a palomino mare. Her black nipples protruded through her white fishnet nightgown, and her tits were so perfect that he wondered if they were real or if they were manufactured. She was wearing a white thong that contrasted against her brown skin. She looked like an erotic goddess form a faraway fantasy island. He just stood and stared at her while she screamed and yelled. He didn't know what she was saying. His ears were still ringing from the report of the gunshot.

The pistolero still had the little dog trying to chew on his leg. Its teeth were locked on the man's pant leg. Instinctively, he pulled out his knife from the scabbard on his belt and slit the pug's throat.

"You bastardo, that was my children's dog! A member of the family!"

The little pup's growls turned into gurgles as it gasped for breath in a puddle of its own blood on the tile floor in the master bedroom.

"Pendejo! You stupid son of a bitch!" Julian blasted.

The plan was falling apart. This was to be simple, a half-hour job, but it was beginning to unravel fast. He could hear the kids' screams at the other end of the house and their mom screaming here and the dead dog. It was pure pandemonium. They were supposed to get in and get out in less than thirty minutes.

"Tie her hands behind her back," Julian told his pistolero. As he did, it forced her tits to protrude out, and now the nipples were poking out through the webbing of her nightgown. *What a lucky son of a bitch her husband is,* he thought.

"Where is the money, senora?" he tried to ask her over her screaming. He was tempted to have the pistolero tape her mouth also, but he needed her to be able to answer his questions. This was getting way out of hand, and he wanted to get the get the hell out of there before anything else got screwed up.

"Where's the goddamn money, cabrona?" Julian's voice was escalating now. He was getting pissed, and he wanted to emphasize that he was serious.

"Tape her mouth," he told the pistolero in Español.

Finally, the only noise was at the other end of the house. Julian went down the short hall that led to the master bath. On the left was a huge walk-in closet and another, identical closet on the right, a his and hers. On the top shelf of the man's closet, there were boxes and boxes of ammunition, bullets of all calibers. Below that was a dresser with a long row of clothes on hangers. Julian tore through all the drawers—nada. Pulled all the hanging clothes back, thinking maybe there was a wall safe—nada. He did the same thing in the woman's closet, nada.

The money has got to be here somewhere.

The pistolero couldn't keep his eyes off the woman's tits. He couldn't resist any longer. His animal instinct overwhelmed his ability to think rationally. He walked over to her, and he drew his knife form its sheath on his belt. She was terrified. She thought for sure he was going to slit her throat just like he did to the dog. And use the same bloody knife. She kicked and squirmed and tried to yell, but she was helpless. The pistolero cut the straps of her gown, and as she struggled to defend herself, the gown fell to her waist, fully exposing her breasts. She was squirming and kicking so much that the pistolero almost cut her neck with the blade of his knife. He moved around behind her and reached down and cupped her breasts, one in each hand. They were firm, almost solid, and jiggled up and down in his grasp as she tried to fight. She was the sexiest woman he had ever seen, the sexiest woman he ever laid his hands on. The only flaw he could see in her, if you can call it a flaw, was the black roots growing out of her platinum hair. But this actually made her more incredible, made her more irresistible to him. He slipped around, very carefully to the front of her, she started kicking and flailing her legs and almost kicking him in the groin. He thought about tying her legs to the chair, but every time she kicked, she spread her legs and exposed her crotch. There wasn't much to her thong, and it gave the illusion that she wasn't wearing anything at all. In his perverted mind, she was doing this purposely, deliberately exposing herself to excite him, and it made him even more aggressive. The urgency building inside him was causing him to drool out of the corner of his mouth and over his partially exposed tongue through his mask. He bent down in front of her, intending on licking her nipples as he caressed her breasts. When his head came down, her knee came up and caught him right under his jaw. He bit his tongue so hard that his blood squirted all over her bare chest. The pistolero let out a roar from deep down in his gut and fell back, almost knocking a hole in the cedar wall.

Julian came running back into the room. "No la molestas pendejo, leave her alone, we are here for the money and that's it, comprende?"

The pistolero was pissed. He wanted the woman more than ever now, but his fear of Julian La Hormiga was greater than his lust for the beautiful blond woman.

Julian was called the fire ant for a reason. His reputation was well earned and wide spread. The pistolero wanted no part of his ire.

Julian looked back at the woman with her breast exposed and covered with blood. She looked good, blood and all. He was having the same lustful thoughts as the pistolero, but he was running out of time. It would be daylight soon, and they had to be long gone before the sun came up. All four of the men tore the house apart. They went through all of the dressers and cabinets, even emptying the dirty laundry basket in the wash room, but couldn't find the money.

Time was quickly running out, and they had to make it look like a burglary, so they stole some jewelry, and Julian decided to take the ammo from the closet. With the new gun regulations in the United States, ammunition was impossible to come by and in high demand on both sides of the border. He'd keep the calibers he needed and trade or sell the rest in Mexico. He grabbed several large suitcases that had been spread open on the floor, and he loaded the ammo into them. Some of the boxes felt empty, but he didn't have time to sort through them, so he took them all.

"Senora, I will free you now, but you must not come out of your room for an hour, or I will kill one of your girls." He told the children the same. They left through the front door, the same way they came in, pissed that he didn't get the money but sure that he would get Juan "Johnny" Williams El Ojo Loco's attention. He didn't worry about the cops; the woman knew better than that.

Juan "Johnny" Williams grew up on a dairy in the small community of Villa Nueva, just outside Brownsville and a stone's throw from the Rio Grande River. Juanito, as everyone knew him when he was a kid, was mostly of Hispanic heritage, and he had a darker complexion than the rest of his family and most of his friends.

At roll call in school, and even at the morning formations in basic training, everyone looked for the white kid when his name was called. The story is that his great-grandmother married a soldier from Fort Brown that she met when they bivouacked for a couple of days near their little ranch in Villa Nueva. They fell in love and, against all odds, married and started a small goat cheese farm. He was killed soon after by a Comanche raiding party not far up river from the town of San Pedro. She was pregnant with his grandfather John, who carried the name Williams and thus passed it down for generations to come.

Juanito hated working at the dairy. He wasn't afraid of hard work. It was the fact that he was a slave to the cows. They had to be milked twice a day, rain or shine, seven days a week. The sick cows had to be separated from the rest of the herd, doctored, and watched around the clock. The baby calves had to be bottle-fed. They were taken from their mothers immediately after birth, not even allowed to nurse the cow for colostrum. The milk was for the customers, not for the calves. There was a golden market for veal at the high-end markets in Brownsville. The calves had to be sold before they were allowed to eat solid food. Seemed cruel, Juanito used to think when he was young, but as he grew older, he realized that they were part of the process. Business is business, and money is the bottom line. He was paid fair for his work, but he was on the job from sunrise to sundown. As a fledging teenager, he needed a social life to spread his wings.

He was riding horseback along the river near Los Fresnos pumps one afternoon, looking for a stray, when he could hear a man on this side of the river trying to coax a young Mexican girl into the river, encouraging her to cross into the United States. "Que paso?" he asked the man. "What are you doing?" He thought the old man was a pervert, trying to get the young girl to cross so that he could have his way with her. Juanito always came to the defense of anyone being bullied or abused. People always took advantage of weaker victims, and Juanito wouldn't stand for it. The man didn't speak English. He told Johnny that she was a maid for a doctor on Palm Boulevard, and he was supposed to pick her up and take her to work. The doctor gave her weekends off, and she would go home to Matamoros but didn't have any papers, so she had to cross the river. She normally walked across the rocks of a little weir constructed to hold back water for the pumping station, but due to rains upriver, the water had risen, and she was afraid to cross in the strong current.

Juanito offered to cross over on his horse and bring her back for twenty dollars. The old man offered ten dollars but told him there were four of them, and that would be more money than he was asking for in the end. Juanito agreed and brought them over two at a time, and it didn't take fifteen minutes. Juanito made a deal with the old man to cross the girls back every week. Word spread, and soon he began his new career smuggling maids. There were only two obstacles he had to watch for, the Border Patrol and the USDA Tick Riders.

The Border Patrol weren't too much to worry about. They changed shifts at the same time every day, and they left this part of the river unattended for two hours at a time. Even if he got caught, he was a juvenile and would just get a slap on the wrist.

The agents that worked this area were more concerned about catching dope than wets. All the agents who caught a couple bundles of marijuana had their pictures taken with their trophies and posted on the walls at the station. Jaunito's uncle was an agent. He would see the pictures hung on the wall in the living room when he visited his uncle's home. Never saw a picture of him with a group of wets. Must be the higher element of danger, adrenaline, with the drugs, he thought.

The Tick Riders were of greater concern. This was an elite group of men who worked for the USDA Cattle Fever Tick Eradication Program. They were officially called mounted patrol inspectors, but all the locals referred to them as tick riders. Some of the Mexicans on the other side of the river thought they were Texas Rangers, because they carried a gun and a badge and wore cowboy hats with spurs on their boots, Rinces in Spanish. These guys patrolled alone along the river on horseback in order to detect and apprehend stray or smuggled livestock from Mexico. They were excellent trackers, and if he were caught crossing his horse back and forth from Mexico, it would mean the family dairy would be placed under quarantine, shutting down the entire operation.

His business expanded to smuggling racehorses into Mexico and then back again. The money was good and the risk minimal. He decided to move his operation to El Jardin pump in Brownsville so as not to risk putting the dairy in jeopardy, and it was much more profitable. He changed his routine, working after dark because the tick riders didn't work at night, and the Border Patrol didn't focus on livestock.

One night just after dark, he unloaded a thoroughbred stud from the horse trailer and led him down to a sand bar below the rocks. He whistled for Julian, his partner in Mexico, signaling him to prepare to catch the rope he would throw him. Just as the horse put his feet in the water, two tick riders stepped out of the Carrizo cane with their 357 magnums drawn. They confiscated the horse and held Johnny until the Border Patrol agents arrived and took him into custody. US Customs confiscated the truck, trailer, and the horse for evidence, and after processing, they would be sold at auction, horse and all.

Thanks to an uninformed judge, he was let go, and the charges dropped. Juanito couldn't believe it. He pled guilty, and the judge let him go anyway. Juanito asked him why, and he explained to the judge that was caught red-handed, and he was guilty.

"Dismissed," the judge growled.

Wow, Johnny thought. *Phew, no record or anything.*

He made a decision after the ruling that he would do no more smuggling. He would graduate from high school in a month and decided to join the Army. He told his father of his plan, hoping to make him proud, expecting to be congratulated and encouraged. To his dismay, his father protested and said no son of his was going to serve under a Republican president! All they were was a bunch of rich warmongers, and he'd be damned if he would let his son be sent to a war and die by a Republican president. Two years ago, when the president was running for reelection, Juanito's class went to hear him speak at the Jacob Brown auditorium near the college, and his father adamantly refused to let him go.

I may never get to see the president of the United States again in my lifetime, I don't care what party he belongs to. He remembered the confrontation. He remembered his dad always putting the president down because he wanted to expand the nukes and build up a strong defense.

"Our money belongs home in the United States. We have no business going into foreign countries."

This was when Johnny knew that he and his parents had different political beliefs. He didn't know anything about politics. The only thing of value he learned in high school history class was about capitalism, socialism, and communism. He remembered the teachers saying that communism would be the perfect form of life; everyone under communism is equal—equal pay, equal assets, equal social status—but that it could never be achieved for two reasons. One is that human nature wouldn't allow it because of greed and power. Humans are naturally competitive, and some always will want to dominate others. The second is that the whole world would have to be communist for it to work. That was the one thing that got Juanito's attention. That was when he realized he was politically different from his parents.

"If we don't fight them on foreign soil, then we'll have to fight them in our own backyard" Juanito would counterargue with his father. "How can you believe anything they say when their intent is to take over the world, one country at a time, and the proof is that they are already trying it." But his argument fell on deaf ears. Juanito never got to go to the auditorium to see the president.

His father finally conceded, realizing it was his future, and he didn't want to hold him back, something he may regret later. Juanito told his dad that he was going to enlist as airborne paratrooper, infantry. His father protested again.

"Those are the first ones called to battle if there is a war. Be a cook or a mechanic or something safe. You BBQ every day at the dairy and can fix any tractor we own. You get the same benefits whether you are a grunt or a pencil pusher."

This time Juanito stood his ground. "I would like to be high speed, and jumping out of a high-performance government aircraft is high speed."

Juanito went to basic training at Fort Leonard Wood in Missouri. He couldn't believe how the cadets complained about everything. One day while they were digging fox holes in soft soil, he'd had enough of this bullshit. Johnny, as he was now called, was used to digging post holes three feet deep by hand in one hundred degrees, 90 percent humidity, baling and loading hay, and a million other tasks. This was a piece of cake.

"Quit your goddamn crying. This is the United States Army, not the Girl Scouts! What did you think you were going to do, bake cookies? You volunteered, nobody made you enlist!"

They all looked stunned, but their attitudes changed, and they all, even the women, realized he was right. Johnny realized right then that he was a leader and not a follower. So did everyone else.

Johnny was assigned to the 82nd Airborne and stationed in Fort Bragg, North Carolina. He first started jumping out of towers to learn the technique and how to land without killing himself. On his first jump from an aircraft, the standby signal was given. All the paratroopers lined up at the door of the C-17. Johnny was second in line at the door of the aircraft. His static line was hooked up and inspected by the soldier in front of him, and in turn, the guy behind checked his. He was nervous, even shaking, a feeling he had never experienced before. He rode a few bulls in the junior rodeos around the valley, and he would get butterflies in his stomach in anticipation of the ride, but nothing compared to this. But it wasn't fear, it was nerves. He couldn't fathom the sensation of jumping out into thin air. That cook job sounded pretty good about now. The paratrooper in front of him was so nervous he was actually visibly scared. He couldn't even speak—his first jump too. Oh well, time to put your money where your mouth is, he reminded them.

The jump light at the door was still red, waiting for the plane to enter the drop zone. The jump master put his hand on the shoulder of the guy in front of Johnny, intending on telling the soldier something—*he jumped!* They were still two minutes from the drop zone. Johnny heard he landed in some trees far from the drop zone, and it took two hours to find him. Maybe he should have been a cook. But now Johnny was hooked. He had never felt anything like it. Smuggling horses and wets didn't even come close. What a rush. It was too quick though. They only jumped from eight hundred feet and didn't get to spend much time in the air. By design though, they were training for war.

Johnny went to Fort Benning, Georgia, to train with the Special Forces. He thought he looked cool in his red beret and battle dress uniform bloused over his boots. Regular solders weren't allowed to blouse their pants or wear berets. That was reserved for the elite, like Johnny.

After attending that training, he knew what his destiny held. Johnny decided he wanted to be Special Forces, trade his red beret for a green one. Maybe even a black Delta Force beret could be in his future. While at Fort Benning, he was sitting outside his barracks, drinking beer and watching some guys climb up to the top of the jump tower. They climbed out hand over hand onto the support beam and did pull-ups, a hundred feet off the ground! These guys were gung ho tough like Johnny had never seen. They were Delta Force. That was what he was going to be.

One afternoon after being released from formation, they were immediately called back into the barracks. "Everyone report to hanger 11—in full ruck. You will receive more information when you get there," the voice on the intercom blurted.

Everyone was issued weapons and live ammo. They lined up in formation and marched out to the tarmac and loaded onto a waiting C-141. They were packed in like sardines. Once airborne, they were told the details of the mission. They were going to Panama to take the airport—this was not a training exercise.

You got to be shitten me, Johnny thought. He could feel the adrenaline rushing through his veins.

The Special Forces were already on the ground. Their mission was to take the president of Panama, Manuel Noriega, into custody and transport him back to the United States on drug charges.

The airborne infantry's job was to secure the airfield. Operation Just Cause.

They encountered heavy resistance from the Panamanian Army, more than they expected from the small country, and unfortunately several paratroopers were shot while still in the air as they descended to the tarmac. The fighting was fierce as Johnny worked his way to safe cover in the pitch-black Panamanian night. The darkness was illuminated by the tracer rounds that were coming at them from every direction. When he finally made it to the cover of the hangar, he tried to get his bearings and determine how many of his fellow soldiers were still with him. As he poked his head around the hangar, a quick peek maneuver exposing no more of himself than necessary, a high-caliber bullet struck the ground, sending a piece of debris directly into his right eye. He was so stunned by the impact that all he could see were stars. It felt like someone had gouged his eye out with a hot spoon. He didn't lose consciousness, but he did drop to his knees in pain. He reached up to cover his eye in the pitch darkness. His hand was wet and soaked with what he thought was blood. He couldn't see even out of his good eye, and he was blinking uncontrollably. He was immediately escorted to one of the Special Forces medics. As it turned out, his eye was still intact, and what he though was blood were tears.

"You are a lucky bastard, you're going home!" the medic told him. "Whatever hit you didn't penetrate completely through your eye. If it did, it would have penetrated your brain, and we wouldn't be having this conversation." He might be lucky to be alive, but he was devastated. This was what he trained for all these months. This was what he joined the military to do, and he was cheated out of the experience before he had a chance to get his feet wet.

"You have been baptized by fire!" the medic yelled over the prop-wash.

He was back at Fort Bragg by noon the next day. He shared the flight home with a couple dozen body bags, and he realized one of them could have been him.

The optometrist told him how he extracted a little pebble from the back of his eye, and if it had a little more velocity, it would have penetrated his brain for sure. He felt a little guilty with what amounted to a scratch when there were who knows how many body bags that would be flown home before the assault was over.

The bad news was that his Army career was over. No green beret, no black beret. No Special Forces. No Delta Force.

Now what. Back to South Texas and the dairy. The thought depressed him.

He did realize he was lucky though. He still had partial sight in his right eye, even if it appeared to be looking off to the right. He looked a little goofy, he thought, but he was alive and could still see. Maybe he'd cross horses and maids again. Who knows, he thought, but he wasn't a juvie anymore. He knew the courts wouldn't go easy on him again.

III

"These sorry bastards!" Johnny yelled as his wife related the episode from last night. He very seldom used profanity with his wife. When he did, she knew he was upset.

She was actually pretty calm when she started to relate the episode, but she became more animated when she got to the part about the dog.

Johnny actually hated that dog. It was cute as a kid goat when it was a puppy but grew up to be a flat-faced slobbering pain in the ass. The dog never did like him, and it growled every time he held one of the girls. The way his tail curled up over his back, all Johnny could see was a puckering asshole. He used to scold the kids about holding the dog and letting it lick them on the mouth. It disgusted him, and he would lecture them about where else the dog's tongue had been. He was wasting his breath. They loved their little black pug. Anyone who would take that away from his kids would pay. As his wife told him how the pistolero put his hands all over her, Johnny became enraged. The thought of any son of a bitch putting his hands on his wife drew rage from deep inside. He was so worked up he thought he was going to puke.

Those bastards! Trespassing into his home, molesting his wife, and terrorizing his kids. They would pay, and they would pay dearly!

But who were they? How did they know about the money?

He tried to calm down so he could comprehend what his wife was telling him. He needed to be able to absorb all the minute details.

He needed to interrogate her the way he learned to do in the Army POW training course. He had to calm down first, but he was having difficulty getting his temperament under control. His personal space had been violated, his family assaulted, and all by someone who knew him. Someone who knew about the money.

He went to the liquor cabinet and grabbed a bottle of Jack Daniel's and took a swig. It burned down his throat as he swallowed, and he could taste the burned-charcoal flavor of the cask on his tongue. He took one more shot and went back into the master suite and sat down in the overstuffed leather chaise. His wife was pacing back and forth on the tile floor, organizing the sequence of events in her head. Everything seemed to run together.

As he waited for the Jack Daniel's to sedate him, he saw some of the pug's bloodstain the maid had missed. The rage started to build again. He had to keep in mind what his wife always told him. Breathe in through your nose and out through your mouth. In with the good and out with the bad.

"Now tell me again what happened," he said to his wife. He was a little more relaxed now. The Jack Daniel's was kicking in, and all his senses were keen.

"There were four of them, four men," she started. "I only saw two, but the kids said there were two in the maids' room with them. The girls said they wore scary Halloween masks. That's all they could remember," she continued. "Oh, they spoke only Spanish. He kept asking me where the money was." She was looking at Johnny like he must know what they were talking about. "What money?" she asked him.

"Don't worry about the money. Who's he?" Johnny asked her again. He intentionally diverted away from the question about the money.

"The one who was wearing a stocking over his head. He must have been the leader because he was asking all the questions. He spoke English, but not really that good, and he would tell the other one what to do. He was giving the orders."

"He told the other one to attack and molest you?" Johnny asked, feeling the rage build again.

"No, he told him just to tape my hands behind my back. And he did after he stabbed the dog. He was wearing a ski mask with two eyeholes and a mouth hole." Her mouth contorted as she was describing the man's face. "His eyes were weird, like he was in a trance, and he kept sticking his tongue out of the corner of his mouth." She quivered at the recollection. "He just stared at me, then all of a sudden he attacked me without any warning. Like he was possessed. He had his knife drawn, and he came up behind me. I thought he was going to cut my throat like he did the pug. I kicked and screamed as he was grabbing at me. When he came around in front of me, my knee caught him in the chin. I thought he was going to throw up on me."

She stopped pacing and was just staring blindly out the French doors to the courtyard.

"Then the man who was giving all of the orders came back into the room. He was yelling and screaming at him in Spanish. He was really upset, and he kept asking me about the money." She had the inquisitive look again.

"I could hear them tearing up the house. The boss returned with a suitcase and went into your closet. He packed all of your bullets into the cases, then he threatened to kill me and the girls if I called anybody. Just to be on the safe side, I waited about half an hour to call you. He was serious, I took him at his word.

"What money?" she asked again.

"There is no money." He lied. "These are just some punks trying to pull off a home invasion," he thought off the top of his head. "They probably got the idea from the news, they glorify these guys all of the time."

"Why would they think there was money then?" She sounded like she didn't believe him. "They must have known something," she added.

"Look where we live," he said. "We have a nice ranch, nice vehicles, nice horses, and we live out in the country. They probably just assumed we keep a lot of cash around. A lot of people around here don't use banks. With the new gun laws, they were betting that we wouldn't be armed."

That was the reason that she didn't call the cops. She had a gun, and she used it. Johnny told her not to ever call the cops unless it was a matter of life or death. By the time they left, the immediate threat was gone. It was too late to call the cops anyway.

"What did they look like, how tall were they, what were they wearing?" He continued to interrogate her.

"They wore masks, so I don't know what they looked like." She felt helpless.

"There must be something. You can't remember what they were wearing?" He felt like one of those cops on TV.

She thought for a moment. "Now that you mention it, the guy who attacked me had a belt that matched his boots…pointed cowboy boots."

"Now we're getting somewhere," Johnny said.

"They both had scales on them, the boots and the belt, snake skin, or lizard, or something, tan, light tan, almost white." She remembered. "And he only spoke Spanish," she continued. "He bit his tongue, he may have bitten it off. He will have a sore mouth anyway." She was kind of bragging now.

"What about the other guy?" Johnny asked.

"He may have had a mustache," she said. She remembered seeing hair through the nylon.

"And he wore a big cross, I could see the chain around his neck and the shape of a big cross under his shirt." She was on a roll now. "And he wore a big gold ring on one of his hands, I don't remember which one." She remembered seeing it right before he left the house. When he was pointing at her and threatening to kill her and the girls. "On his right hand, like it was made out of gold nuggets."

*****

The El Jardin hotel is a nine-story building in downtown Brownsville. It was built in 1927, and in its heyday, it was very prestigious, the place to see and be seen. It was the center of activity in Brownsville, a place movie stars, dignitaries, high-ranking politicians, and even a president once stayed. In the seventies and eighties, as Brownsville spread out to the suburbs, malls came in, and all the businesses built around the expressway. The old hotel became a hangout for the prostitutes and transvestites, a place for them to conduct their business. It was finally closed for good by the city, and all the doors and windows were boarded up. It sat vacant for over a decade while the owners tried in vain to sell it. It became an eyesore, and the city seriously considered demolishing it.

In early 2000, it was purchased for two hundred thousand dollars by an Indian businessman from South Padre Island. Jamial Acharya had the insight to see the value in bringing the old hotel back to life, and he invested several million dollars in renovations. Jamil bet his reputation and his money that with all the violence in Mexico, between the cartels and the Mexican military, he could lure the business back to downtown. He was exactly right. Downtown Brownsville had everything that her sister city, Matamoros, had. Curio shops, gold and silver jewelry stores, shoe and saddle shops, and excellent restaurants. Even the cantinas on market square were becoming a safe place for tourists and shoppers to quench their thirsts. Most of the transactions were conducted in Spanish or broken English. The only difference between Brownsville and Matamoros was the violence.

Downtown Brownsville became a mecca for all the tourists and winter Texans. They could savor the flavor of Mexico without leaving the security of the United States.

This was what Jamil was betting on, and so far, it was paying off nicely. The hotel's banquet room was kept busy with quinceañeras and weddings. The cantina and bistro were very popular with tourists and locals alike. They could drink and dine while the mariachis played through the night. The strumming guitars and blaring horns echoed down the streets and off the walls of the old buildings throughout downtown.

All the hotel rooms were booked full on weekends and maintained steady business during the week. Holy Week, during Lent, and Charro days, the rooms had to be reserved months in advance. Most of the rooms were occupied by rich Mexicans fleeing the violence of their homeland. They were biding their time while their condos on South Padre Island were being constructed.

The timing couldn't have been better for Jamil, or the El Jardin.

"Too bad for Mexico," he would tell his friends, "but good for me."

Jamil was a second-generation Indian. His father and some of their clan came to the United States on a work visa. They pooled their money and started a convenience store in the Kingsville area. They began with one store, where they all worked and they all lived. They were very frugal. Not out of greed, but out of necessity. They didn't hire outsiders or borrow outside money. Everything was pay as they go, and when one store was paid for, they would buy another. They would all help each other succeed, brothers, uncles, or cousins. Their networking was so successful that they expanded into the hospitality business.

Jamil began with a convenience store in Kingsville, sold it, bought a motel in Harlingen, paid it off, sold it, and invested in a beachside hotel on South Padre Island. Times were good on the island, and business flourished, so when the El Jardin became available, Jamil was ready. This was just the kind of venture he was looking for—slightly risky and very challenging.

IV

Gilbert picked his way through the buffet line, not exactly sure what he was putting on his plate.

He passed on the curry chicken. Everybody knows that cowboys don't eat chicken. He loaded his plate with rice that seemed to have some kind of yellow spice, saffron, he guessed. He knew Indians ate a lot of saffron. He was accustomed to eating rice, but it was usually accompanied by frijoles ala charra and fajitas or mollejas. Being reared in South Texas, he was used to eating just about anything, but he always wanted to know what is was first. He was pretty sure that Indians didn't eat beef, something to do with their religion, with cattle being worshipped like a god. So he was pretty sure he wouldn't find any fajitas or costillas here. There was some kind of vegetable that looked like zucchini, too big to be squash though, maybe eggplant. He knew Indians ate a lot of that. It looked good, some kind of chipotle on it, so he piled that next to the rice. There was another warmer with what Gilbert thought was rabbit. Rabbit was abundant in South Texas, but he wasn't sure if it was in the Indians' diet. He put a couple of pieces on his plate. It looked very appetizing. It was smothered in a yellow sauce with green peppers and onions. *Good choice,* Gilbert thought. He loved rabbit.

As he headed to his table in the corner of the room, he noticed how pretty all the Indian women were. Well, most of them anyway. They were all dressed in their native clothing, with bright colors, long gowns, and most of them wore veils. He was surprised to see that many of the women, especially the younger ones, had their bare stomachs exposed. They resembled belly dancers. He was surprised because he always thought the culture was much more conservative, and the men much more protective of their women, in a jealous kind of way. He was pleasantly surprised though. But there were a couple of older ones that Gilbert thought should have been covered from head to toe. He also noticed that out of what he guessed were three hundred people attending, there were only two other couples and himself that were not Indian.

He noticed one young lady in particular. She was wearing a red skirt that started way below her navel and went all the way to the floor. A short sleeveless top that stopped just short of her breasts. She wore a necklace with a huge silver pendant. It was nestled perfectly in her cleavage. Her hair was jet-black and piled high on her head. She wore long dangling silver earrings that matched the pendant, and it bounced back and forth between her breasts.

She looked more Middle Eastern than Indian, maybe even Iranian. Hell, he didn't know the difference anyway. Her skirt was so low on her hips Gilbert was surprised that her pubic hair wasn't showing. She was facing him while sitting at a nearby table, talking with a group of equally beautiful girls. She kept glancing over, almost hypnotizing him with her big dark eyes. He broke away from her spell only to be mesmerized by her perfectly shaped stomach. She had a slight pouch, lightly covered with peach fuzz. He imagined her standing over him, arms rising above her head, slowly dancing and snapping castañuelas while he slipped twenty-dollar bills into the waist of her low-cut skirt.

"Gilbert, glad you made it." Jamil startled him back to life. "Where's Marianna?"

"Son of a bitch, Jamil, you scared the shit out of me," Gilbert shot back at his friend.

"Be glad it's me and not your wife. I saw you checking out the ladies," Jamil told him jokingly. "Be careful, they can put you in a trance, and who knows what they could do to you," Jamil sarcastically said.

"She stayed back at the ranch, she is on the verge of coming down with something," Gilbert explained. "This cold front helped her make up her mind not to come. She promised she wouldn't miss the wedding though."

"Hey," Gilbert said, "I may need to stay here tonight, do you have an extra room? There are Nilgai all over Highway 4 at night, and I may have a few drinks. The alcohol limit is so low now that if you have just two drinks, you'll be over the limit and won't pass the breath test. It wouldn't look so good for the county judge to get thrown in the slammer for DWI."

"I always keep a room available for reasons just like this," Jamil said. "I'll get you a key now before I forget, I've already had a couple myself."

Gilbert always liked Jamil. He played a big part in getting him elected, and he was very generous with his campaign donations. In fact, Gilbert admired all the Indians. They came to a foreign country, learned the language, made a huge effort to assimilate into the American culture. They learned the free enterprise system and utilized it well. All the ones he knew had made something of themselves. They all worked extra hard and were real achievers. All on their own, without any government handouts. *Good for them,* Gilbert thought. Even Jamil's son is getting ready to start medical school. They are still very proud of their heritage and are deeply rooted in their culture. They teach that to their children, even as they are raised as Americans. Gilbert was amazed that even though there were only a few non-Indians here, everyone spoke English. In fact, the ceremony was completely conducted in English. *Amazing,* he thought. And they all excelled. Not only do they speak English, they also speak Spanish and several other languages.

Gilbert wished his own people would adopt this attitude. There were second- and third-generation Mexican Americans here that could not speak English. When a job is advertised locally that requires the applicant to be bilingual, that means that they must speak English also. Even the bus drivers for the local schools do not speak English. The tourists and winter Texans get very aggravated when they cannot communicate with employees of shops, restaurants, or even at Walmart. Not only do they not speak English, but they are indignant when the tourist does not speak Spanish.

As county judge, Gilbert had started a mandatory English language class for all the county employees that didn't speak English. The classes were free and allowed on official time. He didn't want these people to forget their proud heritage and language. He just wanted them to be the best that they could be and not be held back by a language barrier. He wanted them to prosper, live anywhere in the United States, and not be held captive along the border by their lack of communication. Obviously, this wasn't part of his campaign platform. He would never have been elected.

"Here's your key card." Jamil placed it on the table and pulled up a chair and joined his friend. He called the waitress over and ordered himself another drink.

"This is the best rabbit I think I've ever had," Gilbert said "What's in it?"

"Rabbit, you dumb ass, that's chicken!" Gilbert could tell that Jamil had already had more than a couple of drinks. You don't call the county judge dumb ass in public, even if you are just joking. "It's chicken, pendejo! Chicken thighs baked in turmeric."

"Well, it's the best damn chicken I've ever had!"

Did he call me a pendejo? Gilbert wondered. He's just getting loose and having a good time. It's time to join him.

"Whatever you're drinking, I'll have one too," he told Jamil.

"Dos tequilas, por favor," Jamil told the waitress. After a couple of shots, Gilbert changed to Cuba Libra, something he could nurse. He had a reputation to maintain. He couldn't afford to make a fool out of himself in public. As they sat and drank, they discussed the issues the county was facing. Drug violence and gun control dominated the conversion.

"It's bullshit that we can't arm ourselves!" Jamil was starting to get loud, starting to draw attention to their table. It wasn't just the alcohol. Jamil was very passionate about the new gun control laws. In fact, there was a lot of passion on both sides of the issue. Gilbert showed support for the new law in public, to tow the party line and favor votes. Jamil was totally against it, but he supported his friend in the campaign anyway. Having a friend in office helped grease the wheels of bureaucracy. And that was good for business. It was good to have the county judge as a personal friend, even if you didn't agree with everything he stood for. Jamil really didn't think that Gilbert believed in gun control. Maybe he could even persuade him to change his public opinion one of these days.

"It all began with banning smoking on airplanes," Jamil said. "First, no smoking in coach, then no smoking in business class. Then before you knew it, you couldn't even smoke in the airport! Now look. Did you ever think it would come to banning smoking in a bar!" Jamil was wound up. He was passionate. He was on a roll. Like he was pleading a case in front of the Supreme Court. "We used to joke about that, remember? Now look, you can't even smoke in any public place. In some cities like New York and Los Angles, there are laws that prohibit you from smoking in your own apartment or condo!" Jamil looked around and noticed that he was drawing attention. "Now they are telling us what we can and can't eat." He was speaking quieter now, but just as emphatic. "I order the chicken McNuggets from McDonald's now, and the french fries taste like shit! Now our guns." Jamil quit orating long enough to down another shot of tequila.

"Better change poisons," Gilbert told him. "That tequila is going to kick your ass."

"Yeah, yeah, I hear you barking, big dog." Jamil would get comical when he had a few. Gilbert wondered where he came up with these euphemisms. "Did you ever in your wildest dreams think they would outlaw our guns? I know you had to support it publicly, but did you ever really think it would happen?" The law was almost two years old now, but Jamil couldn't believe it could have come to this.

The antigun people argued that a gun in the house was just a weapon of opportunity, a crime in waiting, just a matter of time before it would be used to kill some innocent person, a child. Whether used in an impromptu crime of passion or discovered by a child and used on a sibling. Remove guns, remove opportunity, save innocent lives.

The pro-gun lobby argued that the Second Amendment gave them the constitutional right to possess guns, that if guns were made illegal, then only criminals would have guns.

Neither side was willing to compromise, and with all the recent mass killings of innocent people, the antigun movement was gaining momentum with the majority of the American people. The issue was finally argued before the Supreme Court, and by a small margin, a ruling was made to let the individual states decide for themselves.

"This is embarrassing," one senator said on national TV. "We are the only country in the whole world without gun laws."

Texas has always been a pro-gun state, allowing its citizens the right to carry guns concealed and in the open. The only stipulation was passing a background investigation and a mandatory firearms training course. The newly elected governor from Dallas County was adamantly against guns. Guns of any kind. Handguns, competition guns, hunting rifles, any guns. She was even against hunting altogether, whether it was with bow and arrows, guns, or sling shots—it didn't matter. The momentum for gun control was gaining popularity in Texas, just as it was for the rest of America.

Texas's fate was sealed when a crazed gunman entered a Buckies Bouncey Palace on a Sunday afternoon in Corpus Christi. He opened fire with a shotgun, shooting indiscriminately into the crowded restaurant filled with patrons and children celebrating a birthday party. The shooter killed and wounded kids and adults alike. The blasts from the shotgun inflicted such damage that one reporter threw up on live television describing the scene. Children that were shot at close range were all but decapitated, no features left to resemble what was once their faces. Many just bled to death; the double ott buckshot left too many holes to treat.

The massacre was covered coast to coast. The antigun movement launched a media blitz across the nation and demanded gun control laws be enacted. How many more innocent children needed to die while the politicians bickered back and forth? This was the last straw. SAVE OUR CHILDREN, SAVE OUR FUTURE became their slogan. The sight of those babies' bodies being carried out of Buckies Bouncey Palace in blood-soaked tablecloths drew sympathy from people who before didn't care one way or another about gun control. The graphic images were engraved in the minds of ordinary people. Something must be done. We cannot have our babies slaughtered like cattle. All the mass shootings by crazed gunmen were aired over and over on the twenty-four-hour news cycles and the printed press. The population was demanding action from their elected officials. *Save our children, save our future.*

The NRA argued the same old tiresome argument: Guns don't kill people—people kill people. If you outlaw guns, then only outlaws will have guns.

"The NRA is nothing but a baby-killing organization." The antigun organizations drilled their message into the minds of the American citizens over and over again. Nobody wants to be labeled a "baby killer," and the conservative politicians were feeling the pressure.

Massachusetts was the first state to enact strict gun legislation. All handguns, semiautomatics, revolvers, single-shot muzzle loaders, were outlawed. All nonhunting rifles, any long arm that required a magazine to feed ammunition into the rifle, were now illegal to own. Hunting rifles and shotguns were still allowed but must be stored at the local police station. They were required to be checked in and out when needed, and strict inventory was kept.

Residences were afforded the opportunity to sell their guns to the state at special collection sites where they would be paid fair market value for their weapon. All the weapons collected were destroyed at well-publicized events. Anyone caught not complying with the new gun laws would face felony firearms charges and mandatory jail time for first-time offenders,

New York was the next state to enact strict gun laws. They went a step further than Massachusetts, not only were hand guns and auto and semiautomatic rifles outlawed, but also air guns, BB guns, and pellet guns were also on the list. First offenders would be fined ten thousand dollars and minimum two years in jail.

Gun owners complied out of fear of incarceration. No one, no matter how much they disagreed with the new laws, were willing to take a stand and be made an example of. The penalties far outweighed their instinct to rebel.

As of yet, toy guns were not outlawed, but they may as well have been. Stores quit carrying toy pistols and rifles because of public scrutiny. Children in school could not even point their finger in gun-like manner during play without being chastised by the teachers. One well-publicized episode occurred when a second grader drew a stick figure holding a gun on a piece of paper during class. A little girl sitting next to him told the teacher, and the young child was given a three-day suspension. Another account, a nosy neighbor calling the police on the kids next door playing with toy rifles in their own fenced backyard. Although no crime was committed, the TV cameras parked on the street in front of the house and portrayed the parents unfit and insensitive to all the poor children that had been slaughtered by guns. One news anchor went as far as to suggest Child Protective Services get involved. No mention on the news of any adults getting killed by guns, just innocent children. The headlines always led with child killers. The cameras always scanned the crowd when SAVE OUR CHILDREN, SAVE OUR FUTURE signs appeared.

To the disbelief of many, the state of Texas followed suit. After the massacre in Corpus Christi, no politician wanted to be on the wrong side of the public consensus. Just like Massachusetts and New York, all handguns were outlawed, along with any rifle requiring a magazine to feed the ammo. All carry licenses were rescinded and a registered letter sent to all gun owners to surrender their weapons at the nearest police station. Even law enforcement didn't escape the mass hysteria that was sweeping the nation. All Texas law enforcement officers were only allowed to carry a six-round magazine in their pistol and one backup magazine with the same amount of ammo. This state law applied to the federal law enforcement community as well. Border Patrol, US Customs officers, all agencies along the border, even the coveted Texas Rangers, the elite of the elite, were held to the same standards. The gun owners were reimbursed for their property at fair market value, just as the other states, but it didn't sit well with many of the Texans. Texas gun owners fought the new rule to the best of their ability, but the bottom line is that all the legal guns were registered. This was held over their heads as a threat, all the guns could be traced, and those not in compliance would be prosecuted. The risk wasn't worth the reward. Texans had no choice but to comply with the new but unpopular law.

Within three months, almost every state in the union passed similar strict gun legislation.

To the surprise of everyone, California allowed their citizens the right to carry concealed handguns. After passing the required background investigation and training, Californians were allowed to carry firearms to defend themselves and their personal property, similar to the Castle law, previously allowed in Florida.

"Just like cigarettes." Jamil kept on. "It started with raising the taxes on ammunition." He wouldn't let it go. "Then with limited rounds you were allowed to carry in your gun." He knew Gilbert agreed with him, and he could tell by him not giving a counter argument that the point was resonating. He may even get Gilbert to change his stance on gun control tonight. "What if you fire all of your rounds and the bad guy keeps coming?" Jamil wasn't expecting an answer, just reinforcing his argument. "What if the guy is on PCP, crack, or some other weird drug and just keeps coming? What if he has seven rounds, and we only have six? Who thinks this shit up?" He paused long enough to down another shot of tequila, thinking Gilbert may be right, maybe he should change poisons.

"It's a moot point anyway." Gilbert was finally able to get a word in. "Now you can't carry any ammo, not even one bullet, hell, even Barnie Fife was allowed to carry one bullet." Gilbert chuckled, proud of himself for adding a little comedy to lighten the conversation a bit.

"Like I said, who thinks this shit up and then gets the rest of us to eat it," Jamil continued. "What they do is talk it up and talk it up and then try to convince you that it was your idea in the first place. These goddamn politicians just jumped on the bandwagon, just like you did, just to get votes from all of the people who have been eating this shit for so long it's starting to taste normal to them." Jamil realized he was getting personal now and felt a little bad about it. Gilbert was his friend, and he didn't want to alienate him by making it personal. Even though he was right. Everyone was very passionate, on both sides, but he didn't think Gilbert was ever for it to start with. He was just a politician. And that bothered Jamil.

"Look, you're on your second term. And doing a damn good job, people are even getting on board with this English on-the-job thing you've proposed. Why don't you change your position publicly on this gun bullshit? You should run for governor on a pro-gun platform and get us our guns back. We're Texans, goddamn it. I even consider myself a Texan, and we're going to stand by and let Californians be righter than Texans! I don't think so! There are a lot of people that think like we do." He was trying to get Gilbert to admit his true position on gun control. "You will get a lot of support. You should seriously consider it."

One thing about a politician, they all like power and money. Gilbert already had all the money he could ever need thanks to the family ranch and land holdings. But the Governor has a lot of clout, and with clout comes power. He liked the sound of Governor Gilbert Martinez. It had a nice ring to it. Maybe someday Senator Gilbert Martinez. He liked the idea. "I'll think about it," Gilbert said as he glanced back at the belly dancer who was still watching him. "We'll talk about it."

"Otro round por favor," Jamil summoned the cocktail waitress over to the table again. *He's mixing his English and Spanish,* Gilbert noticed. *If he starts mixing in Hindi, it will be time to cut him off.*

"Got to go and see my cousins off," Jamil slurred to his friend. "They are staying on the Isla tonight, I'll catch up with you later. Watch out for the chiquitas." He laughed as he walked off, obviously enjoying himself.

Gilbert was enjoying himself also. *Better get more of that rabbit to soak up some of the alcohol,* Gilbert thought to himself. He went over to the buffet table, but it had already been cleared. All the food was put away. "Oh well," he said to himself as he grabbed his Cuba Libre and headed off to his room next to the hotel cantina.

As he pulled his room key from his jacket pocket, he noticed his hands had a yellow tint to them. The sight startled him. The first thing he thought of was his liver. He had been drinking a lot over the last couple of years. He used to just have a couple of beers on the weekend, usually while barbecuing something back at the ranch. Now he was finding himself drinking almost every night. Pachangas and parties during the campaign, where beer and liquor flowed freely. It helped put him at ease and more confident when talking to crowds. Now it's committee meetings, luncheons, commissioner court sessions where someone is always trying to buy influence from a politician with a drink. Now when he gets home to the ranch, he drinks a couple of beers while driving around the pastures, checking the cattle, a glass of wine with dinner, and to top it off, a splash of Baileys in his after-dinner coffee. He didn't feel like he was addicted to alcohol, it just became a ritual, and it helped take the edge off the day.

Gilbert went into the bathroom and poured his Cuba Libre down the drain. *I'm in my early forties, I'm too young to have liver problems,* Gilbert thought to himself as he started to realize his own mortality. His imagination was starting to run away with him. He was too young to die. *That's it. Going to make a doctor's appointment first thing Monday morning. Maybe it's not too late.* He had always heard how the liver was the only organ that could rebuild itself. *I hope it's not too late.* He was preoccupied with dying now, as he set the empty high ball glass down on the bathroom sink. He noticed the glass had his yellow fingerprints on it. "What the hell...you've got to be kidding me!" Gilbert almost yelled. He realized that whatever made his hand yellow transferred to the glass. He unwrapped a bar of soap with the El Jardin logo, turned on the water, and scrubbed his hands. "I'll be damned," he said to himself as he watched the yellow substance disappear from his hand and run down the drain. As he dried his hands, he looked at his eyes in the mirror. "As white as the wind-driven snow!" he said to himself. "Turmeric," he said out loud. He remembered that Jamil said the chicken was seasoned with turmeric. It stained his hands as he ate it, even though he wiped them on the napkin. Even after washing with soap and water, he could still see a slight tint of yellow. *Phew, a new lease on life* went through his mind when he realized he wasn't dying.

He sat down on the bed, ready to call it a night. As he reached across to retrieve the remote for the TV, he could hear the music from the cantina bleeding through the hotel room wall. It was only 10:00 p.m., and channel 4 news was just coming on.

"Breaking news, another body was pulled from the Rio Grande River this morning near the Sabel Palm Grove." The anchorette read the teleprompter without much emotion. "The body of a young female who had been brutally murdered and dumped into the river," the anchorette continued. The river had become a burial ground for victims of the drug war. The people of the valley were becoming complacent, and the shock value of these crimes was wearing off. This one seemed different though. This young girl had been gutted like a deer, and her bare abdomen had been eaten clean by the fish and crabs. Anywhere her body was exposed, the marine life had eaten the flesh down to the bone. One would think the Rio Grande was infested with piranha from South America. Her face was almost completely eaten away, and one of her ankles exposed between her socks and pant leg was nothing but bone. The only clue preautopsy that the body was female was the discovery of her bra.

"A body of a young male found at the Brownsville city dump appears to have been murdered in the same fashion. Brian," she said, passing the next story to her coanchor.

"Sounds like someone is sending a message," Brian commented. Channel 4 news never made any commentaries on the news stories, but he was right. Someone sure seemed to be making an example of these two, Gilbert thought. The murders had steadily been becoming more and more gruesome. There had been a body of an adult male found on Southmost Road. He had been hog-tied and nearly cut in half with a welding torch. Another was discovered floating in the river without any hands or feet. They had been hacked off with a machete, and according to the medical examiner, he was alive when he was thrown into the river. The official cause of death was drowning. He obviously couldn't swim without any hands or feet.

He thought about his wife home alone at the ranch and considered going home. It was still relatively early, and he was now wide awake. He thought about it but realized he had way too much to drink. The weather was bad, and there was always a deputy at the checkpoint. With all the deer and nilgai on the road, all he had to do was hit one, and there goes his career. He decided not to take the chance.

The walls of his room seemed well insulated, but he could still hear the music form the cantina pulsating through. The news was almost over, colder and drizzle for tomorrow, too late to call home. He didn't want to wake his wife. *Oh, what the hell,* he decided, *might as well go next door and have another Cuba Libre since I have a new lease on life.* He thought about how ironic human nature was. When someone gets into a bad situation, they pray to God that if he would make things better, they will swear to change their evil ways. Once the bad passes, nothing changes. *Just kidding, maybe next time.* So life goes.

As he shut the door behind him, he noticed four men at the opposite end of the hallway. Jamil and his cousins. To Gilbert, the cousins resembled the three stooges, Larry, Moe, and the other looked like Shep, not Curly. Gilbert thought Jamil's cousins left over an hour ago. It looked as if Jamil was handing something to them.

That's odd, Gilbert thought. *Maybe they changed their minds and didn't want to make the twenty-five-mile trip to the island in this weather.*

The cantina was about half full, with mostly locals. All the Indian guests had already left or retired to their rooms. The old juke-box was blaring Tejano music as Gilbert bellied up to the bar. "Una Cuba Libra por favor," he ordered as his blue eyes adjusted to the dark room. The jukebox was made to look like an antique, to match the motif of the hotel. But it was actually a state-of-the-art sound system. Someone played the "Orange Blossom Special," and the fiddles sounded like a locomotive was screaming right through the middle of the bar. As he ordered another drink, a slow two-step began to play, and a few couples took to the dance floor. Gilbert watched through the mirror that ran the length of the bar, otherwise he would have to crane his neck to watch the couples dance. There were three couples dancing, and one of the women was wearing skin-tight sweatpants, with calf-high lace-up high-heeled boots. She seemed to be slightly tipsy and was rubbing herself all over her lucky dancing partner. She wasn't drunk, but she had enough to drink to lose her inhibitions. Not wanting to miss the show, Gilbert grabbed his drink and moved to a table near the dance floor. Her sweats were so tight he could make out every crease in her muscular body. She was built like a gymnast, and the high-heeled boots made her perky ass move in perfect rhythm with the music. She was just getting warmed up when the song ended. Not wanting the show to stop, Gilbert jumped over to the juke box and inserted enough quarters to play back-to-back George Strait slow songs. He wondered if she brought the guy with her or picked him up here. Just curious, he enjoyed trying to figure out people in the bar.

"Drinking alone, cowboy?" The woman's voice startled him as she came around the table. His back was to the door as he watched the horny gymnast, and he was preoccupied, wondering if she had anything on under her sweats.

The belly dancer. What are the odds, Gilbert thought. "What a pleasant surprise," he said to her. It seemed as if they were old friends. He had been watching her all night. They were watching each other, actually.

"Have a seat, can I buy you a drink?" He hoped his voice didn't give away his excitement. *What are the odds,* he wondered again. "Sit, sit," he said as he got up and pulled a chair out for her. "This must be what you call karma in your culture. Seems everywhere I turn, there you are." He never would have recognized her. She had changed out of her costume and was wearing a pair of cowboy-cut Wrangler jeans and a baggy gray sweatshirt.

"I just came down to borrow a corkscrew from the bartender. I took a bottle of wine from the table, but I couldn't open it. No sense letting it go to waste. My culture?" she asked him.

"Yeah, you Indians believe in karma, don't you?" Gilbert thought he was being suave.

"I have a little Kickapoo blood in me, but I believe the politically correct term is Native American. You're not going to call me a squaw, are you?" She knew what he meant; she just wanted to see his reaction. She also felt as if she had known him for a long time. "I'm just pulling your chain," she said as she took a seat. "I'm not Indian. I'm a south Texas Tejana."

"Wow," Gilbert said, feeling a little stupid. "You easily could pass for Indian. What's your name, little girl?" he asked her as he pushed her chair in.

"I'm not a little girl, I thought you would have noticed," she quipped with a grin on her face. Her black hair was down around her shoulders, and her teeth were so white she could have appeared in a toothpaste commercial. Just a slight gap between her two front teeth.

Sexy, Gilbert thought.

"Erica, my name is Erica, I just came down for the party. I live in McAllen."

Erica, he thought. *Should be Erotica, that will be easy to remember.*

"I'll have a glass of red wine," she said. "Whatever the house wine is."

"Well, what kind did you take to your room?" Gilbert asked her.

"Red Merlot," she said. "I think it was anyway, red something."

What? Gilbert thought to himself. When he drank wine, that was his first choice, red Merlot—karma.

"Then red Merlot it is," he said as he waved the bartender over.

"Where are your friends?" Gilbert asked her.

"Turned in early," she replied. "Busy day planned for the island tomorrow. And you must be what, German, Swedish?" she asked him. "Your bright blue eyes are a rare commodity around here."

"Yes, I am German-Swedish cross actually," he said to her with a big grin on his face. "Martinez is a very old European surname," he replied, laughing.

"Well, where did the blue eyes come from?" she asked, realizing his sarcasm.

"Not sure, my father didn't have them, but his father did. He supposedly was the first in our family tree to have colored eyes, kind of weird if you think about it." He sounded serious.

It was cool, almost cold in the cantina, and Gilbert was pretty sure she wasn't wearing a bra.

"Gilbert! Thought you called it a night." Jamil. Perfect timing. Karma!

"Sit down, Jamil, do you know this young lady?" He was afraid to say her name. It might come out "Erotica."

"Hey, Erica," Jamil said. "Yes, we met tonight."

"Yeah, we just met," she said "I just came down to borrow a corkscrew from the bar, and this kind gentleman talked me into a glass of wine. I know he is a friend of yours, so I was pretty sure he wouldn't bite," she joked as she took the last sip from the glass and stood up. "Thanks," she said. "Early day tomorrow." She headed out the door.

"That was awkward," Jamil said.

"Why?" Gilbert asked. "She wasn't here ten minutes. Completely innocent."

"Be careful," Jamil added. "Remember, a jealous husband is a dangerous animal. Not to mention a jealous wife. Might find you floating in the river missing certain body parts."

"I thought you were in for the night too," Gilbert said. "Was that you with your cousins in the hallway earlier? I thought they left."

"Yeah, they did leave, but they are driving a minivan and wanted to drive down the beach past the riding stables, so I traded vehicles with them. They took my four-wheel-drive pickup, it's never gotten stuck in the sand. I'll trade back with them tomorrow."

"They were gone for a long time," Gilbert said. "Did they go all the way to the island and back?"

"No," Jamil answered. "They went down Highway 4 instead of 48 and didn't realize they were on the wrong highway until they passed the Border Patrol checkpoint. They almost got stuck in the mud when they were turning around. Good thing they had their passports with them, but the agent waived them through without checking. Didn't want to get wet, I guess."

The three cousins were never lost. They intentionally drove out to Highway 4 to locate the Circle M ranch and scout the area. They researched the layout of the ranch on Google Earth, but that didn't reveal what kind of security was in place. They turned off the Boca Chica highway onto Palmitto Hill road and followed it to the first turn. The road was in very bad condition from all the recent wet weather, and they nearly slipped off the wet caliche and into the bar ditch several times. The weather caused the road to erode badly, even though it was lightly traveled. Even the residents that lived on the road had to navigate their way very carefully or become mired in the bottomless black mud of the bar ditch. The cousins encountered similar conditions at home in India during the monsoon seasons. They were experienced enough that they stayed in the ruts created by other vehicles.

The main entrance to the ranch was set back off the road and wide enough to allow long cattle trailers and semitractor trailers ample room to clear the fences while entering the ranch. The gate was constructed out of black wrought iron and was framed by telephone posts with one going across the top, high enough to allow tall trailers with hay loads to pass under easily. MARTINEZ-CIRCLE M-RANCH hung from the middle of the entrance and was carved into a large plank salvaged from an old ship marooned on the beach by some long-ago hurricane. Two antique wagon wheels, one on each side of the top cross pole, balanced out the entrance. They drove past the entrance, to where the road made a second curve, stopped, and backed their van into a secondary entrance to the ranch and turned back toward the direction they came. The cousins turned the headlights off and pulled into the main entrance. The van wouldn't stop and kept sliding on the wet caliche. It slid all the way across the entrance and into the split rail fence that tapered out from the gate to the road. The vehicle knocked the center rail off the fence and the square cattle wire behind the rails hung up on the vans front bumper. As they tried to back out, the van started to slide off the caliche and into the mud. Larry and Shep got out and tried to push the van back into the middle of the driveway as Moe steered. The task was easy, like pushing a hockey puck across the ice. The rain turned into a light drizzle, but the cold north wind was biting to the bone as they pried the wire free from the bumper. The van regained its traction and backed out onto semisolid ground. A light came on in the house, and panic started to set in, afraid they may get stuck again and be discovered if the rancher came out to investigate. The whole operation depended on them not being discovered, no matter the cost.

They drove slowly back to Highway 4, being careful not to get stuck again. Luckily no one from the ranch followed. The cousins had their passports ready as they approached the checkpoint, along with the story that they had mistakenly taken the wrong highway to the island. The agents were preoccupied with another vehicle pulled over for a secondary inspection and just waived the cousins through. They noticed that the other vehicle was occupied by two attractive young ladies seemingly flirting with the agents. Probably a ploy, the cousins thought. The girls were possibly a decoy to keep the agents' undivided attention while drugs or illegals were being smuggled across the flats to the ship channel. Why else would two scantily clad young girls be chatting up the agents in this weather?

"We should remember that ploy," Moe said to his cousins in Hindi. "That would work every time."

Jamil bought their story. He had no reason to doubt them. He didn't know his cousins very well, him growing up in America and them in India, but they were family. They were blood relatives.

Highway 48 and Boca Chica Highway both ran from Brownsville to the Gulf of Mexico parallel to each other but on opposite sides of the ship channel. Highway 48 led to South Padre Island, and Highway 4 went to Boca Chica beach. One to a resort town, the other to an undeveloped beach used mostly by fishermen and smugglers. They were separated at the jetties, only by a narrow inlet from the Gulf into the Laguna Madre and the ship channel. A logical mistake that could easily be made by visitors not familiar with the area.

*****

The three cousins left the El Jardin Hotel and headed down International Boulevard, that eventually turned into Highway 48, but instead of going to the island, they turned onto FM 802 and headed west, out of town. They drove to Villa Nueva, a small community on the old Military Highway, just outside the Brownsville city limits. They shut the pickup headlights off and turned onto a small paved road leading to the Los Fresnos pumps along the Rio Grande. They slowly drove past a gate displaying a sign WILLIAMS DAIRY—TRUCK ENTRANCE. They pulled off the narrow road and parked on the grass next to a canal and shut the vehicle off. They didn't realize how loud the diesel motor was until it was shut down.

The wind was still howling out of the north with light cold drizzle. The air temperature was in the low forties, but with the wind chill, it felt like the low thirties. The only good thing about the weather was the gusty wind drowned out the noise from the diesel motor.

Larry was sitting in the back seat of the pickup, studying Google Earth on his iPhone. They wanted to get a good layout of the dairy. The map showed a main entrance to the dairy from the Military Highway, with a paved road that wound around to the main residence and then back to the milking parlors and the feed lot. The truck entrance, where they were, followed the levee, bypassing the residence, and led to the working area of the dairy. There were three barns, a milking barn, one storing hay, and another where the pregnant cows were brought to have their calves. Two trailer houses were conveniently located near the calving barn, where the workers and their families lived. Google Maps did not show any kind of security, so the cousins decided to leave the pickup and walk the short distance to the trailer houses. The plan was to go to the first trailer, the closest one, and kill anyone they encountered, then on to the second one and do the same. Then Moe and Shep would walk to the main residence and take care of the owners and his family, while Larry retrieved the pickup and met them at the main entrance on the Military Highway. They were counting on everyone being asleep this time of night and taking everyone by surprise.

The service road was lined with native mesquite trees, and as they rounded the corner, the barns came into view. The three barns were identical to each other, separated only by a narrow lane, wide enough to drive a vehicle or tractor through.

Security lights were strategically placed at the corner of each barn and lit up the area like a sports arena. The drizzle had tapered off to a light mist, and as the precipitation was passing through the lights on the top of telephone poles, it gave the illusion of being in the eye of a hurricane.

The first barn on the left was open on three sides and was half filled with huge sweet-smelling hay bales. The barn on the right was completely enclosed and had oversize sliding doors on either end. On one side, the doors were partially slid open, and the cousins could hear cattle bawling and heard some kind of activity taking place inside. There were two tall silos standing sentry next to the hay barn, casting just enough of a shadow to give the cousins the cover needed to approach the barn unseen. The barns appeared to be as big as a football field, and the tall metal walls amplified every little noise.

The barn had four rows of corrals extending from end to end, an alleyway between each row, and a catwalk that ran above them. The light fixtures hung from the ceiling by chains, and a simple low-watt light bulb dangled below, covered by a tin saucer for illumination. They cast an eerie dim light inside the barn, just enough to see your way around without difficulty. The far end of the barn, where the activity was happening, was much better lit, and the cousins could hear muffled voices and the echoing of metal gates being slammed. There were just enough cows in the corrals to block the cousins' view, not allowing them to see what was happening at the other end. The cows were bigger than the cousins had ever seen in India. hey were as tall as the men were, and their udders were as big as beach balls with human-sized fingers protruding out. The bags were as tight as a snare drum, and if you were to thump one, it might explode. The cattle were nearly all identical, black with patches of white. Just a few were solid black, and they were all the same size and shape.

They seemed to waddle uncomfortably, coping with the unnatural bag between their legs.

The cousins quietly worked their way down the row of corrals, intending on getting close enough, undetected, to see what kind of activity could be taking place this time of night. The cows became alarmed as the cousins snuck down the alleyway. They lined up like cavalry soldiers at the far end of their corrals, ready to draw their sabers and defend their territories. Their big black eyeballs reflected what little light there was. Their ears protruded out of their pointed heads, alerting them to every movement the men made. The cousins realized that to the cows, their posture must resemble predators, like coyotes or mountain lions, and the cows were just acting instinctively.

They made the decision to back off and go down the farthest alleyway, hoping that the cattle hadn't already given them up.

The far alley was lined with little wooden crates, and there was a baby calf in each one. There was only enough room in each pen to allow the calf to lay down, and a pail of milk was fastened to the head gates. There seemed to be hundreds of them, all the same size and color—clones, just like the cows. The calves made little noise as the cousins passed by them, except for the occasional bawl, barely audible, weak-sounding moans from the small pens that didn't even allow the calves enough room to turn around.

At the end of the alley was a tractor hooked up to a trailer loaded with cattle feed and a round tube sticking out from each side. This gave the cousins a good concealed observation post and allowed them to see what all the activity was about.

Two men were forcing a big black cow into a chute, far too small to accommodate her large body. The cousins were surprised that the cow was complying so easily; then, all of a sudden, she balked and started to back up, trying to turn around and go back to where she came from. The man at the rear of the cow picked up a yellow stick, placed it against the metal of the corral, and sparks seemed to fly as the sound of electricity filled the barn. Then the man turned the stick on the protesting cow, and she lunged forward as the electricity penetrated her body. She crashed into the front of the small confined chute, where the second man slammed the front gate, catching her head, and a half gate fell behind her, trapping her in the chute. The worker at the rear of the chute slid a long clear glove on one of his arms, it extended all the way up to his shoulder, and they watched in disbelief as the man forced his arm into the vagina of the protesting cow. They watched as the man pushed and pulled, over and over, until a pair of legs emerged out of the rear of the cow. The other worker carried some chains over to the rear of the chute and attached one end to the protruding legs. The other end was hooked up to a winch. They switched the machine on, and when the chains slowly tightened and began to put pressure on the cow, she bawled in agony.

The winch pulled, stopped, chains released, then reattached, pulled again, over and over, as the man with the glove continued to push the legs back into the cow, intentionally prolonging her agony. After what seemed like hours to the cousins, a calf plopped out of the cow and landed on the hard concrete behind the cow. The calf was wiped clean by the worker, as the other man stabbed a yellow tag into each ear. The little calf was trying to stand on his wobbly legs and flee but was held tight between the legs of the worker. The ranch hand then lifted the calf, grabbing him by one of his newly pierced ears and the scruff of his flank, and threw him to the ground again and pinned him down, placing his knee on the newborn's neck. The other man drew a knife from the scabbard on his belt, cut a slit in the calf's scrotum, and squeezed the testicles out of the helpless calf, scraped his knife blade back and forth, slowly, deliberately, severing the vesicles until they detached. He held the bloody testicles in his gloved hand for a few seconds then tossed them over to the patiently waiting dog.

Larry sprung up from his covert position, unable to contain himself, let out a yell, and started to scale the fence separating him and the ranchers. Moe grabbed his cousin by the nape of his neck and jerked him back down behind the tractor. The ranchers didn't hear the yell over the howling wind and lowing cows, but the blue cow dog did and ran over to the fence and started barking uncontrollably.

The ranch hands looked over to the dog but didn't walk over to investigate his distressed warning. The cold winter weather had driven the possums and raccoons inside to escape the cold, and they had been wreaking havoc on the feed trailer. They hollered at the dog to back off, but she wouldn't let up. The ungloved man threw a pair of tagging plyers at the dog, missed his target, but caught Larry on his chin, just under his bottom lip.

The workers turned their attention back to the baby calf. They stuck a large needle into the calf's neck, grabbed a fistful of salt, and rubbed it into his open, bleeding scrotum. They grabbed the calf by both ears and dragged it down the alley to a waiting wooden cell, where he was rewarded with a pail of fresh milk from the tortured cow.

The cousins knew that a calf's instinct was to suck milk from his mother, not lap it up from a pail like a dog. To the cousins, this was just another form of cruelty, one they had not heard before, and they watched as the other worker approached the still-contained cow, holding a small piece of broom handle, wondering what was in store for her now.

Larry started to rise to his feet again in defense of the cow, but Moe was ready for him and grabbed him even before he had a chance to move. His swollen lip prevented him from yelling. They watched intently as the hand walked over to the cow, stick in hand, grabbed the placenta that was barely visible, wrapped it around the stick, and started rolling it up like a ball of kite string. The tissue slowly unbuttoned itself from the protesting cow and wrapped into a ball on the stick. As the man rolled the stick, the cow would wrench in pain, just as she did when the men ripped the calf out of her. The men laid it out on the concrete and studied it, baffling the cousins, wondering what sort of torture they would perform with this bloody mass.

Finally, the cow's head was released from the front gate. One of the men followed her down the alley to a waiting corral and slammed the metal gate behind her, the sound echoing through the barn like a clap of thunder.

The other man grabbed a pitchfork and turned his attention to the still barking dog and headed to the feed trailer where the cousins were still crouched in the shadows. The ranch hand remembered how much easier it was to dispatch the varmints with a .22 rifle and rat shot rather than chasing them down and impaling them with the tines of the pitchfork. With the gun, even if he didn't get a direct hit, the animals would go off into the brush outside to die. Now he would have to stab them bloody, usually still alive, and carry them outside to the brush line himself. The possums would growl and hiss like a mad cat, fighting and baring their teeth all the way, before their half-bald bodies were flung into the brush. The coons were much more of a challenge. They were as big as the dog and would put up a vicious fight right up to the end.

As the worker neared the corral panel to go around the feed trailer, the dog took the shortcut, ran under it, and latched onto Larry's lower leg. Startled, the ranch hand froze then raised the pitchfork and ordered the cousins, in Spanish, not to move. It wasn't uncommon to occasionally have illegals hide in the barn as they waited to be picked up on the Military Highway, and the hand mistakenly thought this was who he was dealing with. Before he could alert his coworker, Shep grabbed him from behind and put him in a chokehold, a sleeper hold, held him long enough to stop the blood flow to the brain until the man passed out. The timing had to be right. Held too long, the man could die. A tactic learned from law enforcement, now outlawed. The other worker came up the alleyway yelling at the dog to shut up. Realizing the pitchfork was gone, he assumed his coworker was tending to the varmints.

The dog yelped and then went silent. The man called for him then called for his partner and did not get a response. He rounded the feed trailer to see the dog lying on the ground with the pitchfork pinning him to the floor, dead. He froze as he let his eyes adjust to the shadows. He could sense something was wrong and called for his partner again. The fight-or-flight instinct came over him, and as he turned to run, he came face-to-face with Moe. He turned to run the other direction, only to be blocked by the other two cousins. He was trapped, blocked in on three sides by the men and by the feed trailer on the other side.

"Que queres," the hand stuttered in Spanish. "What do you want? Where is my amigo?"

The cousins did not say a word. Larry hit him in the gut with a piece of pipe, and the ranch hand doubled over. Larry wanted to hit him across his head with the pipe, still sore from his injury by the pliers. Shep knocked the man to the ground and came down with both knees into the middle of his back, right between his shoulder blades. The hand was paralyzed with both fear and lack of air caused by the full force of Shep's body impact.

The time had come.

This was what they had been indoctrinated with from the time they were little boys back in India, as were their fathers and grandfathers. They were taught that all the cattle in Texas were descendants of their holy cattle, stolen and smuggled out of India decades ago. The stories had been drilled into the cousins from a very young age, as far back as they could remember. They were told how the Texans would torture the holy cattle, mutilating their gentiles, cutting their ears completely off, burning them with white-hot irons, and even sawing the horns off, spewing blood into the air. They were told how the cattle were hung upside down, their throats slit, and after they bled to death, they were skinned and the flesh eaten. They were told that the cattle were usually still alive while their skins were being ripped from their bodies.

They were not told about the calves being ripped straight out of the cow vagina before it had a chance to be born, testicles sawed from its scrotum, stabbed with needles and impaled with ear tags. Either the ancestors didn't know about these new forms of torture, or the Texans had just evolved into creating new rituals.

These stories had been instilled in them for years. It had almost become folklore at home in India, but to witness the torture first-hand, to actually see with their own eyes, enraged them beyond their wildest dreams.

Now they would carry out their duties with gusto, a new driven purpose. Everything they had been told had been witnessed with their own eyes. They were born again. Driven.

They dragged the unconscious man over to the chute previously occupied by the cow and stripped him naked and tied his hands behind his back with bailing twine. They dragged the other man over, jerked him to his feet, and tied his hands behind his back and then to the cattle chute.

The cousins hoisted the unconscious man, feet-first, to where his knees met the top rail of the chute. They doubled his legs back at the knees and secured them to the rail with the bailing twine. His stark-naked body, except for his boots, hung upside down, his head just a few inches from the ground. Larry pulled his jackknife from his pants pocket and approached the unconscious ranch hand. The other man, tied to the fence, started yelling and screaming, "Que queres! Que queres! What do you want!" He was yelling in both English and Spanish. He had no idea what the cousins wanted from him and his coworker. They were mere ranch hands, just working hard to feed their families. They had no cash, no assets, no anything. They couldn't understand what the cousins could possibly want from them. They witnessed illegals and narcotics come across the river and through the dairy many times, but they never reported it. They always looked the other way. They never wanted to get involved with any illegal activity that would put them and their families in danger. They had heard the rumors of what the cartel did to snitches. They heard stories about men being tied up and forced to watch their wives and daughters raped before their eyes, and they were allowed to live, to tell others of their experience, what would be in store for them if they crossed the cartels.

"Shut up! Callate!" Moe yelled at the terrified ranch hand. They were glad the rain was now pounding down on the tin roof of the barn, along with the gale-force wind. Any calls for help would be drowned out by the weather. But it was an added nuisance that Moe couldn't tolerate. Like a barking dog, it penetrates to the core. "Shut up!" Moe yelled again, this time just in English, and he pointed his pocketknife at the cowering prisoner.

The unconscious man resembled an upside-down crucifix, his penis and testicles dangling freely on his lower abdomen. Larry grabbed the man's testicles and scrotum together in his left hand and, with his knife in his right, made one clean cut, removing the organs and tossing the body parts on the ground in front of his coworker tied to the fence. The man began to scream and yell again, shaking uncontrollably, losing control of his bladder, urinated, and soaked his blue denim pants.

"Shut up!" This time it was Shep yelling. Filled with adrenaline and revenge, he picked up the dirty, bloody scrotum and forced it into the convulsing prisoner's mouth.

"You want to scream! Then scream! Scream!" Shep yelled.

The naked victim never moved. He didn't even flinch as he was being gelded, but he was bleeding profusely, blood dripping down his penis, onto his chin, around to his eyes, and finally forming a puddle on the ground beneath him. A sign that he was still alive.

Larry went to the feed trailer to retrieve the tagging plyers that hit him in the mouth earlier. He cut an ear from the upside down victim and used the plyers to fix it to the man's nipple, just like was done to the calf.

The tethered man managed to spit the scrotum out of his mouth and began screaming uncontrollably, incoherently again.

Shep started toward the quivering man, brandishing his knife. As he leaned over to cut the twine that held the prisoner to the fence, the man lost control of his bowels. The stench was unbearable. The cousins hadn't included this in their scenario. They didn't calculate what fear would do to the human body's uncontrollable reflexes. He was to be sacrificed, like his partner, like the innocent bull calf.

Shep folded his jackknife and put it back into the front pocket of his pants. Moe came over to the man, pistol in hand, looked at the man for a second, then he stepped back and shot the cowhand in the forehead just above his left eye. He was back far enough not to get any bone or blood splatter on his clothes. The semi-jacketed hollow-point round made a small hole in the man's forehead but blew the back of his head completely off. Pink and white brain and bone hung from the rails he had been tied to. He then went to the castrated man, still hanging upside down, and shot him under the jaw, leaving brain matter, bone, and a pile of black hair in the pool of blood created by the castration.

Larry drew his pocketknife and carved the words *El Dedo* in large letters on the dead man's bare chest. He cut the other man's T-shirt open, from the tail to the collar, exposing his upper torso. He started carving the same message into this man's flesh but only able to get *El D* before the stench overwhelmed him, before he could spell out the complete message.

As they walked down the alleyway, leaving the barn, they opened all the gates, freeing the cattle. The loose cattle would cover their footprints, critical evidence the investigators would need, and it would give the sacred cattle a little bit of freedom.

Now, they were going to start at the nearest mobile home and just execute anyone and everyone there, then move on to the second trailer, and then take on the main residence. Even if the others didn't directly participate in the torture of the cattle, they were complaisant, accomplices. They did nothing to stop it, and they profited from it one way or another. Guilt by association.

As they stepped out of the barn and into the shadows of the silos, they could hear sirens off in the distance. They listened carefully, over the wind and rain, and it seemed as if they were getting louder, closer. If they could be heard over this weather, they must be close. They must have been detected. Someone must have heard the screaming. Or the gunshots.

They hurried back to the pickup, pulled up to the levee, turned around, headed back to the Military Highway, and on their way to the island.

It had begun!

The prophecies set by their ancestors all those years ago were finally beginning. This had been their purpose in life, to avenge all the atrocities committed against their sacred cattle, to see it through, and make the Texans pay for their crimes.

Many had come to America with the intention of carrying out the mission, and all had failed for one reason or another. But now it had begun. The stars had aligned for the mission. The timing could not be more perfect. Never before in history had the circumstances been better. They could never have predicted a more perfect scenario, allowing them to fulfill their obligation, and if done correctly, they would not even be suspect.

With the different cartels fighting each other and the Mexican federales for control of territory, drug routes, and most of all power, combined with the brutal, morbid methods used to kill each other and their enemies, the cousins' mission would most likely be focused on the drug wars. The message *El Dedo*—"the finger" in English— carved into the corpse at the dairy, should lead the law enforcement and the cartels to the conclusion that these were contract killings, sending a message. If you rat on the cartel, this is what will happen to you. No mercy. It would just be considered spillover violence, something the politicians had been denying for years.

As the cousins pulled back onto the Military Highway, they passed an ambulance, lights and siren blaring. Close call. Not the police. They considered going back and finishing the project but decided not to push their luck. The point had been made, and the mission begun.

*****

The first sign of the new day was peeking over the horizon. Dawn was breaking as they crossed the Gateway International Bridge and into Matamoros. Julian handed the Mexican border guard his Tamaulipas driver's license along with a hundred-dollar bill, American. The suitcase of ammunition that they stole was spread out across the back seat of the pickup truck. One hundred dollars went a long way when crossing the border back into Mexico. Julian didn't need the border guard looking through his truck and asking questions of his pistoleros. Especially Kiko. He didn't want to explain the blood all over his clothes or why he was unable to speak. The guard handed the license back and discreetly palmed the hundred-dollar bill then waved the vehicle safely through the port of entry.

Julian had a temper tantrum. He went into a tirade. He was furious about the failure of the raid at "ojo locos" ranch. He scolded each of the pistoleros, especially Kiko, for not being able to control himself with Johnny's wife. He held his temper during the drive from the ranch back to Mexico, but he was fuming, surprised he was able to contain himself until they crossed the river. Not a word was spoken by anybody. The only sounds were groans of pain coming from Kiko. This added to Julian's ire, infuriated him almost beyond control. Every moan was testimony that the pistolero could not follow simple instructions, lack of self-control, lack of obedience, lack of respect. The whole operation turned out to be a waste of time and, in the end, an unnecessary risk. All that money was somewhere in the house, Julian was sure of it, and none of them could find it. He knew it wasn't the pistolero's fault, but he was taking his anger out on them anyway, and his anger was genuine, especially toward Kiko. He knew that you never broke rank and act on impulse. Julian's face turned as red as his hair as he ranted and raved, shaking his fist, pounding the dashboard, and punching the headliner of the car as he drove down Calle Primera toward the villa. He would turn around as he drove, his left hand on the steering wheel, his right hand in the face of Kiko. He would have grabbed him around the throat if he were able to reach him. As he ranted, he sprayed saliva all over the pistolero sitting in the front passenger seat. This was why he was known as La Hormiga, the fire ant. His temper was quick, and just like the fire ants that plagued South Texas, you could be stung before you even knew they were there. His complexion would change as fast as his mood. His light-complexioned skin would turn red every time his temper flared. La Hormiga, as he was referred to behind his back, but everybody knew who La Hormiga was.

Mexicans tagged everybody with a nickname, El Pelon, the bald one; El Panson, the big belly; El Chappo, shorty; or Gordo, fatso; and even Ojo loco, crazy eyes. The majority of the time these names were used behind their backs and rarely to their face, especially if it was someone of power, because the nicknames usually accented the person's flaws, either physically or characteristically. Most of the time the names were not flattering. There were exceptions though. El Professor usually reflected someone's intelligence. El Jefe was the boss, or Maestro. La Hormiga Roja or La Hormiga Brava were neither flattering nor insulting, just fitting. But still, no one would dare call Julian by his nickname to his face.

As he drove on Highway 2, the Playa Baghdad Highway, toward his villa, his temperament changed. He was once again calm and collected. The modest villa, once considered way out of town, now sat in the shadows of one of the many maquiladoras built in recent times. Julian ordered the pisteleros to bring the suitcases into the villa and place them on the floor next to his mesquite dining room table. Even Kiko was required to help. Julian showed him no mercy. Any agony he was in was his own fault. There were five suitcases, and they were heavy. Everyone needed to pitch in. The ammunition was made from brass and lead, and all those boxes made the suitcases heavy and bulky, except for one of them. It was much lighter than the others. With all the commotion and confusion back at the ranch house, and the adrenaline, Julian hadn't realized the size of the cache of ammunition his old friend Johnny Ojo Loco had amassed. Johnny should be grateful it was he that found the stash and not the ATF, or DEA. That much ammo would get him a lengthy sentence, maybe even life nowadays. Johnny had enough ammunition stored to start a war. If found by the police, he would certainly be considered a terrorist plotting some mass operation against the United States. Yeah, Johnny should be grateful. La Hormiga chuckled to himself at the irony. He actually did Johnny a favor, but somehow, he didn't think he would see it quite that way.

Julian was amazed. There were boxes and boxes of ammunition, .223 caliber, perfect for fully automatic long guns, 9 mm and .40 cal., a lot of it, the two most common semiautomatic handguns carried by drug dealers, law enforcement, and even by the common citizen before the new gun laws. There was a whole suitcase full of .357 jacketed hollow points, labeled "For law enforcement only." This was used in the .357 and .38 revolvers no longer carried by law enforcement. Julian still had one of the old wheel guns, a Ruger .357, one of his favorite weapons and one of the best he had ever shot. They were loud, with a lot of recoil, like shooting a cannon, compared to the newer semiautos. He may carry the old faithful again now that he had plenty of ammunition. The revolver never jammed, unlike the new pistols. This would sell well on the street. The raid wasn't an entire loss after all.

He opened the lighter suitcase. It was full of ammo boxes, but they were not as heavy as the others, maybe just brass, to be used as reloads, Julian thought. He shook the first box, something inside, but not ammo or brass. It didn't rattle like bullets would. He opened the end of the box, intending on slipping the plastic ammunition retainer out, but what he saw instead stunned him. Pleasantly stunned him.

The pisteloros were standing near the table, watching their boss, patiently waiting for their next orders. Kiko was sitting on the floor in the corner of the room. He was in misery. His eyes were almost completely closed, his lips were shut, but his bottom jaw was sagging, like he had a mouth full of something. He had dried blood that had trickled out of the corner of his mouth.

"Kiko," Julian said. "I am going to send you to my doctor." He motioned to one of the pisroleros and handed him a piece of paper.

"Here is the address to my doctor," he told the pistolero. "Take him." Then he whispered to the obedient man, "Bring me back his tongue."

The pistolero understood completely as he escorted Kiko outside to the waiting pickup.

Julian immediately knew what he was looking at. He slid the stack of cash out of the box and just stared at it. The stack was bound by a single rubberband around the middle. Julian picked it up, held it over his head as if he could see through it, then he thumped it like a deck of cards and sat it back down on the table. It was all fifty-dollar bills. He picked up some of the other boxes from the same suitcase and shook them. Same thing, something inside, but not ammunition. He opened two more boxes. Cash, more fifties. He was getting excited. He counted the boxes—fifty.

He went over and locked the entry door. He called down the hallway and asked the housekeeper if there was anyone else in the house. "No, senor," she replied, "but it is still early, they should be here soon." She was afraid she was getting her coworkers in trouble for not being available when the boss asked for them. She knew La Hormiga also.

"Tam Bueno," Julian told her. "Do not let anyone bother me, no calls, no nada."

"Si, senor," she replied, surprisingly relieved.

He counted the stack of fifty-dollar bills. There were 225 of the bills per stack, $11,250. He did some quick math in his head, times fifty, that would be over a half million dollars.

He thought about Kiko briefly. The man had worked for him for several months. *Bastard,* he thought. He should have learned self-control.

He counted each box and left it in its own stack, 225 fifty-dollar bills. It made the math easy. He wrote the totals on stick 'em notes and tagged each pile.

He opened another box—hundred-dollar bills! He counted the bills, same as the fifties, 225 of them per box. He excitedly opened all the boxes and lined them up on the table, twenty-five stacks of fifties and twenty-five stacks of hundreds. Over $800,000! Just short of a million. What a stroke of luck. The money *was* in the house! His money! Plus, interest! Very ingenious of Johnny to put the cash in the ammunition boxes. If not for the United States government shutting down the ammunition manufacturing plants, creating a shortage, and driving the prices up, Julian would never have taken the boxes of bullets. The ammo itself was almost worth its weight in gold!

"I'll bet Ol' Crazy Eyes is pissed off!" Julian said with a wide grin on his face.

Julian knew Johnny long before he was El Ojo Loco. Johnny used to bring him racehorses to smuggle across at the rocks at El Jardin Pump. He would whistle for Julian when he unloaded the horses on the river bank, and he would appear out of the brush on the Mexican side. Johnny would wade out into the river, throw Julian a long coil of rope, return to the bank, and coax the horse from behind as it was guided across the river into Mexico. Very seldom did the horses jump right into the water. Johnny would place a rope around the hindquarters and apply pressure, as Julian guided the horse's head. It was quick and almost always worked. Speed was essential, and time was of the essence. Periodically, Julian would delegate the head rope to one of his accomplices, who would pull on the head rope instead of guide, causing the horses to resist, costing valuable time. Once, one of the horses pulled free and was apprehended by the tick rider patrolling the area. The horse was confiscated by the government and sold at public auction.

"Never pull on a horse's head." Julian remembered Johnny would lecture. "When you pull, his natural reaction is to pull back. Just guide his head, guide it." Caution needed to be taken into consideration with the racehorses. If they were injured or spent all their energy fighting the crossing, then they wouldn't run to their full potential. Needless to say, the owners wouldn't take too kindly to that.

Most of the owners were shady characters, and Johnny didn't know how they made their money, and he really didn't care to know, but he had a pretty good idea. Most of them dressed alike, dark slacks with loud shirts, usually unbuttoned halfway down, high-heeled pointed boots and matching belts, with silver buckles big enough to eat off. They all wore perfectly shaped felt cowboy hats of all colors, black, silver-belly, mustard, with various styles of hat bands, usually plaited from the mane and tail of their favorite horse. Normally felt hats were only winter wear, straw hats were worn in the summer months, but that didn't matter to these caballeros. It was felt hats year-round. And gold. Huge gold chains hung around their necks, usually adorned with medallions of some sort or another. Many of the men wore crucifixes, maybe to ease their way through the pearly gates. Gold rings. Gold watches. Even gold teeth. Macho. The more gold they wore, the more macho they were. Even the horses had to be macho. Horses added to their virility. And the horses had to be stallions. Stallions were macho. Stallions of all colors, there were bays, grays, blacks, and even some pintos, but the palominos were by far the most popular. A palomino stallion was macho. One with a golden coat contrasted by a white mane and tail, long and perfectly groomed, painted black hooves, and you were the center of attention. And the women. A pretty young girl hanging on their arm was macho. There were wives, but they stayed home and took care of the children, cooked, and maintained the household. The wives went to the quinceañeras and the weddings and the birthday parties. But not to the horse races. The pretty young girls, the *movidas*, they went to the horse races and to the after-parties, the Pachangas. They were as flamboyant as the men, their skintight jeans, high-heeled boots, fancy gold dangling earrings, and gold bracelets coiled up their arms from wrist to elbow. They wore enough makeup to last for a week, with bright colors of mascara and liner exaggerating their eyes, and black lashes matching the dyed mustaches and side burns of their macho sugar daddy.

The races were held at what was no more than a plowed-up dirt road, with starting gates at one end, pickup trucks and cars lined either side, blaring ranchero ballads from the open doors. Everyone brought their horses and horse trailers, whether they were going to match someone for a race or not. It was show-and-tell time at the track.

As the day would progress, the beer would flow. The more beer, the more races would transpire. These weren't Kentucky Derby–type races, with formal betting. These were unregulated tracks, where horses were injected with various performance-enhancing drugs, and it was done in plain sight, out in the open for all to see. It was an accepted practice. Everyone did it.

The money flowed freely, and betting took place between different groups. The machos took pleasure in displaying their wads of money, always pulling it out and flashing it for all to see. There were no lights, so all the races needed to be run before dark.

There was always a fistfight before the day was over. Someone always cheated, left the gate early, bumped the other horse off the track, whipped the other jockey with their quirts, always something. Many times, it was just for pride. It bruised the macho image to lose a race, especially in front of the *movida*. To stand up for your honor was one way to regain your machismo, your respect.

And everybody was armed. Macho. Guns were macho. There were no rules for the jockeys or for drugging the horses, but there was a rule about guns, an unspoken rule. Weapons were pulled all the time, guns, knives, even machetes, but they were never used. Everybody knew and understood the unspoken law. Sometimes people would disappear, show up dead in a back alley, or found floating in the river, but never at the races. The races were sacred.

Johnny went to his first race when he was seventeen, and at first, he was intimidated by all the boisterous strangers and the loud music, but it didn't take long to become seduced by the festive carnival atmosphere and all the beautiful young ladies. He was glad to run into Julian, his horse-smuggling partner in crime. It was good to see someone he knew. The races were held every Sunday during the long days of the summer months, and Johnny made sure he was there. He and Julian made quite a name for themselves as reliable horse smugglers, always delivering the horses in sound racing condition, never losing any, except for one, to the Tick Riders. They were well-known and welcome into all the cliques at the track, never had to buy beer, and always had a pretty girl to dance with at the Pachangas.

Back then, Julian was known as El Gallito, the little rooster, because his light complexion and red hair, they joked, resembled a rooster's comb. They would tease the two of them because Julian Gonzales-Gonzalez looked like a gringo, and Johnny Williams looked like a Mexican and spoke Spanish with a Texas drawl. Neither took offense to it. They thought it was ironic also.

But El Gallito would fight at the drop of a hat. Even as a young man, he would display his quick temper and, as he grew older, earned him the nickname La Hormiga. The fire ant.

After the races, late one Sunday night, as they drove back from Mexico, toward the B and M Bridge, Johnny was teasing his friend that the girl he was kissing all night was really a man.

"You've seen those transvestites at the Zona Rosa," he teased his friend. "The only thing that gives them away is their Adam's apple." Johnny was a little drunk. They were both a little drunk. "Your girl-friend had an Adam's apple." Johnny laughed.

Julian slammed on the brakes and jumped out. "Get out, you son of a bitch, I'll beat your ass right here!" Johnny didn't realize his friend didn't see the humor. He must have struck a nerve. Maybe it had actually happened to him before. These transvestites could actually look like women, especially if you were drunk. Maybe it was just the macho in him that he learned from hanging around the track. It was not macho being accused of making out with another man. Johnny should have anticipated his friend's reaction, but he was drunk, his judgement and sense of humor clouded by the alcohol. "Get out, you son of a bitch," he repeated. Julian was yelling and pointing to the sidewalk. He had stopped the truck right in the middle of the street and almost threw Johnny through the wind-shield when he slammed on the brakes. Johnny was taken aback. He had witnessed Julian lose his temper many times, but he had never turned on him, drunk or not. Julian was overreacting. This set him off, but something else must be bothering him for him to react like this, something must have been building up in him for a while. The bomb had gone off, but the not-so-obvious fuse had been burning for a while.

"Get back in the truck before the Federales show up!" Johnny yelled back at him. "If you want to whip my ass, then you can do it as soon as we cross the bridge." Johnny had enough common sense not to get out of the truck. There was no traffic this time of night, but there were apartments on both sides of the street. Someone would surely call the police. "As soon as we cross back, pull into the

Amigoland Mall parking lot, and we will settle this there. I'm not going to jail here in Mexico."

Julian stood there for a minute and looked up and down the avenue. It must have sunk in. He got back into the pickup, shifted the truck into gear, and sped off toward the border. Not a word was spoken. Silence. Julian drove with both hands on the wheel and stared straight ahead, didn't look at Johnny even once. Johnny was a whole head taller than his hotheaded friend, and at least thirty pounds heavier. He was sure he could take him. He had seen Julian fight men bigger than him though. His hands and feet were as quick as his temper. He fought like the martial arts actors in the movies. Johnny once saw him punch a guy in the stomach and the throat simultaneously. The guy went down and didn't move. He may have died. He wasn't seen around the tracks again. Maybe his pride wouldn't allow him to return. Machismo.

Johnny was sure he could take him though. Well, not so sure. His reflexes were affected by the beer. He decided that when they'd stop at the mall, he would grab him and drag him out of the passenger door and wrap him up. No sense taking a chance of getting his wind pipe crushed.

They pulled up to the booth on the US side of the border and presented their IDs to the customs officer, Johnny his Texas driver's license, Julian his Tamaulipas driver's license along with his green card. They explained their business in Mexico to the officer, that they had been to the horse races, hoping that he would not ask how much they had to drink. US customs rarely asked about alcohol consumption, unless it was obvious you were too drunk to drive.

There was a Cameron County deputy parked nearby. He would ask, if he were to pull them over.

The agent asked the usual questions, if they brought any alcohol or tobacco into the country. The agent held them there for a few more minutes while they ran a k-9 around the pickup. They watched as the dome light of the deputy's car came on. He got out, walked to the front of the vehicle, and stood staring toward their pickup. Johnny and Julian looked at each other for a second. They made it out of Mexico without going to jail, through customs, now to be arrested by the county for DWI. The deputy stopped just past the front of his vehicle, spread his arms out, like he was flapping his wings, twisted his torso a couple of times, bent down, touched his toes, and got back into his vehicle.

Julian drove down Mexico Boulevard toward Amigoland mall, came to the intersection of Palm Boulevard, turned right, and kept going. Johnny relaxed as they drove past the Montgomery Wards parking lot, relieved Julian didn't stop. He must have changed his mind seeing the deputy at the port of entry. Johnny almost told him he made the right decision but decided not to relight the fuse. They turned left onto Jefferson, right onto Central, hit the Military Highway, and back to the dairy.

"Manana bro" was all Julian said. He drove to the bunkhouse, in the back, where he usually stayed when they returned home late from the races.

*****

Johnny sat at his desk reading the morning issue of *El Día*, the local Mexican newspaper. It was late afternoon. He rarely showed up at the office before three, if he showed up at all. His "firm" consisted of himself and his secretary, located in the front half of a leather goods shop at the El Mercado Juarez in Matamoros. His customs brokerage firm clients were mostly buyers and sellers of livestock, mainly horses but also cattle and sometimes hogs, and anything to do with them, feed, vehicles, and any supplies needed to support the industry.

Since the United States outlawed the slaughter of horses, for humane reasons, his faux business was actually doing very well and producing a nice revenue. His job was to facilitate the paperwork between the Mexico department of agriculture and the USDA. He made sure all the certificates were current, all the bureaucratic forms were filled out properly, and most importantly, made sure all the right people got paid. If all the palms weren't greased, the right *mordida* paid, then the animals would be rejected at the Mexico port of entry and sent back to the United States. They would be held there indefinitely, all at the cost to the livestock owner. This would cost everyone involved, cost time and money, time he didn't have, time he needed to devote to his other, more lucrative business ventures. His secretary ran most of the brokerage business. She processed all the paperwork, handled all the money, and made sure everything ran smoothly.

Since the closing of the horse slaughter plant in Palestine, Texas, his business had been booming. He never could understand the logic behind the humane society's decision to push to close all horse-slaughtering facilities in the United States. With all their money and clout, they ran ads on TV and radio depicting horses being herded into corrals and pushed into chutes and punched in the forehead with hammer guns. Pictures of horses biting and kicking each other in the holding corrals added to the sensation of their plight. Their campaign was successful, and all the slaughter plants in the United States were closed. Not taken into account was that the slaughter of horses would continue, not in the United States, but in Mexico and Canada. The society didn't realize that most other countries of the world ate horse meat and paid high prices for it. In the United States, these plants were closely regulated by the USDA. Inspectors were on sight to ensure the humane treatment of the horses and made sure the product was processed properly and the facilities were maintained in a sanitary condition.

Now, all the horses are packed into crowded tractor trailers and shipped to government holding facilities near the border, held for inspection before allowed into Mexico.

They were unloaded, reloaded, then spent hours and hours in the overpacked trailers and waited in long lines to enter Mexico, then endured the long journey to their final destination. If they arrived when the plants were closed, they were put into corrals with no feed or water, sometimes for days, waiting for the facility to reopen. Electric cattle prods were used to push the horses to the front of the chute to meet their executioner, then dragged over to the hoist, skinned, and gutted. Some of the animals were not dead, just immobilized. Mexico had no Humane Society.

Johnny rocked back in his leather diamond tuck-and-roll chair, unfolded the *El Día* on his lap. He was greeted by large front-page graphic pictures of a bloated corpse floating in the river, arms extended, and jet-black hair waving around his head like a peacock spreading his tail feathers. The big bold headline at the top of the page read (in Spanish), "Another Victim Discovered in the River of Death." He turned the page, and two more huge graphic color pictures showed the decomposing body of an adult male, still fully clothed, big green flies in the nose and mouth, and a single bullet wound in the center of his forehead.

Mexico newspapers didn't edit anything out. Dead animals, dead people, violent traffic accidents, the more gruesome the better. The graphic, uncensored pictures sold newspapers.

The accompanying article went on to explain that the unidentified man was obviously a victim of the cartel wars. He was clearly executed by one bullet to the head and his body dumped into the river. The newspaper went on to surmise that the man must have been an informant because his tongue had been cut out of his mouth, clearly meant to send a message.

Johnny looked at the pictures again, more closely. Did he know this guy? There was nothing recognizable on the body's face. It was grotesquely bloated and wrinkled like a large prune. The two holes that once held his eyes would forever mask any secrets his soul may hold. He went over the pictures, from the man's boots to the collar of his Guevara shirt. There was no jewelry or visible tattoos on the body, nothing Johnny recognized. But there was something. Something Johnny couldn't quite put his finger on.

The dead man's pockets were turned inside out, evidence that the body had been picked clean of any identifying jewelry or trinkets. The poor children of Matamoros barrios ascended on bodies dumped in the river and stole anything of value, even the clothes, right down to the socks. The chickleros, as they were called because they swamped the vehicles waiting in line at the bridges and tried to sell them gum, must not have been able to retrieve the clothes due to the body's bloated condition. Johnny walked three stores down from the leather shop to use a pay phone. He'd rather conduct his business like this with certain people. He was less likely to be eavesdropped on. Sensitive conversations wouldn't bleed over to another phone. Once, he listened in on one side of an entire conversation of a married woman setting up a rendezvous with her lover. He never trusted using a cell phone after that. He was even suspicious of the landline in his office. Someone could tap the phone, and he would never know.

"Bueno," the voice on the other end of the line answered.

"Meet me at Garcia's in a couple of hours," Johnny told the man on the other end of the line. As he walked back to the firm, he noticed how few people were browsing the market these days. The violence had driven the tourism business down to almost nothing. Two gunfights took place in Reynosa last week in the middle of the afternoon and killed four Mexican citizens, including an infant. The American tourists were afraid to get caught in the crossfire in some of these border towns. It was like the OK corral in Tombstone, Arizona, and the ones paying the price were the restaurants and shops that relied on the tourism. The people were just scared. Johnny missed the old days when you had to push your way through the crowds in the Mercado. The elbow-to-elbow shoppers haggling over the prices of sombreros and guitars allowed him to blend with the tourists, made him incognito when he would choose to conduct his business on the public phones.

The bells on the shop doors jingled as he reentered the store. The sweet aroma of oiled Mexican leather on the saddles greeted him with a smile. The smell reminded him of when he was a boy. It relaxed him, made him feel at home. Mexican Charro saddles with their big white rawhide saddle horns were lined all the way down one side of the store, American-style roping and pleasure saddles lined the other. Leather head stalls with silver Conchos hung on the wall behind the saddles, and bits and belt buckles were on display in the showcase. Rawhide riatas and nylon-blend lassos hung on the walls behind the counter, and spurs with rowels of all sizes were spread around the store in the many smaller showcases. There was a boot shop in the rear of the store where handmade boots would be fitted and ordered or an old pair of broken-in favorites could be repaired and spit shined. To the left of the front door was a half wall separating the firm from the popular leather shop, partially concealing Johnny's secretary and his small office enclosed behind her.

"Senor," the secretary started speaking to Johnny before he was even all the way through the door, "a man called and needs you to help him get his burro to Belize. He said it was very urgent." She explained as she followed him into his office. As he sat down at his desk, before he had a chance to reply, she leaned over and was handing him the man's contact information. She wore a flowered blouse, unbuttoned just far enough to show her cleavage, and a skintight navy-blue skirt with a slit high up the side exposing her entire thigh as she moved. Her high-heeled stilettos made his feet hurt watching her gingerly bounce around the office. She resembled a trotting horse shod to intentionally give him an unnatural gait. He couldn't decide if she looked more like a hooker or a supermodel.

"He tried to cross it through the Rio, but he got caught, and it was confiscated by the Garapateros," she explained.

"Okay, I'll take care of it," he told her, intending on blowing it off. He had more important things on his mind right now and didn't need any distractions.

But his curiosity got the best of him. He couldn't understand why anyone would want to take a burro all the way to Belize. Burros were common animals. They are everywhere. Why wouldn't the guy just buy one when he got to Belize. And why would he take the chance of getting caught smuggling a burro. Smuggling across an international border was a felony. Was this guy an idiot? Johnny wondered. Maybe he should offer classes on how to smuggle livestock, or anything, for that matter. So out of curiosity, Johnny called the man. As it turned out, the animal was a mammoth jack, an extralarge breed of donkey used to breed mares to produce large mules, like Missouri mules. Now Johnny understood why, but why not do it legally, why take the chance? Curiosity satisfied, Johnny told the man to pay his fines, get all his certificates and required paperwork in order, then call back and make arrangements with the secretary.

Johnny arrived at Garcia's a little early, planning to down a couple of Modelos and take the edge off the day. The cantina was dimly lit, and it took Johnny a few seconds for his eyes to adjust. He could see that Julian was already here, sitting at a table in the corner of the room with his back to the wall. The cantina was empty except for two men sitting at opposite ends of the bar. Another sign of the times, Johnny thought to himself, sadly, as he walked over to the table. Julian stood, and the two men shook hands, bumped shoulders, and gave each other a slap on the back. Johnny didn't expect to see his old friend there for at least another hour. Everyone ran late in the relaxed culture. Across the river, it was referred to as South Texas time. If your appointment was for two o'clock, you would show up at three o'clock, or later, and it was completely acceptable to most people, but Johnny hated it. He liked promptness, but he came to realize that no matter how much he protested, things weren't going to change. South Texas time was South Texas time, even in Mexico. The visiting winter Texans and other tourists thought of it as part of the relaxed, laid-back culture. Johnny thought of it as "I don't give a shit" attitude.

"Mucho tiempo, amigo," Julian said with a serious expression on his face.

"Yes, it has been a long time, my friend," Johnny replied, still gripping Julian's hand and clutching his elbow with the other.

Johnny did not tell why he wanted to meet, and Julian didn't ask.

But Johnny could tell that his old friend was curious. He showed up much earlier than expected, and he seemed edgy, his eyes darting back and forth.

"Things are not going well," Johnny continued, trying to look his old friend in the eye. They hadn't seen each other in over a year, and Johnny mistakenly thought he could confide in old campanero.

"Sientate," Julian said as he gestured toward the chair across from his. Instead, Johnny took the chair next to him, cocked it around, and sat next to Julian. They both now had their back up against the wall, looking rather awkward. Neither man wanted his back to the door. In this business, they had to be aware of their surroundings. Sometimes they had to step on some toes, and sometimes they had to stomp on some heads. Never let your guard down, scrutinize everybody, sleep with a gun under your pillow, and always sit with your back to the wall. Life's lessons learned from their horse-smuggling days.

"The other day, two rancheros were tortured and executed at the dairy, did you see the pictures in the paper?" he asked Julian, as the waiter set a frosted mug and a bottle of Modelo on the table. Julian was already nursing a short glass of some sort of clear liquor.

"Anything else?" the waiter asked.

"No, gracias," Johnny said and waved the man away. One thing about the waiters in Mexico, you never had to ask for anything. A glass never went dry, and an empty plate never sat long. They almost hovered over the table. It was nice to be doted on when you were just relaxing, but at times it could be bothersome, especially if you wanted some privacy.

"Those two rancheros were meant to send a message to somebody," Johnny said as he stared straight ahead toward the bar.

"Do you think that I had something to do with that?" Julian asked, with an indignant tone in his voice.

"No, amigo, I don't think you were involved!" Johnny barked back. "They obviously ratted on somebody, and I need you to help me find out who.

"My ranch was invaded a couple of days ago. My dogs were poisoned, and my worker was tied up and gagged, the bastards broke into my house and terrorized my wife and kids." He had to stop and catch himself. He was reliving what his family went through. He motioned the waiter over and ordered a shot of bourbon. He had to calm down. He was going to tell him about his wife being molested, but he needed to calm down first. "Someone is trying to send me a message." He tried to look Julian in the eyes again, but he just darted around the room, wouldn't make eye contact. On second thought, he decided not to mention his wife or the money. He didn't want anyone to know that another man put his hands on his wife, and whoever took the money would expose themselves eventually. Whoever the trespassers were knew who they were messing with, and their machismo wouldn't allow them to keep the secret to themselves. They'll have too much to drink and boast about it in a cantina like this one or whisper it to their movida after a night of sex to let her know what a macho man she had chosen.

"These people don't know me well, or they would know that the dairy hasn't been in our family for a long time. All I know is that there were at least four of them at my ranch, and one of them was injured." He chose not to reveal how. "Put the word out to your gentes, and help me find these bastardos, por favor."

La Hormiga was relieved that Johnny hadn't suspected him. He would find out eventually though, and Julian would be ready for him, but not yet. He still needed more time.

"We will find them," Julian assured him. "It may take a while, but we will find them." Julian really would try to find out who the killers from the dairy were. He wanted to know himself. He didn't see the connection between Johnny and the dairies, but he could understand how Johnny would think they were related. Better for him that Johnny felt that they were connected. There was no word on the street about the dairy murders, no drug loads lost at the pumps, and no one had been busted. He was curious. Two 9 mm shell casings found at the scene, it had to be Mexicans. Nobody in the United States had any ammunition, or guns for that matter.

Johnny got up to leave, and the two shook hands again. "I almost forgot," Johnny asked, sounding a little like Lieutenant Colombo. "Do you know anything about the body pulled from the river yesterday? There is something about that man, but I can't figure out what it is." Julian just shook his head no.

Johnny promised his wife that he would be home early. Since the incident at the ranch, she didn't want to be alone after dark, so he didn't want to press the issue. He'd find out one way or another.

As he walked to the door, he noticed that the two men were still at the bar, still at opposite ends, and he could see that they were watching in the mirror, looking back and forth between him and La Hormiga, in unison, almost like the trained dolphins at sea world.

Johnny got into his Dodge dually pickup truck, made a U-turn on the Alvaro Obregon Boulevard, and parked about a half a block from Garcia's, just far enough away that he could watch the restaurant without being seen. Julian's white Cadillac Escalade SUV was parked in front of the cantina, where Johnny could see it easily. Something was bothering him. Something just didn't sit well, so he decided to sit and watch for a while. He considered going back into the restaurant, with the excuse that he had to relieve himself, he had too much beer, but then decided against it. He would just wait patiently for a little while longer. Just a few minutes went by, and Julian appeared from the front door, got into his SUV, and started the engine.

Oh well, Johnny thought. Maybe he was wrong, just a little paranoid with all the recent events. Johnny was just starting to pull out onto the avenue when he saw the two men from the bar come out of the cantina together. They looked toward the Gateway Bridge and stared in the direction of the port of entry for several minutes. Johnny could feel the hair on the back of his neck standing up. That uneasy feeling was returning, and for good reason. The two men got into La Hormiga's Caddie, one in the front seat and the other in the passenger side rear. "Well, well." He knew something was off. He sensed something about these two men still at the bar when he was leaving.

V

Gilbert got up before dawn, splashed some cold water on his face, and brushed the stale alcohol from his teeth with his finger. The ice-cold water felt good on his face. He couldn't decide if he was hungover or not. He had just the slight hint of a headache. He walked out to his truck in the parking lot. The air was cool, almost cold. He was only wearing a brush jacket and wished he had thought to throw his parka in the truck before he left the ranch. The starlit morning sky was a welcome sight. The cold front had finally passed through the valley, and as soon as the sun came up, the temperature should rise quickly. Last night's weather report was wrong again. As typical in South Texas, the day after a front passed through, the weather was very comfortable. No wind and low humidity, and most of all, no rain. He reached into the glove box and grabbed a bottle of aspirin, kept for just such an emergency. He shook out three pills and popped them in his mouth before he realized he didn't have anything to wash them down with. He considered spitting them out but instead chewed them up and tried to swallow. The sour, chalky texture almost stuck in his throat, and he gagged and thought he was going to throw up. He opened his door and leaned out, just in case. The sensation passed, and he finally was able to get them down, so he pulled out onto Elizabeth Street and headed home to the ranch. The lingering taste of the aspirin was still making him gag. He pulled into a Stripes convenience store to get something to rinse the taste form his mouth and opted to grab a cup of coffee to cleanse his palette. He was greeted at the door by the aroma of fresh coffee and homemade tortillas. The smell triggered his appetite, so he filled his coffee cup, ordered two chorizo and bean breakfast tacos to go. He was waiting in line to pay, when his stomach grumbled, and he broke into a cold sweat. The urge to throw up again hit him. He set the food and coffee down on the counter, went back to the walk-in, and got a ginger ale from the cooler, paid for everything, but left the food on the counter. He took his soda with him to the truck and headed home again. He decided that he was hungover after all, probably from mixing the tequila and the Cuba Libre. It seemed like a good idea last night.

Dawn was breaking, and the sun was emerging above the sand dunes on Boca Chica beach, blinding Gilbert as he approached the Border Patrol checkpoint. Normally he would check in with the agents, ask about any activity in the area, and just visit with them to maintain his friendly rapport, but not this morning. He was going straight to the ranch. The ginger ale gave him gas, and every time he burped, he could taste the aspirin again and wanted to puke. He hasn't been sick to his stomach since college and didn't want to break that streak now.

He turned off the pavement and onto Palmitto Hill Road, still sloppy and covered with water. The road was in dire need of repair, but being county judge and living in his own precinct, he had to be careful of the public perception. Caliche was like gold, and it didn't take much to start a scandal in Cameron County politics. There were a lot of roads in the county in need of maintenance, a favorite topic for candidates running for office. "Vote for me and I will caliche your road." That's why in South Texas, it is known as caliche politics. Some incumbents have even gone as far as to steal caliche from one road, scraping the top layer off and putting it on another, just to garner votes. As if no one would notice.

As Gilbert negotiated the last turn, he was greeted by one of his mature Zebu bulls standing in the middle of the road. Zebu cattle were an impressive breed. Their massive bodies and intimidating horns curled around their heads like a devil's claw, long ears, and with the huge humps on their shoulder, the bulls could easily tower over six feet, as tall as a grown man.

"How the hell did he get out," Gilbert mumbled under his breath. He hadn't had a hangover in years, and this bull picked this morning to go gallivanting. Gilbert took pride in the excellent condition of his ranch fences. The corner posts all had a telephone pole for a deadman, two more smaller ones on either side as braces, cedar used for the line poles, and fifty-two-inch-high ranch wire topped with two strands of barbed wire. The ranch was fenced and cross-fenced the same way. There was even a fence along the Rio Grande to prevent the cattle from watering in the river, lessening the odds of becoming infested with cattle fever ticks. A narrow lane was left, just wide enough to allow the Border Patrol and the Tick Rider's access to the area. Now, with all that, here was this bull standing in the middle of Palmitto Hill Road, like the billy goats gruff, collecting a toll to cross the bridge. A full-grown Zebu could easily jump the fence, flat-footed, from a standstill, if he desired, but it was highly unlikely unless he was stressed, if somebody or an animal was chasing it.

In the ranching business, cattle got out from time to time for one reason or another, but Gilbert's "law" was if an animal got out of the pasture more than twice, it was sent to the auction barn. If they got out that many times, they must have learned a trick to escape, and not only would they keep getting out, but teach other cows to do the same. The grass was always greener on the other side. Two-strike limit, then adios.

Gilbert pulled up to the bull and honked his horn, hoping to push the bull back to wherever he escaped from. They usually went back to the same spot. Instead, the bull backed up a few steps and stood his ground. "Shit," Gilbert said out loud. He stepped out of the pickup, on to the wet caliche road, and his feet slipped right out from under him, landing on his rear in the slimy muck. "Shit!" he yelled at the defiant bull, and he rolled over onto his knees, grabbed the door handle and the steering wheel, and pulled himself back to his feet. Caliche was like ice when it was wet and needed to be respected, and now his pant legs and rear end were covered with the red mud. He reached down and grabbed a caliche rock, gingerly stepped around the truck door, holding on for dear life, hoping not to fall again. He squared off to throw the rock at the bull. The beast threw his nose up in the air twice and snorted, blowing snot into the morning air. The bull lunged forward, regaining the ground he had given up. Gilbert released the rock, like a ninety-mile-per-hour fastball, hitting the bull in the center of his forehead. The bull pivoted on his hindquarters like a reining horse and headed back down the road. "Shit!" Gilbert yelled out loud again as he carefully maneuvered his way around the door and back into the cab of his truck.

All his ranch bulls and a lot of the cows had been loaned out to FFA students as projects, tamed and halter broken. The cattle were entered in the spring prospect shows, and by the time the final live-stock show in Mercedes came around, the cattle were as gentle as a saddlehorse. But most bulls, especially those with Brahma blood-lines, were turned back into the pastures and used for breeding. They reverted back to wild and unpredictable animals. Sometimes they were bluff, and sometimes they were ruff, Gilbert lucked out; this one was bluff. He followed the bull down the road, back toward the ranch, and watched him turn into the main entrance. Gilbert hoped that maybe someone had left the gate open or the wind from last night's norther blew it open during the storm, then no repairs would be needed. As he turned the corner into the driveway, to his disappointment, the gate was securely closed, but the split rail fence on the right was down, one of the posts broken off at the base, and the square wire was pulled out into the entrance and coiled like an accordion. He wondered why the bull would run through the fence instead of jumping it. Something must have really stressed him to cause him to plow through the wire. But he didn't appear to be stressed, and the tracks coming out and returning were fresh, and after the rain, the bull hadn't been out for very long and would not have calmed down that quickly. If he were stressed enough to tear through the fence, he would still be running off, not sauntering down the road exploring his newfound freedom. Gilbert thought that a nilgai may have run through the fence, escaping a pack of coyotes, or a cat. They were known for running through or going under fences rather than attempting to jump. But even a big Nilgai bull wouldn't have been able to damage a fence like that, and there were no tracks, no sign, but the fence didn't fall down by itself. He got out of the truck, careful not to repeat his mudslide, holding on to the bed and around the back and out to where the end of the wire lay. He laid the wire out, stepped on the strands, trying to unkink the squares and straighten the fence out enough to put it back in place temporarily, until he could repair it properly. The heavy gauge wire was difficult to work with, especially with a hangover. He noticed that the wire was bent into a V in the middle, the point of contact. This wasn't the result of an animal, Gilbert thought, it appeared to him as if someone had hooked a chain around the fence and intentionally pulled it down. "Goddamn punks," Gilbert said to himself. He dragged the wire back in place and tied it to the remaining posts with orange bailing twine left in the bed of his truck. He noticed a rut in the mud, the impression from a vehicle tire, and confirmed his theory that someone had done this intentionally.

He could see his wife pull back the drapes as he approached the house. She met him at the door with a hug and pulled back when she felt the mud all over him.

"What the hell happened to you?" she asked.

"Well, good morning to you too," he replied as he stripped his boots and pants off, tossing them onto the front porch. "These goddamn punks pulled the fence down by the gate last night, and I found one of the bulls walking up the road." He explained the mud all over him, how he slipped and fell into the wet caliche, and he felt like a klutz as he related the story to her. "These punks sleep all day then go get high at night and destroy other people's property." His stomach grumbled again. "They damn sure don't have to worry about getting up early and going to work."

"I heard the dogs barking last night. I don't even know what time it was," Maryann told her husband. "I went out on the porch, thinking a cow may be in the yard, but I didn't see anything." She said, "But all I had was that old 410, and I don't even know if it works."

"Good thing you didn't have to use it," Gilbert said sarcastically. "You would be in more trouble than the vandalizing punks." Then he added with a more serious tone, "We're going to need to address this gun issue soon." As Gilbert told her, he realized he was starting to sound like Jamil.

"It's better to be judged by twelve than carried by six," she quipped back. She heard someone say that once, and it made perfect sense to her. "Let me get you a cup of coffee before you get in the shower," she offered as she headed to the kitchen.

"No, I'm good," Gilbert told her. "I bought one at Stripes on the way home." His stomach grumbled again. He wasn't really lying. He didn't say he drank it. He didn't want to let on that he was hungover.

"Do me a favor, don't leave me home alone at night anymore," she said as she handed him a cup of coffee. Gilbert took the cup from her and sat down on the breakfast bar. He pulled her close and wrapped his arms around her. She had always been strong, self-assured. He had never seen her show any sign of insecurity. She never appeared vulnerable. He felt guilty. He was sitting in the cantina all night, making small talk with the belly dancer, and here she was, home alone, scared. He should have been there to take care of her.

"I thought about it last night, as I went out on the porch with a gun that I don't even know works." She put her cup down too and put her arm around his neck. "With all of this bullshit going on in Mexico"—she often used colorful language—"wets and drugs coming across down river at Port Isabel pumps every night, and now these kids, if it was kids, are tearing down our fences." She was holding his face between her two hands and looking him straight in the eyes. "Times have changed, and I don't think they are going to return to normal anytime soon." She released her grip on his head and rested her forearms on his shoulders.

"I'm afraid this is the new normal," Gilbert told her. "From now on, if I go out of town, then you go with me, and if you can't go, then I can't go."

"Deal," she said. "How come your eyes are bloodshot, asshole?" she asked him with a grin in her face.

"Come wash my back." He grabbed her hand, and she willingly followed him to the shower. Gilbert knew a good cure for a hangover!

Gilbert stretched out on the couch in the den and turned the television to the Arnold Palmer Invitational. Tiger was playing terrible, but Gilbert was rooting for him anyway. The Masters was coming up, and Gilbert was really hoping Tiger could win another major.

"Goddamn it!" Gilbert yelled at the TV.

"What's the matter now?" Maryann called from the living room. She was watching a girly movie on LMN. "Tiger just hit one in the rough. He's going to get a double bogie." He sat up and punched his knees. His hangover was all but gone. Too bad he couldn't bottle his cure. He'd be a gazillionaire.

"I know what his problem is!" his wife yelled back. "All he can think of when he hits the ball is $750 million! $750 million!"

"Yeah," Gilbert said, "he got screwed by his girlfriends on the weekend, now he getting really screwed by his ex, every day!" Gilbert was pulling for him anyway.

Gilbert's cell phone rang. He read the caller ID, the sheriff's office. "Shit," Gilbert said. It had to be important for the sheriff to call on a Sunday.

"Afternoon, Sheriff."

"Gilberto," the sheriff said with a heavy Tex-Mex accent. "There was a double murder at the Williams Dairy last night." The sheriff sounded tired. Murders were not uncommon in Cameron County, in the entire valley for that matter, especially on the weekends, when tequila and Miller Lite flowed freely at the Pachangas. The county judge was basically just an administrator, not a coroner. Gilbert had never been called out to a murder scene or even consulted about one.

"The old Williams Dairy in Villa Nueva?" Gilbert asked. He knew the Williams when they owned the dairy. Everyone in the cattle business knew each other. Their son Johnny, or Juanito, as everybody called him back then, used to help at the ranch, gather and dip the cattle at vat 49.

"This is more than just a double homicide," the sheriff said. "These two men were, like I said, tortured and brutally murdered. They were found, you know, by one of the wives early this morning when her husband did not return from the calving barn. A cow was having a calf come out backwards, you know, beech, I think they said, and her husband and his brother went to deliver the calf, you know, and they did not come back." The sheriff continued to describe the incident. "Like I say, you know, she went to look for him, when she called 911, the operator could not even understand her." The sheriff had seen a lot of gruesome crimes in his long law enforcement career, but this must be really bad. Gilbert had never heard the sheriff speak with such urgency in his voice.

"I'm on my way," Gilbert told the sheriff.

"No, no, Gilberto," the sheriff replied. "We are almost finished here. A few more crime scene photos and we will be finished, you know, except for the security guard on site, we will be completely finished. The coroner is going to do the autopsies today. We are fast-tracking this one, Gilberto, it is obvious that they were killed by a gunshot to the head, or finished off that way, you know."

Sometimes Gilbert was called to approve overtime, when extra people, like the coroner, were needed, but a blanket approval had already been approved by the commissioner's court, and justification could be made after the fact.

"There is a message as to how they were killed, and we must try to figure it out. It's like a puzzle, you know," the sheriff explained to Gilbert. "Gilberto," the sheriff continued, "you must call an emergency meeting." The sheriff wasn't asking, he was telling the judge. "We need to get everyone involved, the Border Patrol, the Brownsville Police Department, the FBI, ATF, and even the USDA. The tick riders have a stake in this too, you know. So far all of the executions have been connected to the wars in Mexico. Now we are getting more and more spillover. Something, you know, is not right with this one." The sheriff was adamant.

Gilbert's mind was racing as he absorbed all the information the sheriff was relating to him. There was an emergency management plan in effect, but it was more for natural disasters, like hurricanes or floods, and didn't involve the federal law enforcement community.

"We need to have this meeting tomorrow," the sheriff said.

Gilbert was still trying to digest all that the sheriff was telling him. No way tomorrow. Gilbert still had to call an emergency management meeting with the commissioners and formulate a plan and designate a liaison to communicate with the feds, someone to coordinate with the city and another to deal with the press, a special public information officer. He needed to consider tourism and the affect it will have on the local economy. The valley couldn't afford any worse publicity. The RV parks were already reporting losses for this winter. The snowbirds wanted to go to Mexico to buy cheaper medications and stock their liquor cabinets while they were here, but the bad publicity was keeping them away. Take away Mexico and all they have is the weather and the beach. Florida has that.

If word got out about the spillover, it could do some serious damage to the economy of the entire valley. Good economy was what got politicos elected, and Gilbert was a good politician. He liked bureaucracy. Every decision had to be made by a committee. Every project had to have a special project manager. He micromanaged the county to a fault and had to make the final decision on every issue, something that didn't sit well with most of the commissioners. Some projects took weeks to receive final approval because Gilbert was busy with other business, while the paperwork sat on his desk, awaiting his signature. The commissioners recently approved a short list of applicants for the position of chief deputy for the Cameron County sheriff's office. The sheriff made his recommendation to Gilbert, and most of the department leadership agreed. At the last minute, Gilbert decided the position should be rotated, each applicant to serve thirty days, giving him a chance to observe each one's management styles. After the three completed their rotations, Gilbert decided not to hire any of them. He told the sheriff that the two not selected would have the right to sue the county. He didn't want to take the chance. The sheriff was pissed, and he challenged the judge.

"On what grounds would they sue? If you select the most qualified, they don't have a legal leg to stand on," he argued. The county judge held his ground and appointed the chief jailer to fill in when needed. This backfired on the judge. Four major narcotic smuggling and one murder case were thrown out of court, guilty parties released from custody, never to be tried again because of the double jeopardy law. All these cases were under investigation during the rotation of the candidates, evidence was lost, and witness testimony was misinterpreted by the different applicants. Because of the lack of consistency, the county attorney decided not to prosecute, afraid the county would look like a bunch of buffoons.

"Tomorrow is out of the question," Gilbert said, the wheels still turning in his head. "I must meet with the county legal team, the CFO, and the head of all of these other agencies first. No, no way tomorrow, let's see if we can set something up for Wednesday."

"Bullshit, Gilberto!" The sheriff wasn't going to let this case get mired down with bureaucratic red tape. "Tomorrow, we will have the meeting tomorrow, first thing in the morning. Call whoever you need to today and set this up for first thing in the morning. You make a list, you know, and I will make a list. When I get back to the office, we will compare the names and divide them up, like I say, notify them, don't ask."

Gilbert wasn't used to being challenged. Jamil called him a dumbass and *pendijo* last night, even though he was trying to be funny. Gilbert wasn't accustomed to being challenged. He better get a handle on this before it got out of hand and became a habit.

"I'll call you in the morning, and we'll see what we can do." Gilbert was letting the sheriff know he was in charge of the county.

"Bullshit!" the sheriff's voice was escalating now. All of a sudden, he didn't sound so tired. "Yesterday, the Mexican newspapers reported a body pulled from the Rio, you know. He was tortured, shot in the head, and his tongue was cut from his mouth while he was still alive. According to the Mexican coroner, he was shot with a 9 mm bullet, you know, the same caliber used here at the dairy." The sheriff was speaking emphatically now. "I think these murders are connected, like I say, you know, these rancheros have 'El Dedo' carved into their chests, and the body from the Rio had his tongue cut out, you know, do I need to spell it out for you?"

Gilbert realized that the sheriff was right. He was on to something. If these were connected, then the county better get on top of it.

"We will need to meet with these other agencies to compare notes, you know." The sheriff's voice was almost back to normal, not tired like earlier, normal. "They may have intel on other incidents that could help us. We can help each other, you know, we need to get a handle on this."

The sheriff was actually making a lot of sense, Gilbert realized. "Solve this, and it will be a great résumé enhancer for a politician." The sheriff slipped this in, knowing Gilbert's ambitions. Governor Martinez, Jamil, and the sheriff may be on to something.

"Ten-four, let's get to work," Gilbert conceded.

"Ten-four, hasta manana, Gilberto," the sheriff said as he hung up the phone.

*****

Moe was the first of the cousins to wake up. He looked around, not sure of where he was. He hadn't quite gotten his bearings and was disoriented. The room was dark, and the clock on the nightstand by the bed read 12:00 p.m., and as the fog in his head cleared, he realized he was at cousin Jamil's hotel on South Padre Island. He lay in bed for a while, just staring up at the textured ceiling. With a little imagination, it resembled the surface of the moon. A single ray of sunlight peeked through the closed drapes and cast a shadow on the peaks and craters of the ceiling, as if it were the sun setting on Earth's satellite.

As his mind cleared from the short night's sleep, and he adjusted to his new, unfamiliar surroundings, he recounted the events of last night at the dairy. He felt euphoric, jubilant beyond his anticipation as he recalled the long-overdue mission. Finally. He felt like a mighty crusader fulfilling the prophecies made long ago by his forefathers. In his mind, he was a proud crusader. Many of his countrymen had come here before him to cast revenge on the heathens, the infidels, and all had failed for one reason or another. Some had become Americanized, like his cousin Jamil and his family, others just didn't have the fortitude needed, and some were just never afforded the opportunity that the cousins were given.

To Moe, it was karma. To be sent here at this perfect moment in history, when the leaders and protectors of the free world deprived their citizens the right to carry, even own a firearm. America's independence from the British was obtained through the use of firearms, the Native Americans were conquered with the rapid-fire Winchester rifle and the Colt .44, the West was won by gun-toting cowboys, and every war fought since that time, even until today, was won with guns.

Who would have believed that the Republic of Mexico, the country with some of the strictest gun laws in the world, would have their very sovereignty threatened at the hands of armed criminals. The cartels were armed just as well as the Mexican military, and running gun battles in the streets of the cities had become a common occurrence throughout Mexico. Every organized crime syndicate, every street gang, and every common thug in Mexico was armed to the teeth, despite the strict Mexican gun laws. At every port of entry, there were large signs posting the penalties for bringing guns or ammunition into Mexico, leaving the naive tourists to believe they were entering a gun-free zone. Quite the opposite. Very public examples were made of the tourists, who paid the high price when they were found to have a firearm or ammunition in their possession, most of the time unintendedly, absentmindedly, left in their vehicles.

A young couple from McAllen were going to Progresso, a popular tourist town on the border, to celebrate the wife's birthday at a local restaurant. They were pulled over at random for secondary inspection by the Mexican customs, a soda bottle containing three .22 bullets was discovered in the door pocket of the vehicle. The husband explained that a .22 rifle was kept in his truck and used at his ranch to kill snakes and shoot rabbits. He removed the rifle but over looked the ammunition. He pleaded his case to the officer, only three bullets, an honest oversight. They have been in jail for almost a year and have yet to go to trial. Not only did they lose their freedom, they lost their expensive heavy-duty pickup truck and everything in it. The strictest gun laws in the world were selectively applied against those that support the border-town economy, depicting them as law-breaking criminals, while the real criminals had free rein to wreak havoc on the population.

The spillover into the United States had been denied for a long time, referred to as the "ostrich with his head in the sand" syndrome.

To others it reminded them of Amity Island, in the movie *Jaws*, when the city elders tried to explain away the shark attack as just a big fish bite, or the swimmer stuck his foot into the shark's mouth, absurd excuses to save the summer tourist season. Municipalities will do or say any anything to keep the money coming in. Simple economics, money keeps the wheels turning. Money is the bottom line.

No, to Moe and his cousins, this was karma, their destiny. How else could the perfect timing be explained. The stars had aligned, and to the cousins, this was divine intervention.

The heathens would pay for their atrocities, all of them, and they had started to. The dairy was just the beginning.

The crusade would be carried to the feedlots, starting in the panhandle of Texas and expanding to Kansas City, St. Louis, and Chicago and ranches and sale barns in between. A small army of like-minded crusaders would be recruited.

The infrastructure had been in place for years. The cousins' relatives had been accumulating legitimate businesses along the border, buying convenience stores and motels, affording them the perfect voyeur used to monitor the targets.

By the time the crusade gains momentum, PITA, the Humane Society, and the vegans and vegetarians should be on board and support the effort to sabotage the cattle industry. The anti-beef community would be easily infiltrated by the crusaders, sympathetically supporting their cause, easily persuaded, prodding their beliefs, the basic creed of their organizations, the mistreatment and slaughter of innocent animals.

The next target must be the Circle M Ranch, where the campaign was supposed to begin. The ranch of the original sin, the final destination of the holy cattle stolen from the homeland.

The weather circumstances dictated that they divert from the primary plan, but that won't happen again. They would be more disciplined, more focused. The Circle M Ranch would be the next target. If anything had gone wrong at the dairy, had they been stopped, the whole project, the whole crusade would be in jeopardy.

Moe got out of bed and found his way to the living area of the suite. Cousin Jamil did good. They were in the penthouse on the thirtieth floor, the top floor, facing the Gulf. The suite was like a small house, three bedrooms, each with its own bathroom, a full kitchen, complete with a marble island in the center. The living room faced the Gulf of Mexico, ceiling to floor windows, with double glass sliding doors in the middle that opened out to the balcony. Moe found a teapot, filled it with water, and turned the electric stove burner on. He was afraid that the high-pitched whistle from the escaping steam would wake the other two cousins. It was almost dawn when they arrived at the island, so Moe decided to let them sleep; they earned it. He opened the cupboard and found a tin of Darjeeling, black tea. Jamil thought of everything, and Moe admired him for the extra effort to make them feel at home. He wished he could divulge the mission to Jamil, but his cousin was more American than Indian, but he didn't blame him. America had been very good to him, but he could never put the mission in jeopardy. Jamil was doing his part anyway, even though he didn't know it.

Moe poured the strong black liquid into a small teacup and went out to the balcony to absorb some of the fresh sunshine and salty sea breeze. The balcony was surrounded by a stainless steel railing, several round tables with real glass tops and wicker chairs, and lined with potted ornamental palm trees, creating a comfortable Caribbean atmosphere. Moe went to the railing to take in the panoramic view and enjoy his tea. The day was beautiful, not a cloud in the sky. The top floor suite offered an excellent view of the gulf. The surf was calm, small waves lapping at the pristine beach below, and from his vantage point, Moe could see the waves approach the beach from one angle and return to the sea at the opposite angle. This was odd to him. He always assumed that waves came straight, never thought about how they went out. As he watched the wave action, he became mesmerized. The motion of the sea was hypnotizing. As he stared at the ebb and flow of the waves, he could hear the god of the sea, Poseidon, calling him. Jump! Jump! He could feel his body leaning over the waist-high railing. Jump! Jump! Poseidon was persuading him to climb up on the rail and soar with the pelicans to the serenity of the sea. Jump! Jump! Like a moth drawn to a flame,

Moe could not break the spell. The lure of the sea had complete control of his mind and body.

The glass doors slid open behind him, interrupting the trance the god of the seas had placed on him.

"What is the matter, cousin?" Larry asked as he drug a wicker chair over to the railing. "You look as white as the Americans, are you afraid of heights?"

Moe had never experienced a feeling like this before in his life. The ocean was like a magnet, pulling and pulling at him, almost taking complete control of his mind and body. It made him wonder if anybody had actually jumped. He would ask Jamil. He was curious.

"Nothing is the matter," Moe snapped back. He feared nothing. That was the face he wore. He was embarrassed and a little ashamed that anyone would think otherwise. Fear and sadness were two emotions that a fearless crusader like himself could never reveal.

"I feel euphoric, like the endorphins in your blood after a prayer," Moe told his cousin. He could feel the color returning to his face. "Our mission was a complete success, and we have begun to restore honor to the Hindi nation." Shep appeared through the glass doors, balancing two cups of the hot black tea, and he handed one to Larry. The three cousins raised their cups in the air and tapped the rims together in unison. Not a word was spoken as they toasted each other, as if it had been rehearsed, scripted. They were proud. Their faces glowed as they sat in silence, sipping their tea, each lost in their own thoughts.

"Let's go and celebrate," Moe said as he headed back inside the suite. "I'm hungry, we can eat and relax at the lounge downstairs by the pool."

The sand was wet all the way up to the dunes separating the long line of hotels and condominiums from the Gulf. The high tides exaggerated by the cold front was Mother Nature's way of housekeeping. Not a single piece of seaweed, foul-smelling kelp, or trash thrown overboard by the fishermen on the shrimp boats could be found. Pockets of bright white seashells and an occasional bright blue man-of-war jellyfish riding in on the turquoise waves and becoming stranded on the beach added contrast to the wet brown sand.

They sat at a table under the canopy of the cabana, ordered a seafood botana of peel-and-eat shrimp, fried oysters, and snow crab legs. Moe decided to order a dozen raw oysters on the half shell to nosh on while they waited. They weren't sure what drink. They asked the waiter to help them select something, It had to contain alcohol, and because they were at the beach, something tropical.

The waiter suggested a tequila sunrise. It was tropical, and it had orange juice in it. He mistook their lethargic demeanor for a hangover.

"The hair of the dog," the waiter told them.

"What dog?" Shep asked the waiter, craning his neck to look up at the man. "I do not want any dog hair in my drink! No dog hair!"

The waiter chuckled as he placed napkin-wrapped utensils down on the table. "You know," the waiter continued, "the hair of the dog that bit you last night." He could see that the cousins had no idea what he was talking about. "Just an old joke," he told them, opting not to explain. "No dog hair then," he sarcastically said as he headed toward the bar.

The hotel pool was next to the cabana and extended under the canopy and right up to the bar. Swimmers could float in on their rafts, or tubes, and order their drinks without getting out of the water. All the drinks were served in clear plastic cups, designed to resemble real glasses, champagne glasses, whiskey tumblers, water goblets, and even plastic shot glasses used for body shots made popular by the young wild college students.

There were three girls sunning themselves, lying on the lounge chairs just outside the protection of the canopy. Two of the ladies were lying facedown, appearing as if they were not wearing anything, giving the illusion of being completely naked, and the third was sitting up in her chair, rubbing cream on her arms. Their bodies were bronzed by the sun, all except for the cheeks of their asses and a thin line where their bra straps crossed over their shoulder and across their backs. The pink skin contrasting with the rest of their tanned bodies added to the illusion of them being naked. The girl in the middle started rubbing suntan lotion to her companions, alternating back and forth between the two. She looked up and noticed that she had drawn the attention of the cousins. She brought her left leg over to the right side of the chair and leaned over to pick up another tube of the sunscreen, intentionally entertaining the cousins, giving them full view of her breasts, all the way to her nipples. She poured a stream of the lotion down the back of the girl closest to the cousins. She slid the straps completely off her friend's shoulders and let them fall from her body. She spread the lotion evenly, from the girl's shoulders to just above her rear end. She poured a palmful of the lotion in her hand and began applying it to the girl's neck, using both hands to rub it in. She moved to her shoulders, massaging the sunscreen into the girl's body using the heel of her palm. As she migrated down the girl's back, she stopped, rose from her chair, and knelt down at her friend's head, facing the cousins. She applied pressure down the sleeping beauty's spine and pulled her hands out to her side, exposing the side of the girl's breasts. She looked up at the cousins again as she applied more lotion to her hands. She rubbed it down either side of the girl's waist then pulled back toward her shoulders, pulling the content girl's head into her crotch with each motion. As she slid her hands back down the girl's body, she rubbed the side of her bare breasts. As she pulled back, she subtlety slid her fingers inside the cup of her bikini bra in one smooth motion. She came back over to the girl's side and knelt down beside her. She dribbled cream on the cheeks of her bare ass and down the back of her legs, spreading the lotion evenly, as she did before, then moved to her feet and calves. Her friend flinched and raised one leg as the masseuse ran her fingers across the bottom of the girl's feet. She skipped the thighs and started rubbing the pink skin around the motionless girl's bare ass. She squeezed each cheek simultaneously, one in each hand, and when she would release them, they jiggled like underinflated water balloons. Then she moved down again and started rubbing the back of the girl's thighs, her patient raised her head up from the chair then laid it back down in the opposite direction, facing the third girl. The other girl seemed to be enjoying the show as much as the cousins and looked as if she was going to get up and join in.

The masseuse put her hands between the girl's knees, and she voluntarily spread her legs without any prodding, responding to a subtle cue, one she seemed to be familiar with.

The cousins were completely transfixed with the ménage à trois. They could not believe it. Here they were in a public place, watching girl-on-girl porn being performed live, seeming just for their pleasure. They were alone except for the waiter, not that it would have mattered to the girls. To the cousins' disappointment, they could see the girl's crotch was covered. A thin strap ran up between her cheeks and high over her hips. The masseuse started rubbing the lotion on the inside of the girl's thighs and drew her hands up the girl's ass, dragging her manicured fingernail along the girl's crotch, following the strap of her thong, all the way to the small of her back. She paused, applied more lotion to her finger, and looked over at the cousins and rubbed the cream over the lips of her partially open mouth. She started over at the small of the girl's back. This time she spread the girl's cheeks; as she did, the girl pushed up on her knees, her ass in the air, her head down, and looked back between her legs toward the cousins. She looked like a cat just waking up from a nap and stretching its body, extending its claws. They could almost hear her purr.

Another couple arrived at the pool and sat at a poolside table across from the masseuse and her friends. People were starting to emerge, like bears coming out of hibernation after a cold winter, to take advantage of the long-overdue sunshine.

The masseuse slapped her costar on the ass, got up, and dove into the swimming pool. The cousins couldn't tell if she was being playful with her friend or if she was frustrated that she couldn't continue with her performance.

The waiter arrived at the table with three colorful drinks on his tray. He sat one down in front of each cousin. The goblets were half filled with a red liquid, topped off with what looked like orange juice. A rainbow-colored umbrella, two impaled red cherries protruding out of the plastic cup, and an orange slice garnished the brim.

"What is this?" Moe asked the waiter with disgust.

"Tequila sunrise," the waiter happily replied. "It has grenadine, orange juice, and tequila. You said you wanted something tropical, try it, it's good." The waiter could sense that Moe was upset about something. "It is our most popular drink, very good quality tequila."

"Popular with the girls?" Moe said as he grabbed the umbrella from the cup and tossed it under the table. "This is a girly drink, do we look like girls?" he said as he handed the drink back without even looking at the waiter. "Bring me something with one color and no bows or ribbons or flowers and no umbrella…bring us a man's drink."

The culture here was much different than he was accustomed to. Girls having sex with each other in public was unheard of in India. You could buy it, enjoy it in private, but never in public.

If a waiter brought a man a drink with an umbrella in it at home, it would be considered an insult and taken as a challenge. A man would be within his rights to defend his honor on the spot, by any means available. In some provinces, even murder was an acceptable punishment to defend his virility. Larry and Shep followed suit. They surrendered their drinks to the waiter, just as the masseuse was swimming up to the bar.

"Waiter!" Moe called to the man as he was retreating back to the bar, before he could disappear again.

"Si, senor?" the waiter asked, expecting to be chastised again. He knew the cousins were special guests of the owner and were to receive the VIP treatment.

"Put a new umbrella in those drinks, and send them over to the girls outside. Tell this one in the pool, she is with them." The waiter went over and spoke to the masseuse as she was stepping out of the water. He turned and pointed to the cousins' table. She stood there looking at the cousins as he spoke to her. She tugged on the straps of her bikini, pulling up on the thong, showing off every crease in her anatomy. She smiled at the cousins, gave a half wave, and dove sideways back into the pool, splashing water at the foot of the table.

The waiter returned with drinks for the cousins and fresh umbrellas in the tequila sunrises for the porn stars.

The waiter passed on the thanks from the girls. He told them that they were college girls from the Midwest here for spring break. They appreciated the gesture.

The cousins felt confident. They were empowered by last night's events, and they were excited. They had heard the tales of the promiscuous college girls. They traveled miles away from home to party, and they were able to act out their fantasies without inhibitions. Moe sent another round over to the girls, and they were giggling and pointing back at the three men.

They guzzled down another drink, to bolster their courage, then divided the girls amongst themselves before they approached the table. It would be awkward to compete against each other for the same prize.

Moe stood, electing himself to approach the girls first and invite them back to join them at their table. He was about halfway to the girls' table when three men arrived. The girls stood, retrieved their towels, and headed off toward the beach with them. One of the girls, the masseuse, turned and mouthed "Thank you" to Moe. Not wanting to look foolish, without breaking stride, Moe headed to the restroom.

"Oh well," he said to the other two men when he got back to the table. "We need to get more ammo anyway. I will ask Mr. Julian to get us some girls too, maybe we can meet him tonight. I will call him," he told his cousins, trying to make a bad situation better. "We need to wash Jamil's truck and return it anyway."

*****

Julian sat at the mesquite table in his villa, nursing a bottle of Topo Chico. He was just sitting, staring at the suitcases stacked in the corner of the room. He was surprised at how much money was there, a lot more than there should have been from that one deal. Well, it was supposed to be his money anyway, he justified, and now it was, so La Hormiga would consider it interest paid on the account.

Julian was putting this deal together for a few weeks, and he had done business with this client before. Normally he would receive partial payment up front, earnest money, and collect the balance after the product was delivered. But not directly. The payment was paid through different mules, allowed to take their predetermined cut, and by the time the money changed hands, three and sometimes up to five times, everyone was paid. What was delivered to him was his, his bottom line after expenses. Julian was a businessman, not much different than those running corporations. He knew what his profit line was, and any expenses above that would be passed along to the buyer, who in turn passed it along to the consumer. Supply and demand. Simple economics applied to his business as well.

When Julian started out, he would offer his product at a discount. At that time, he could do most of the work himself. He was physically involved in every step of the process, keeping his overhead low. Now, he was well-known in the business. He had become a reliable, dependable supplier, and his clients were willing to pay a premium for the service. He was becoming well-known to everyone, his competition and law enforcement, on both sides of the border, the price of fame. But with his notoriety, he had to take extra precautions. He rarely went anywhere now days without his pistoleros, his bodyguards. In this business, you had to be willing to kill or be killed. There were few, if any, retired drug dealers. They were either in prison or in the ground, but the financial rewards outweighed the consequences. The attitude "This won't happen to me, I'm different" is common to all.

Now he rarely got his hands dirty. He set up the deals, did all the logistics, and saw the job through, not unlike the CEO of Walmart. He has had to keep up with the times. The early days was just marijuana. Now it was anything in demand, anything from methamphetamines to black tar heroin and anything in between, even human trafficking. Julian could see the trend was pointing to smuggling illegal aliens, and this worked well for him. They could serve a dual purpose. He could use them as mules, especially on the flats. The illegals would be perfect to carry the product across the wetlands from the river to the ship channel. Some of the young girls were preselected at the stash houses in Mexico and cut out of the group, like cattle being culled from the herd, some to be used as domestics, as maids; the others, the prettiest ones, would be sold into the sex trade.

He was looking at a lot of money, his money, and he didn't have to split it with anybody. The pistoleros thought the boxes contained ammunition, and it would stay that way, and most of them did, but they had no reason to know about the money. Julian spent a lot of his time putting the deal together, but just as any well-laid plan, there were unforeseen circumstances. The marijuana was late from his supplier. The product had to be rerouted from Chihuahua because the cartels were having turf wars. The territory disputes were affecting the timely deliveries. The gangs had to avoid each other's roadblocks and the ones set up by the military. Traveling the roads in Mexico has become a risky venture for everybody. The roadblocks were becoming commonplace, and buses were being boarded by cartel members in search of rival gangs, and any suspects were taken off the bus and executed on the spot, right out in the open, in front of everybody. Sometimes all the able-bodied men were taken off the busses and forced to fight each other, the winners forced to join the cartel; the losers were shot, murdered. One bus was taken to the outskirts of Matamoros. The passengers were taken into a barn and executed, men, women, and children, even the driver, all innocent with no apparent motive. No judge. No jury. No trial. There wasn't one. They had no resistance from the populace. People feared that if they spoke up, they would be targeted, and they were. The lack of resistance only served to empower the cartels. The cartels were using Middle Eastern tactics to carry out their executions. Bodies were commonly found decapitated, posing with different victims' heads in their arms, headless bodies hung upside down from overpasses on busy city streets and major highways, usually displaying a banner warning of what would happen if you crossed them. They were becoming more brazen, bolstered by the unchecked reign of terror on the country, challenged only by rival cartels and law enforcement.

The government would get on their soapboxes and declare the country safe and the military in charge, parading prisoners before the cameras, their black-and-blue bodies on display and producing their confessions for all to see. But the public wasn't fooled. The evidence proved otherwise.

The load Julian was supposed to deliver was a week late at its final destination near Playa Baghdad. There was an advance look-out leaving Chihuahua, looking for rogue patrols and pop-up check-points. They had to turn around and return to their point of origin or risk losing the merchandise. Julian, tired of the delays, hired a small cargo plane to transport and drop the merchandise on the wet sands of the beach. The pilot had to contend with clouds concealing the rocky peaks of the Sierra Madres and the overcast skies along the coast, but finally he delivered—a week late.

The plan was to transport the load twenty miles inland and smuggle it into the United States near where the levee ends. The dope was packaged in fifty-pound bundles, wrapped in black plastic and duct tape, with two rope loops entwined into the bale, used as arm straps and carried like a backpack. The mules would carry the bundles north from the river, following the drainage ditch across Highway 4, right under the nose of the Border Patrol checkpoint, all the way to the Brownsville city landfill. The drugs would be loaded into a parked city brush truck, identified by a number to be given to Julian by the contact, passed on to the mules, and delivered to the client first thing in the morning. When the drugs were safely across the river, Julian contacted his client. Just as he had to be paid in layers, his client had to be contacted the same way. A lot of the times their identification was never discovered. Julian was sure he knew who this one was. They had done business before.

"The horses have left the gate," Julian said to the contact. He was using a throwaway phone, readily available at any convenience store. Used once, then tossed, no way to trace the number back to the caller.

"The horses are neck and neck," Julian told the contact, letting him know that everything was going smoothly.

"What is your speed index?" Julian was asking for the number of the brush truck, there were at least ten trucks parked at the land-fill, and each had a number painted on the fender. Somebody would sure be surprised if the drugs were put into the wrong truck.

The speed index is a number given to a quarter horse, indicating his speed at a certain race track, almost similar to the handicap given to a golfer, not exactly, but similar. Julian liked to use racehorse metaphors; they came naturally to him, growing up around the brush tracks in Mexico.

"Bought new horses last week," the voice on the line replied.

"Que chignon!" La Hormiga yelled into the phone. "I have horses leaving the gates ahora mismo."

"I told you your horses are too slow," the voice said without emotion. Julian knew that the man on the other end of the line was just a peon. It was like calling about a defective product and speaking to someone in China. They had scripted answers and can't, or won't, think for themselves. You can argue until you are blue in the face, you can yell and scream at them, but it won't do a bit of good. They're just going to give you the scripted, unemotional answers.

"You get El Jefe to call me now!" Julian kept yelling at the voice on the other end of the line, hoping to intimidate him to convey his message to the client, his boss.

"I am telling you that we have already purchased different horses." The voice was calm and deliberate. "A racehorse must be fast and reliable," the man said, emphasizing *reliable*.

Julian had run into a situation beyond his control. He was aggravated with himself. He should have had the foresight to predict the problems with the roadblocks in Mexico. They had been all over the news and graphically depicted in the newspapers like *El Dia*. It was getting more difficult every day to do business in Mexico, on either side of the law. In the past, the different cartels would do business together. As long as the "tariffs" were paid, all was good, but that isn't the case any longer. Greed is a powerful motivator, and because all the factions were becoming more and more greedy, doing business was getting harder and harder. One side didn't want to see the other side succeed. "If we can't have it, then they can't have it" seemed to have become the creed. This cultural mentality is compared to a pot of boiling crabs. When the water gets hot and a crab tries to climb the side of the pot to escape, the other crabs grab him and pull him back into the boiling cauldron. If I can't have it, then neither can you.

This is the way things are done now, a sign of the times. If you think someone has your back, think again. He probably has a knife in his hand.

It's not much different from when the settlers passed through the Indian territory. They had to be very careful not to be detected. If they were discovered, they paid the high price for trespassing. The women were raped and scalped, and the men were tortured and scalped. The children that looked like good prospects were taken prisoner and used as slaves, and some, used as breeding stock.

The times have changed, and the motives have changed, but the consequences remain the same. Enter my backyard, and if I catch you, you pay a price. The penalties are just as horrific now as they were over a hundred years ago. Maybe you won't get scalped, but you will get decapitated, disemboweled, sexually mutilated, cut into pieces, or all the above. Scalping may be on the list; it just hasn't been applied yet.

Julian was pissed. But what was done was done, no sense looking back at what might have been. Look forward and see what must be done to correct it. First of all, he had to get his load back to Mexico without getting caught, then his inventory needed to be secured at a safe place, one he had in mind for just an occasion as this. He used small vans to transport his narcotics instead of pickup trucks because they were less obvious, bland vehicles that didn't draw much attention. The vans split up and headed to a ranch outside Matamoros, and the bundles of marijuana would be stacked in a barn of alfalfa hay. Alfalfa is a perfect disguise; it has a sweet aroma that will mask the strong smell of the weed. If for any reason there was a fire, burning marijuana and alfalfa smelled exactly alike.

And it added another element of risk to the deal gone bad. The more he had to handle and store the drugs, the higher the risk, the better the odds were of getting caught. And it was very labor intensive. The pistoleros hated it. The heavy alfalfa bales had to be unstacked, and the marijuana bundles placed in the middle, then the hay was restacked around the dope. The alfalfa bales would blister the soft hands of the pistoleros, and the stems would chaff their arms. Then when it came time to move the load, the process had to be done all over again, in reverse. Julian would be forced to get rid of this load in a hurry. Time is money. The longer he held on to it, the riskier the deal became. He was pissed at himself for using the overland route to start with. He knew that the law of averages was against him. He became complacent, and there was no room for complacency in this business. The bottom line was he lost his client, and not only this sale, but any future sales with this dealer. In this business, there weren't any TV commercials or newspaper ads to advertise your product. You relied on your reputation; your reputation was your business card. Actions spoke volumes. Words meant nothing without the actions to back them up. Talk was cheap. If this client started spreading the word that Julian Gonzales-Gonzalez did not come through as promised, then his business would suffer drastically. And to have his old friend El Ojo Loco be the one to cut him out of the deal, to steal his client, just added salt to his wound. He was betrayed, and he took it personal. He gulped down the last of his Topo Chico and slammed the empty bottle down on the table. The impact of the glass bottle hitting the hard surface of the mesquite echoed off the stucco walls of the dining room and snapped Julian back into reality. He looked at the positive side. He had the money and the drugs, so even though he will have to sell at a discount, it will all be pure profit. In the short run anyway, he will still need to regain his reputation.

He must keep in mind that when Johnny figures out it was him that raided his house, there will be trouble, big trouble. And he will figure it out. He will know not to cross him again, steal his business, and pay the price. He got off easy this time. But he knew his old friend well enough to stay prepared, watch his back, and sleep with one eye open.

"Bueno," Julian said into the receiver of his third phone. This was the final day for this one. It would soon join the dozens of others at the bottom of the Rio Bravo.

"I need more food for my dragons." Julian immediately recognized the cousin's heavy accent.

The Indians had purchased their weapons from him a few days ago. He threw in just enough ammunition to let them try out the guns, and he banked on them being return customers.

"They are almost out of food, and they have a heavy appetite, and the dragon slayers are lonely." Julian knew that the dragons were guns, and food was ammunition. The cheap throwaway phones were supposedly untraceable, but codes were still used just in case.

"Are que? What?" Julian asked the cousin. "Dragon slayers?" He understood English better than he spoke it, but when a heavy Indian accent was added, he really had trouble deciphering the meaning.

"Lonely," Moe emphasized. "We want girlfriend." To hell with the code words, the cousins wanted to get laid! The spring break sirens back at the pool dominated their thoughts. Getting laid was now a priority.

"Oh mujeres, senoritas," Julian cackled back into the phone, disregarding the codes also. "Ladies," he said.

"Yes, yes," Moe answered before Julian finished his sentence. "Yes, ladies. But not here, at the El Jardin. We will meet you over there."

"Same comeda for the dragons?" Julian asked.

"Yes," Moe responded, "and some desert for their faster big brothers."

Julian knew what he meant, 9 mm and 223 for the AKs. "Ta Bueno," he said.

The cousins hurried back to the suite, changed from their beach attire, and donned more fitting clothes to go clubbing in Mexico. They crossed the causeway and stopped at an automatic car wash in Port Isabel to wash all the mud and crusted caliche from Jamil's truck. Someone had placed a SOCSOF sticker on the back window. Must have been some of those drunk spring breakers, they guessed. They excitedly drove the twenty-five miles to the El Jardin hotel, left Jamil's keys at the front desk, jumped into the Astro van, and headed across the Gateway Bridge to Garcia's with a new purpose. They were driven.

The cousins stood at the entrance of the cantina and let their eyes adjust to the dimly lit bar. The majority of the patrons appeared to be young spring breakers from the Midwest, ignoring the State Departments travel advisory not to go to Mexico. The alcohol boosted the young college kids' false sense of security and reinforced the "It won't happen to me" mentality. Garcia's and several other Mexican establishments were advertising heavily on South Padre Island, desperately trying to lure back the lucrative business they once enjoyed from the vacationing spring breakers. The local government in Matamoros ordered the police to be lenient on the tourists. Absolutely no arrests were to be made. Worst-case scenario, the students will be transported back to the port of entry and released, with the intent of spreading word of mouth advertising. By the time Texas week comes around, the island's busiest, Matamoros should be known as a safe place to party, and the American money would once again flow freely. Garcia's was even offering free shuttles from the island to the Gateway Bridge, but not across the border, just in case someone tried to cross some contraband.

Julian was sitting at the corner table with his back against the wall, the same table he and Johnny were at earlier. Moe led the trio across the room. He had his chin in the air, and his arms extended with his palms up, expressing his disappointment at seeing Julian alone at the table. He looked to the tables on either side of Julian and didn't see any women, just men at the nearest ones, and they weren't sharing with any women, and the table closest to Julian was empty.

"Sientate," Julian said, gesturing to the chairs. He didn't stand to greet the cousin. "Sit," he said.

Julian didn't like the Indians. They were coming to the United States in droves, and Julian didn't like it at all. They were taking over a lot of the businesses, businesses the Mexican should have. It aggravated him when they would speak in their native tongue right in front of him. To him it was intentional rudeness. It made him feel insecure that they must be saying derogatory things about him. Most of them spoke many languages, and they were fluent in both English and Spanish, so why else would they speak Hindi in front of him, unless they had something to hide, or they were speaking badly of him, insulting him. And they were very pushy. They would interrupt the waiter when he was busy taking orders from other tables, with total disregard for the other customers. No, he didn't care for the Indians or their culture. It was just a matter of time, he surmised, before they would be coming to Mexico, bringing their families, their culture, their language, and they would demand you do business with them in their native tongue. Yeah, they were pushy, Julian knew, but they had money, and money they wanted to give to him. So he would tolerate them and do business with them, but he would never like them. Or trust them.

"Where are the ladies?" Moe asked, standing at the table, his arms still extended. Moe did all the talking for the cousins, all the time, especially when doing business. Larry and Shep knew their place, their stature in the pecking order. They completely understood that there could only be one front man, one voice. This was good for business and left no room for misunderstandings.

"Sit," Julian said again. This time he rose from his chair and extended his hand to Moe. He didn't want to stand, but he did. It was a show of dominance over the Indian, who was just a little shorter than him. He shook hands with all three of the cousins and gestured to the chairs again. The cousins sat facing the wall, facing Julian, a strategy he used to disadvantage unsuspecting clients, just in case anything was to go wrong. Julian thought the Indians were naive, especially when it came to their surroundings, but he didn't mistake that for stupidity, they were far from that. They acted non-chalant, lackadaisical, but Julian could see through the facade. He could tell that there was something cold and calculating about them. He could tell that they were purpose driven.

"Ladies?" Moe asked again with a hint of disappointment in his voice. Julian looked over at the other two cousins. They looked like two little children, promised ice cream by their mother if they behaved. "We've been good! We've been good, Mama!" their expressions conveyed.

"Aye vienne," Julian answered him. "They will be here soon." He considered leading them on a bit, lift them up, then let them down, just to watch their expressions. He enjoyed having the upper hand. He could work them like marionettes.

"Let me sell you some food for your dragons first," Julian told them. He wanted to take care of business first and then have a couple of drinks to consummate the deal. He wanted something besides the Topo Chico. He always waited for the alcohol until the deal was finished. He was always clearheaded during negotiations. Alcohol loosens the tongue, makes people promise things they can't deliver. It minimizes obstacles that the sober mind will have to hurdle. In this business, you must deliver, as Julian well knows.

The cousins ordered enough ammunition to start a small war. Julian had sold them ammo before, so he knew they were reliable customers. They offered a prepared cover story, that they were going to supply Indian guerillas to defend themselves against Pakistani incursions. Julian really didn't care one way or another. As long he was paid in US currency, they could take over all of Asia as far as he was concerned. They haggled over the exorbitant prices of the ammunition, many times what it used to cost legally in the United States, but they paid it. They had no choice. Supply and demand. Free enterprise. Anyway, money was no object.

The details were worked out, new phone number, delivery date and location, and drinks ordered.

"Ladies?" Moe asked again, raising his chin and turning his palms up on the table.

"Por ahi, mira." Julian pointed to the bar and made a circle motion with his arm. "Look over there," he said. All the barstools were occupied by women, except for the two bookend men. "The one in the middle is for me," he told the cousins, turning around in unison, not appearing to be listening. "Take your pick from the others, anyone you want, and I will call them over." He pointed to the vacant table next to them, but they weren't paying attention.

"Any of them?" Shep asked, not turning around.

"Any or all of them, todos." Julian laughed as he stood and raised his glass. "Salude."

*****

Johnny's mind was going a hundred miles an hour as he drove home to the ranch. "What is that son of a bitch up to?" He reran the meeting with Julian over and over in his head. The two men at the bar, why didn't Julian tell him those were his men, was he expecting trouble? It was common to have security around, but the two of them had known each other for a long time, and Johnny would have let him know if he had people with him. If for no other reason than they wouldn't be mistaken for the enemy if something were to go down. Professional courtesy, Julian should have told him those were his men. And he seemed edgy, and especially when Johnny was relating the episode about the ranch. He seemed defensive. "Why would he think I was accusing him?" Johnny wondered. And Julian wouldn't look him in the eye. He would look at the floor and the ceiling, and his eyes darted back and forth uncharacteristically. Edgy. And he was really evasive about the floater. Something was off with him. Johnny had dealt with a lot of unscrupulous people around the tracks. He had a good instinct. He was a good judge of character. La Hormiga always looked him in the eyes when they spoke, not stare, but eye-to-eye contact, especially when he was confronted about something. Johnny wasn't challenging him, but he was acting like he was being accused. He was defensive. Too defensive.

And the floater. The floater still bothered Johnny. Besides the torture and execution of the man, and the obvious connection to the random murders at the dairy, there was something. But what. It consumed him all the way home.

Johnny drove down the long driveway to the house. The giant spiders created by the shadows of the sentinel palm trees were still waiting patiently for their prey.

It was odd not having the dogs greet him, barking at the tires as he approached the house. The blue heelers weren't an aggressive breed, and their size wasn't intimidating, but they would always bark an advanced warning to anyone, friend or foe, approaching the house. They were very persistent and wouldn't give up the alarm until someone from the house came to investigate and reassure the dogs that the danger had passed. Many times, Johnny had to run off lovers who used the isolated road to the ranch as a rendezvous point for their tryst, a sad reminder of the invasion, and he could feel the angst building up again. He replaced the dogs, with a larger, more aggressive breed. He knew he would have to replace the pug too, and he knew he would have to get over his distaste for the slobbering, asshole exhibitionist that the pup would grow into. He could do that for the girls. He did it once, he could do it again. He replaced the heelers with Blue Lacy's. They were the state dog of Texas, bred for hogs and deer and used as excellent catch dogs for wild cattle. They are very good family pets, loyal and protective, and just the right size. They were mostly gray, with a star on their chest, and if he cropped their ears, they would look like an intimidating Doberman Pincer. Intimidation is an excellent enforcement tool, and anyone, any sane person, should stay in their vehicles thinking the dogs will eat them alive, when actually, they would probably lick them to death.

Johnny called his wife on the cell phone to let her know he was home. He didn't want her to hear him coming through the door, thinking he was an intruder. She was still walking on eggshells, and the odds of her shooting and missing again were slim to none. She greeted him at the door, half asleep and wearing his heavy bathrobe. He wrapped his arms around her and squeezed her hard. He held on, not wanting to let her go. He pulled back, put his fingers to his lips, and pointed down the hall. He grabbed her shoulders, turned her around toward the bedroom, and slapped her on the ass, admiring her as she retreated.

He stood at the door of the bedroom, watching his little girls sound asleep, the purest form of innocence, he thought. He was rarely around them when they were asleep. He cherished the limited time he had spent with them, realizing that they were little angels. He wasn't hard on them, but he was firm. They were going to pull their weight around the ranch and learn a good work ethic, not grow up like the other kids spoiled by their parents and no respect for authority. They were going to learn, like he did growing up on the dairy, that you have to work for what you want. Nothing in life is free. Johnny Williams' kids will not be spoiled.

He watched them as they slept, lost in dreamland, not a care in the world. And as he looked at them, he realized they were just little babies, small frail babies, totally dependent on their daddy to protect them. As he stood there admiring his daughters, a lump swelled up in his throat. It sunk in that he wasn't here when it counted the most. He wasn't here when they needed his protection. He was tempted to sweep them up out of bed, one in each arm, and just squeeze them and never let them go. A little bit of innocence was stolen from them, and he vowed it would never happen again. It was as if he had an epiphany. A feeling he had never felt had swept over him, infiltrated his soul.

He had no choice but to work hard at the dairy. His parents weren't poor, but they weren't rich either. When Johnny was a boy, he thought his father was just mean, just made him work to make him work. He could never see the justice, that he had to work and the other kids could play all day, no responsibilities. Now as an adult, he understood that he had to work. It was just part of the dairy lifestyle. The animals relied on him for all their needs. They couldn't care for themselves. It was up to him to assure that they were fed and watered every day. But he couldn't see that as a kid. At that time he considered himself a slave. He wanted a way out. It was the drive for an easier life, easier money, and a stroke of bad luck from Mother Nature that landed him where he was now, on the wrong side of the law.

He made up his mind right there. He was going to spoil his little girls. They would have the rest of their lives to deal with all the challenges life would deal them. He had plenty of money now; he could afford it. He felt a huge wave of relief come over him. He imagined this was what being born again must feel like. He could have stood there all night, thinking of a million different ways he was going to make it up to them.

His wife was lying facedown on the bed, sound asleep. Her hair was covering most of her face, and she was drooling on the pillow through her half-opened mouth. She shed his bathrobe in a pile halfway between the door and the bed. Her nightgown was hiked up around her waist, her right leg was straight and the other bent at the knee and crossed over, looking like the number four, and her panties had ridden up on her butt like a thong, exposing one of her smooth, soft baby cheeks. Johnny was tempted to wake her up and indulge himself in long-overdue pleasure they both deserved. And he knew, even though she was fast asleep, she would willingly oblige him. He let common sense win over his animal instincts, knowing how exhausted she must be to fall so sound asleep this quickly. It made him feel good. She must feel safe now that he was home. Morning will be here soon, and he could make up for lost time then. Johnny stood there and admired her, realizing what a lucky man he was, to have a beautiful woman love him and want to spend the rest of her life with him. He was very self-conscious about what he considered his deformed face, and to have her choose him, yes, he was a lucky man. She had spent too much time alone, and that was going to change. Johnny vowed that he was going to devote the rest of his life to his family. He had enough money, a nice herd of cattle, and some fine horses. He would never need to work again. He just had one more thing he must do first.

The wind was beginning to blow out of the south again, indicating that another cold front was on the way. The humidity and heavy dew had returned, and both of Johnny's socks were soaked just from the short walk through the lawn to his truck. Some summers were extra hot and extra dry, and everybody prayed for rain. The pastures and lawns were brown from lack of moisture. Even the tropical ornamental plants were suffering, but not this year. It had rained every week since September. Every time it started to dry out, it rained again. The rain was good for the ranchers. There should be good spring pastures for a change, and good for the farmers, if it dries out enough for them to get their crops in the ground. Like the old-timers say, be careful of what you wish for.

This time of the year, the spring fronts will produce severe thunderstorms with drenching downpours and wind and hail damage, unlike the cold overrunning rains of the winter storms. But like another euphemism from the old-timers, never cuss the rain; you never know when you will see it again.

Johnny reached under the console of his truck, retrieved a copy of *El Dia*, and headed to his retreat in the barn. His hideaway was intended as a storm shelter for the family in case of a hurricane. The bunker was constructed of steel rebar-infused concrete block walls, the roof built with I beam purlins and lightweight concrete and tied to the foundation with one-inch rebar. Nothing was going to blow this bunker away. It was equipped with its own generator and plumbing. It had all the comforts of home, bathroom and kitchen and heavy-duty air conditioner. Johnny finished one of the inside walls with old corrugated tin and weather-worn cedar planks. The room had a regulation-sized pool table that could be converted for ping-pong. On the other side of the room was his desk and diamond tuck-and-roll executive chair, just like the one at his firm at the Mercado in Mexico. The wall behind the desk was adorned with pictures of paratroopers jumping out of c-130s and c-17s. They were file photos, but Johnny circled a paratrooper in each one and swore it was him. Other pictures of his army days, him carrying the company flag as Guidon, sharply clad in his class A uniform, bloused pants, and red beret. Others of him in the field, in full ruck, on patrol with his buddies. He was proud to be a soldier and reminisced about what could have been if it wasn't for Panama.

The hay barn was built around the bunker as an afterthought. Strangers to the ranch would never know it was there, the perfect camouflage, hiding in plain sight.

Johnny rocked back in his chair, put his boots up on the desk, and opened *El Dia* and spread it out on his lap. He stared at the grotesque pictures of the blood-soaked corpse, the full-color blowup concentrated on the dead man's face. Johnny didn't like looking at the lifeless decomposing head with its mouth agape, big green flies inside and out, but there was something familiar about him, and this was the only way he was going to figure it out. The nostrils were almost completely gone, eaten back to the cartilage by the fish and crabs, and two black holes revealed where the eyes had once been. The bullet wound was centered perfectly in the middle of his forehead, right between the scalp and his eyebrows, which were amazingly preserved in perfect condition. The killer wanted him to know he was going to die, cold, hard, matter-of-fact, here it comes. Boom, you're gone. Johnny wondered if he was killed on the river bank or somewhere else. He wondered if the victim knew he was taking his last ride. Between the decomposition and the consumption of the flesh by the marine life, most of his cheek was gone, exposing the inside of his mouth. This picture didn't trigger anything. He didn't get the feeling about him he did earlier. He turned the page to view some of the other pictures. They were panned out further than the front page but were just as graphic. Johnny thought about how sadistic these editors and photographers must be, showing every minute detail just to sell a copy of their paper for a few pesos. They didn't care. This could be a child killed in a car accident, and the pictures would still be just as graphic. One of the pictures showed the fully clothed body floating facedown in the water, arms and legs extended, his hair surrounding his head like a black halo. Another picture showing the police on the bank, throwing ropes at the corpse, like they were tossing a cast net to catch bait fish. A picture of the uniformed men pulling the lassoed man toward the shore, and yet another, a final picture showing a boot with a bone protruding from it. The decomposing foot had become detached from the rest of the body as it was being reeled to the bank. Johnny went over the pictures on the second page, time and time again.

There was something there, but he couldn't put his finger on it. He looked at the picture of the boot again. The noose of the rope was tight around the boot, and a loose coil was wrapped around the bone, still partially attached by the decomposing flesh, like an over-cooked drumstick. The police probably discarded the contaminated rope, only to be claimed by the poor kids from the *ejidos* and used as a jump rope or some other form of entertainment. Johnny looked closely at the boot. It appeared to be green, but he realized that it was covered with moss from the river. He went back to the other picture of the man floating facedown in the river. He could only see the heels of the boot. He studied the photo and could almost make out the belt on the bloated body. The body looked like a balloon with a string tied around the center, covering either side of the belt, revealing only a portion across the small of the back. His eyes darted back and forth between the pictures, only one boot visible. He studied it. He studied the belt. He went back and forth many times, looked at the pictures on the other pages, but he kept coming back to the boot and the belt. He didn't recognize anything on what was left of the man's face, but there was something about this guy. He looked at the boot again, then back to the belt. That was it! He could barely make out the scales on the boot, and the belt had the same pattern, scales. He went back to the front page and studied it again. He was beyond the gruesome aspect of the pictures. He was beginning to think like a forensic medical examiner, looking past the blowflies and the maggots and concentrating on the evidence. He could not see a tongue. Was the tongue eaten by the fish and crabs, or was it gone before he went into the water? The tongue is soft tissue and would be the first to decompose or be eaten. He knew this from growing up on the dairy. Farm animals would quickly decompose if they were left in the open on dry land, in the hot sun. But the body had been in the unusually cold water of the river. He looked back at the picture of the head on the front page. He could make out part of the tongue still in the victim's mouth.

That was it! This was him! The description his wife gave of her attacker, his belt, his boots, his tongue! This was the guy. His brain recognized the subliminal clues that his conscious mind could not see. He could not be positive, but his suspicions wouldn't let him leave it alone. Johnny felt a new rage infiltrate his body. He felt cheated that he wasn't the one to let this guy know he was going to die. Johnny never would have let him die from a bullet wound. He would have taken a long time to die! Put his hands on his wife! On his children! He would have died slow! He would have died knowing he was going to die and why.

Finding out who he was and his accomplices would be easy.

He vowed to himself and his sleeping family that he would become a changed man, a better man. He meant to keep that vow, to be the father and husband his family deserved. But first, he must give this stinking, rotten body's accomplices what they deserve. And he will!

*****

The small parking lot at the Fort Brown Border Patrol station was full when Gilbert arrived. He forgot how bad the road from the ranch to the highway was, and it took longer than he calculated. There was a group of protesters blocking the intersection of the expressway and East Avenue, carrying signs displaying a circle with a pistol and a line through it, chanting, "Save our children, save our future." All the local television stations had camera crews filming the small gathering of antigun protesters, some posing for pictures and selfies under the SOCSOF billboard.

A Border Patrol unit punched in his code at the gate to enter the secure area. It stayed open long enough for Gilbert to follow in behind him before the gate closed again. The agent slammed on his breaks, almost causing the county judge to rear-end the government vehicle. The agent approached Gilbert's truck with his hand on his weapon. The other agent came up on the passenger side, yelling at him to keep both of his hands on the steering wheel where he could see them. Another agent appeared out of nowhere, flung open the passenger door, and immediately his truck was surrounded by agents with their guns drawn and pointed at him. Gilbert slowly got out of the vehicle and identified himself and showed the agents his credentials. When they were verified, two agents escorted him to the conference room. With all the violence and cartel activity, strict security procedures had to be followed, and the agents had trained for unauthorized vehicles breaching the security gate. Everyone was on heightened alert.

The room was abuzz with people, most just standing around in small groups, gripping Styrofoam cups and eating pan dulce. Gilbert looked up at the clock on the wall, seven fifty-five. Technically, he wasn't late; the meeting was scheduled for eight o'clock, but he knew he should have been there at least half an hour early. There were several uniformed Border Patrol agents. He could tell by the insignias on their lapels that one of them was an A chief, two were supervisors, and the other three were line agents. The Brownsville Police chief was here with two of his commanders, and Hidalgo and Willacy County sheriffs were present and in uniform. One of them had one star on his collar, and the other had four. Gilbert never could quite understand how they determined how many stars to display. Politics. There were six men all wearing identical gray suits. Gilbert knew all of them. Two were US Customs special agents, two marshals, and two FBI. There was one man wearing a black felt cowboy hat with a Tom Mix crease in the crown, another wearing a ball cap with the USDA Mounted Patrol logo on the front of it. Both wearing blue denim jeans tucked into their high-top cowboy boots and each with a silver belt buckle fastened on their hand-tooled leather belts, badges hanging from the pocket of their khaki shirts. Gilbert knew one of them. He was a tick rider who patrolled the river near his ranch, the other obviously his coworker.

Cameron County sheriff Juan Aguliar was huddled with his chief investigator, the city attorney, and two council women deep in discussion about this morning's agenda. The sheriff looked at his watch then up at the door, just as Gilbert was coming in.

"Ah, Gilberto." He walked over and shook the judge's hand and gestured to the table at the front of the room, no time for discussion. They were going to be behind schedule. There were four place cards at the table, one for the sheriff, one for the county attorney, one for Gilbert, and one for his secretary.

"Let's get started," the sheriff bellowed to the audience. "Everyone, please take a seat." There were plenty of folding chairs, more than were needed.

"I want to thank everyone for showing up on such short notice," Gilbert said, opening the meeting. "It looks like all of the agencies are well represented." Gilbert rose from his chair at the table and stepped out into the open to address the audience. He was an excellent politician and knew how to work a crowd. He had the kind of voice that mesmerized people. He wasn't boisterous or monotone, just a natural speaker, a natural politician. His comfort and confidence connected well with the crowd. He could recite the alphabet, and the audience would probably hang on to every syllable in anticipation of the next. "I'm sure by now y'all have heard about the ranch hands executed at the dairy on 281 over the weekend." Gilbert was strolling back and forth, seemingly making eye contact with each person, making them feel as if he was only speaking to them. "Sheriff Aguliar and I spoke yesterday about the increasing spillover of violence into the Valley from Mexico. It has seemingly been subtle, sneaking up on us, and although we knew it was coming, nobody would say it. It's like the joke about the number we don't talk about...what number is that? Is the natural response...I said we don't talk about it! As the sheriff recounted all of the violence that occurred over the last year, it is obvious that something is going on." The judge was standing directly in front of the first row, his hands folded in front of him, like he was leading his congregation in prayer. He was so close that he was almost stepping on the police chiefs' toes. "When the sheriff called me yesterday to inform me about the killings at the dairy, it was like a slap in the face, like a bucket of cold water was poured over my head. How could we have overlooked something so obvious." The judge walked back over to the table and stopped right behind the sheriff. "Again, I want to thank y'all and apologize for the short notice. I know that everybody had to rearrange their schedules, but as I told the sheriff, we cannot put this off any longer. This meeting had to be held as soon as possible. We collectively need to put our heads together, share intelligence, and see if we can get a grip on this, sooner rather than later. And with that, I am going to turn this back over to the sheriff. Sheriff Aguliar."

While Gilbert was speaking, he had his hands on the sheriff's shoulders, a subtle gesture that conveyed the message of how much confidence the two had in each other. While not exactly true, they did have a lot of respect for each other. Gilbert knew the sheriff was a good and honest lawman, with the best intentions of the county in mind. Unlike his predecessor, who gave law enforcement in Cameron County a bad name. He was serving a five-year sentence at what was no more than a country club. He was on the payroll of the county and the cartel.

The sheriff liked Gilbert too, but he knew him for what he was, a politician. Just like he took the credit for calling this meeting. The sheriff knew that by making Gilbert think it was his idea in the first place, it would yield better results. And results are what count.

"Thank you, Judge," the sheriff said as he rose from his chair and followed Gilbert's lead, stepping out from the comfort of the table. "These two young men at the Williams dairy were not just murdered last night, you know, they were brutally tortured."

The sheriff was at a disadvantage following the judge. He wasn't nearly as eloquent a speaker. His speech pattern was soft and slow and, at times, hard to hear. The sheriff was starting to show his age. His short-cropped military-style haircut was almost completely gray, as was his pencil mustache, barely visible on his upper lip. He stood before the audience, his shoulders drooped, his hand at his side with his thumb in his pocket. His right hand was flipping the thumb break back and forth on his obviously empty holster. A nervous reaction from a seasoned law man not accustomed to being without his weapon. As the sheriff spoke, his chief investigator was pinning blowups of the crime scene photos on the wall.

"Like I say, you know," the sheriff said as he stepped back and pointed to the last four pictures on the wall. "El Dedo was crudely carved into the torsos of these two men, an obvious statement that they have betrayed the cartel, you know, a warning to anyone who may want to do so in the future. Which cartel did this, we don't know yet. It's like I say, you know, these guys want to be famous." One of the line agents walked up from the back of the room and handed the sheriff a laser pointer. "Plus, like I say, you can see from the other pictures that this man was sexually mutilated." The sheriff pointed to the picture of the naked lifeless body hanging upside down on the squeeze chute. "As you can see, his ear has been cut off and nailed to his body." He then aimed the laser at the other man with the partial message carved into him. "Like I say, they must have been spooked because they did not finish the message on this guy." Then he pointed the laser down to the scrotum on the ground. "We think they were going to make him eat the other man's *huevos*," the sheriff continued, his face contorted, clearly disturbed as he related the pictures. The sound of someone throwing up at the back of the room drew everyone's attention. As they all turned around to see what the distraction was, a young line agent was throwing up in the waste paper basket. "They were wet with his saliva, you know, and had possible teeth marks. The lab will determine for sure." He was flipping the strap on his holster more aggressively, louder, to the point of distraction. He realized what he was doing and snapped the strap back to the empty holster. The sheriff never acknowledged the person getting sick to his stomach in the back of the room. "Whoever did this was angry, very angry, but like I say, you know, no one has claimed responsibility. We have not taken any big loads, no big arrests, like I say, everybody must keep their ears on and listen." Everyone knew he meant *open*. "Listen for anything. Someone will talk. These machos will want to show their muscles." And with that, the sheriff went on to relate all the other murders that had occurred in the valley, brutally carried out like the one in Mexico. The murders at the city dump, the bodies found gutted in the river. They were all to be looked at again and see if there was some common denominator. "Like the body pulled from the Rio, you know, with his tongue cut out, most of these people were mutilated while they were still alive," the sheriff added.

After the sheriff spoke, everybody broke into small groups again, mainly to exchange names and phone numbers so that they could stay in contact with each other. They all had a positive attitude and a shared confidence that collectively they would be able to solve some of these gruesome murders and put an end to the killing fields that the valley had become.

The three sheriffs were together in the back of the room, when Sheriff Aguliar urgently motioned Gilbert over to join them. The four of them were huddled together in the corner of the room as if they were plotting the final winning play at the Super Bowl. Gilbert broke from the group, urgently clapped his hands as he headed back to the table at the front of the conference room.

"Everybody please take their seat again, just for a minute." He was hoping he caught everyone before they left. "The sheriffs of the neighboring counties, Willacy and Hidalgo, have heard rumors around the sale barns and feed lots that something bad was going to happen to the cowboys. At this point it is just speculation, but everything is on the table. We aren't ruling anything out. A body was found on a ranch in Raymondville last week with the letter W carved into his forehead. This may just be a coincidence, but we are looking into everything. The sale barn in Edinburg has reported several strange men hanging around the loading area after hours, nothing illegal yet, but they are probably staking out the area. We are not going to put this out to the public yet. We don't want panic in the streets. Keep your eyes open."

The tension in the room grew, now everyone realized that this could be a much larger epidemic of violence than earlier thought and not just isolated to Cameron County.

Gilbert looked around the room at all the agents with eerily empty holsters, some nervously tapping on them, exhibiting the insecurity of being unarmed in these uncertain times. What if someone got through security and came blasting into the station? No one could defend themselves. All their weapons were checked into the armory. How would that read in the newspapers?

Gilbert recalled the conversation he had with Jamil and realized that there was something seriously wrong with this picture.

"This is exactly what we hoped to accomplish here today," Gilbert was shouting excitedly to the crowd. "Let's put our intel to work and see if we can ID some common denominators." He sounded like a coach at a high school pep rally. "Let's get to work. We have set up a hotline at the Sherriff's Office, let's make it pay off."

Gilbert made the rounds, thanking each one personally for showing up on a Monday with such short notice, and leaving with an enthusiastic attitude.

The room thinned out. Gilbert, the sheriff, and a handful of agents were still milling around.

"Sheriff," a Border Patrol agent stopped the sheriff and Gilbert just as they were leaving, "I almost forgot all about this, but on the night of the dairy murders, one of our units was involved in a vehicle accident on 281." The agent related, "One of our patrol agents responding noticed a white 4x4, not sure of the make, but a crew cab, four door, pulling out of the Los Fresnos Pump road. He got a partial on the plate, SPI, the truck was covered with mud, so that was all he could get."

As he related the information, he could tell by the look on the sheriff's face that this was more significant than he thought. "I'll get his report and CC it to you ASAP," the agent told him.

"This is what we are doing here." Gilbert grinned and slapped the agent on the back. "Get that to the sheriff today."

*****

The three Astro vans left the Baghdad Highway and drove down a small, well-drained path, straddling a thin brushy loma. The small, barely visible road dropped down to a low grassland submerged in standing water by the recent rains and the tidal flow from the Gulf of Mexico, five miles to the east. Four men were waiting there, standing under a lone ebony tree, swatting at the mosquitoes with willow branches. Four saddled horses and eight burros were staked out, tethered to the scrub brush, swatting at the mosquitoes with their tails and kicking at their bellies with their hooves. The salt flats were spillovers from the river and the bay, normally dry in the summer months and wet in the winter, and excellent mosquito hatcheries, keeping the swarms well stocked year-round.

No time was wasted. Everyone had a job, and they knew what to do. The vaqueros led the burros, one by one, over to the vans, and the three drivers helped the men transfer the marijuana from the vehicles to the donkeys. The first seven burros were loaded, the dope secured to the pack saddles with ratchet straps, each animal carrying four fifty-pound bundles—two hundred pounds per burro.

Each bundle was wrapped in a layer of burlap and a layer of black plastic, and due to all the rain and standing water, a third layer of clear cellophane was added as a precaution. Wet marijuana will mold and spoil rapidly, ruining the product, making it unsellable. Julian didn't want to injure his reputation further, so he took the extra precaution of the third wrap, making the effort to regain the respect he once enjoyed. The first donkey was stomping his hooves and pawing at his lowered head as the last bundle was being secured to the packsaddle. As the vaquero reached under the burro to grab the strap, the animal's broom tail swatted him right in his open eyes. Blinded, eyes burning, the vaquero instinctively kicked the donkey, making contact in the rear belly, near the animal's flank. The burro jumped in the air, kicked the vaquero in the elbow, unloading all four bundles of the marijuana into the wet grass and one into the mud created by the pawing hooves. The vaquero screamed in pain, holding his bleeding elbow, blood dripping through his fingers onto the ground. The three pistolero van drivers scrambled to pick up the marijuana and get it up off the wet ground and back into the van. The three bundles that landed in the grass were wet on the outside, but dried off easily thanks to the cellophane. The other one didn't fare so well. It was torn open by the sharp hoof of the panicked animal.

"Pinche pendejo, you stupid son of bitch," Julian said in a low but commanding voice as he started toward the wounded vaquero. One of the pistolero van drivers grabbed him by the sleeve of his windbreaker, breaking his momentum. He ushered his boss over to the van, long enough for him to regain his composure. The body-guard was lucky that La Hormiga didn't turn his anger on him. He had killed his employees for a lot less reason. Julian watched as the men dried off the bundles that had fallen in the grass, but the other one was going to need to be rewrapped. The water had enough time to penetrate into the weed before it could be retrieved from the mud hole, and the outside was caked with black slimy clay, and all the cellophane and black plastic had to be removed. They were able to reach through the torn burlap and pull out the wet marijuana by the fistful and toss it out onto the ground. The burlap was pulled back into place and rewrapped with the black plastic, but the cellophane kept sticking to itself, sticking to the wet grass, and coating itself with the black slimy clay. No matter how they tried to reattach it to the bundle, it wouldn't cooperate. When it was finally spread out symmetrically, one end would coil back and reattach to itself like it was magnetized. Finally, out of frustration, and due to the time con-straints, one of the pistoleros crumpled it into a ball and tossed it into the mudhole that created the problem to start with. The rewrapped bale was obviously damaged, and no matter how they tried to hide the defect, it was out of shape and not uniform with the rest of the load. It resembled a present that the children had rewrapped after peeking at it before Christmas.

The pistoleros weighed their options, keep the bale and maybe peddle it themselves later, throw it in the brush and blame it on the vaqueros, or just hope that the customer wouldn't notice. They agreed that the last option wasn't going to work. If all the wet dope wasn't removed, it would contaminate the rest of the bale. The bundle was obviously misshaped, obviously tampered with, and obviously missing most of its wrapping. Julian decided to haul it. The load needed to be balanced on the burro anyway. He would explain to the buyer and sell it to him at a discount or just keep it and toss it in the brush.

They still had to trek a half mile to the river through mud and sacahuista grass, then unload the burros, cross the dope, repack the animals, and travel another five miles to the ship channel, then repeat the process all over again. The odds of the bale making it all the way to delivery without getting wet were pretty slim, and that was if they didn't encounter any rain or drizzle that hovered along the coast this time of year.

The pistoleros watched the three vaqueros load the marijuana onto the burros. The injured man stood aside, holding his elbow, still dripping blood onto the ground.

"Vente pa ca," Julian called to the wounded vaquero, his voice still low but firm. "Come help your friends load the burro, pendejo"

The vaquero just stared back at La Hormiga, with dark defiant eyes.

"Vamos, let's go," Julian told him again. "I'm not going to tell you again." Julian told him in Spanish, "You work like the rest of them, you let the burro get the best of you, pendijo, that's your fault, your problem, vamos!"

The vaquero didn't budge. He just stared back defiantly at Julian. He was a cowboy; he was used to working alone in his nomadic lifestyle, tending to his herd of cattle that free grazed the Mexico salt flats, rarely encountering any people except for the occasional shark fisherman who camped along the Rio Grande. He made his own decisions and suffered the consequences when he was wrong, like kicking the burro, and he was paying for it. He did not know who he was challenging. He had no idea who the man ordering him around was. In fact, he hardly even knew the other vaqueros he was working with. They approached him about trailing some burros across the river and offered him enough money he would be able to buy more cattle for himself. He didn't even need to think about it. The easiest money he would ever make, he thought.

Julian stared back into the man's cold black eyes, the man defiantly standing his ground and holding his bleeding elbow. "Para te jefe," the pistolero urged Julian to stop. "We need him"

Julian closed the gap, and the two stared at each other, face-to-face, like two prize fighters before a bout, each trying to intimidate the other. Julian took a half step back, kicked the vaquero right in the ass, knocking him to the ground. "Vamos pendejo." This time Julian's voice was raised, and it carried off into the distance. Before his foot was back on the ground, the vaquero drew his knife with his good hand and stepped into Julian's space.

The report of the 9 mm was deafening. The weather was calm, and the evening air was cool. The 9 mm gunshot sounded like a cannon going off on the coastal plain. One round caught the vaquero in his good shoulder, spinning the man around and knocking him to his knees. The other missed its target altogether.

Julian looked back at the pistolero, the one holding the gun. Neither man said a word, but it was understood that Julian was grateful.

The donkeys and horses tried to bolt, startled by the gunshots, but they were all tethered to each other and didn't get far. The vaqueros had their work cut out for them constraining the spooked animals but were finally able to gain some control.

Everybody's senses were acute now. The gunshots blasting off into the distance even startled the wildlife and waterfowl. The birds that were settling down in the shallow water to roost for the night all took to the air in unison. It was as if they had been choreographed, white pelicans, with their eight-foot wingspans and distinctive black flaps, great egrets, that could easily be mistaken for pterodactyls, flocks of migrating Canadian geese and sand hill cranes all took to the skies together as one huge flock.

The vaqueros still busy settling the burros, were amazed by what they just witnessed. Living the isolated lifestyle of the Mexican cowboy, they had escaped all the violence that had become endemic along the border. They were scared.

Julian stepped back toward the wounded man, who was trying to get back up on his feet. The vaquero couldn't use either arm now. He just made it up on one knee, when Julian's boot connected with the side of his head and knocked him back to the ground. The vaquero's knife was lying beside him, but with two bad arms, he wasn't able to reach for it. As Julian bent down to retrieve the knife, the vaquero spat on his golden crucifix that was dangling in his face. The vaquero's cold black pupils dilated as the knife blade severed both of his jugular veins and windpipe as if they were made from Manteca.

One of the vaqueros threw up as he watched his campanero thrash around on the muddy ground convulsing in his own blood. The gurgling sound of the pink fluid oozing out of both sides of the man's severed esophagus was more than the seasoned vaquero could take. Julian ordered them to drag the lifeless body off the trail and stash it behind a stand of prickly pear cactus. The men jumped up without hesitation and dragged the corpse to his grave, knowing the consequences of questioning their boss.

Julian told the men that he would be taking the dead man's place and would ride his horse and trail the burros to the river. The vaqueros fell all over themselves getting the horse and burros ready for him. They didn't know who this ruthless killer with the quick temper was, but they weren't about to cross him. La Hormiga. The fire ant. A man they will never forget.

*****

The judge was on a conference call with commissioners from precincts 1 and 7, finalizing agenda items for next week's commissioners court hearings. They were reviewing standard items that needed the courts blessing, lights for a soccer field on Browne Avenue, paving some of the rural roads—caliche was once good enough, but now the people were demanding asphalt—and approving a memorandum of understanding for a Customs Border Patrol radio tower to be built on county property. The radio issue was a high-priority item. Communication on the border was an absolutely essential necessity for officer safety and protection. Most of the areas the border patrol agents patrolled were isolated and remote locations, and when backup assistance was needed, it was needed immediately. Communication was a vital lifeline for the agents, who for the most part, patrolled alone. After the 9-11 attacks on America, an executive order was issued mandating that all agencies have the capability to communicate with each other and share intel between themselves and their civilian law enforcement counterparts.

The MOU between the county and CBP was already approved once, and construction of a three-hundred-foot radio tower was well underway. The foundation had already been poured, electric supply installed, and the ten-foot-high security fence was complete. Everything came to an abrupt halt when the county attorney received an urgent phone call from the director of the Brownsville-South Padre Island International Airport.

The construction caught the eye of a FedEx pilot on final approach to the airport. The prevailing winds were normally out of the south, but there was still a slight breeze out of the north from the lingering cold front, so the landing pattern was from the opposite direction than it normally was. Otherwise the construction error may have continued indefinitely, going unnoticed until it was maybe even completed.

When the plane was taxiing to the gate, out of curiosity the pilot asked the tower about the construction on the airport perimeter, assuming it was an upgraded navigational aide being added to the airport. The FedEx pilot informed the tower that the construction was directly in front of runway 31. Any tall structure would interfere with approaches and departures from either direction and prevent the runway from being used.

The air traffic controller immediately notified the airport director, who in turn notified the city and county engineers.

Gilbert couldn't believe that this major detail was overlooked by everyone involved. It would have been discovered long before any aircraft or lives were risked, but that was not the point. All the time and money that had already been spent on the project was all for nothing. Not to mention the twenty-year lease contract signed by the land owner. Hopefully, a settlement will be made, Gilbert hoped, but what a waste of taxpayer money. The cost would ultimately be absorbed by the county.

The blame was shared by all involved. Even the FCC and the FAA didn't catch the error.

But that didn't ease the political pressure that was coming in from all directions, and now they needed to find a new location for the tower. The county-owned property on Southmost road, next to the levee, and it may be the only option at this point. The two acres were passed over the first time due to the proximity to the river and the high amount of illegal alien traffic. The Border Patrol and the county law enforcement would need to step up to the plate and make sure the site was secured at all times. There were no other options.

Gilbert's cell phone was ringing. It was Jamil. The judge excused himself from the conference call for a few seconds. "Hey, Jamil," the judge said, "I'll call you right back, I'm on a conference call."

"Don't forget, Gilbert, it is very important." He could hear the urgency in Jamil's voice.

"Give me twenty minutes at most," Gilbert replied.

The judge got back on the call and apologized to the commissioners and resumed the agenda discussions. Gilbert looked at his watch, 4:58 p.m. He was hoping to be at the ranch by 5:00 p.m. Not going to happen. The commissioner from precinct 1 was having a problem with the new proposal site, and he was a stickler for details. He wanted to dissect every word and rehash points that had already been resolved.

Gilbert could hear someone trying to call in but decided not to look. He could check the caller ID and return the call later, hoping to get this call over with. The commissioner was now proposing the construction of a bullet-proof building to house the radio and the repeater. "We have received gunfire from across the river, some rounds striking the buildings at the college, even hitting a vehicle and breaking out the windshield." He was right about that, Gilbert knew, but luckily no people were hurt. "Border Patrol agents and the Tick

Riders are routinely pulled back to the US side of the levee because of these running gun battles in Matamoros."

Gilbert's cell phone rang again. Sheriff Aguliar.

"Excuse me again, I need to check a call on my cell. Give me a second." With that, Gilbert put the land line on mute. "Hey, Sheriff, can I call you right back, I'm just finishing up a call on the office line," Gilbert told him.

"Call me right back, we have a very serious situation," the sheriff said.

"I will," Gilbert replied, looking at his watch, 5:20 p.m. *Damn!* he thought. It would be dark by 7:00 p.m., and he still had calves to feed at the ranch.

"Sorry about that," the judge apologized again. "Look, get some figures together on the cost of the building, and we will take it from there. I really doubt that we will have that for the court by next week, but we will toss it out there anyway," Gilbert said, hoping to put this issue to rest.

"I think it should be constructed out of concrete, something that will stop a high-powered round, maybe even a .50 caliber. These cartels have all kinds of weapons at their disposal." The commissioner was still insisting on discussing the minute details of the project. Gilbert looked at his watch again, 5:30 p.m. Damn, his cell phone rang again. Jamil. Gilbert let it ring and go to voice mail. He texted back and told Jamil to give him a few more minutes; he was about to wrap this call up.

"Look, get the numbers together, ballpark figures, and we'll weigh the options." Gilbert knew it was overkill, but he didn't want to lead him into further discussion.

His cell rang again, 5:40 p.m. The sheriff. The judge let it go to voice mail again.

"We will need to do soil samples before we pour the foundation." The commissioner just kept on with his line of thought. Gilbert knew this guy. This was how he was with everything. Anyone else would have thought it was a deliberate act, trying to piss him off. The commissioner had tunnel vision. He just wouldn't let it go, and this was just one item. There was still the dairy. He was hoping to discuss it with the commissioners before the hearing.

"I'm going to cut this call off for tonight," Gilbert told the two men. The commissioner from precinct 7 sounded relieved. He wasn't able to get a word in during the last half of the call anyway.

"My wife said a horse is colicing at the ranch," Gilbert lied. "That's who keeps calling in," he lied further. "Let's meet here tomorrow." He did not wait for a reply and finally ended the call.

Gilbert called Jamil back as he walked out to his truck without checking his voice mail first.

"Hey, sorry about that, I couldn't get this pain-in-the-ass commissioner off of the phone."

"Have you talked to the sheriff?" Jamil asked.

"No, but he has called a couple of times," Gilbert told him. "Like with you, I told him I would get right back to him."

"He called me in this afternoon." Jamil was obviously shaken. "I thought he wanted to discuss Mexico and the El Jardin." His voice was low and barely audible. "When I showed my ID at the front desk, I was immediately escorted to an interview room by two deputies. I told them…I told them, they must have me confused with somebody else, I have an appointment with the sheriff." Jamil sounded like he was going to cry. "The deputy said the sheriff would be right in to talk to me…then he read me my rights!" His demeanor went from broken to excited. "'What the hell are you charging me with? You are making a huge mistake,' I told them!"

"What!" Gilbert yelled in disbelief. He knew Jamil. He knew him as an honest, trustworthy business and family man.

"The sheriff came in with two detectives wearing suits and their badges pinned to their neckties. The sheriff was very apologetic. He said he planned on having an off-the-record discussion with me in his office. But his detectives convinced him that due to the seriousness of the evidence, everything has to be done by the book."

"What serious evidence?" Gilbert hollered into the receiver.

"They told me that a witness placed my truck at the scene of a murder near the Williams dairy."

"What!" Gilbert said again, not believing what he was hearing.

"A border Patrol Agent came forward and said he had seen my truck parked on the road to the pump house next to the Williams dairy. He said he was responding to a vehicle accident on 281 or he would have stopped to investigate," Jamil continued. "I told the sheriff I was at the El Jardin hosting a party and that you were there too, and you could vouch for me."

"Let me call the sheriff," Gilbert replied. "That may be why he's been calling. Don't worry, we were together, along with a lot of other people. Relax, you can't be in two different places at the same time."

Gilbert looked at his watch, 6:15 p.m. There was about an hour of daylight left, and it was still a thirty-minute drive back to the ranch.

As he pulled out of the parking lot, his cell phone rang again, his wife. "I'm on my way," he told her in a hurry. He was just getting ready to dial the sheriff's number. "We still have enough time to feed, if not, I've got my spotlight.

"I know," she said. "The calves won't starve to death if they don't get fed tonight, I'm concerned about the gunshots. I think they came from across, but I'm not positive."

"I'll speed, I'll be there in twenty minutes," Gilbert reassured her.

"Sorry, but after the other night—" She stopped for a second, thought she heard the dogs barking. "I think I'm just edgy, I'll feel better when you're here."

"On the way," he said. His thoughts darting back and forth from Jamil and the sheriff to his 410.

The cell phone rang again and snapped him back to the present. "Sorry, Sheriff, I was just getting ready to call you back. My phone hasn't stopped ringing all afternoon."

"I need to talk to you about your friend Jamil," the sheriff told Gilbert matter-of-factly. "Can you come by the office?" he asked.

"Now?" Gilbert asked.

"Yes, sir," the sheriff demanded.

"No way tonight," the judge replied. "Marianna heard some gunshots, and she thinks they came from across the river, but she's not sure, she is really spooked lately."

"I'd rather speak to you in person, like I say," the sheriff said.

"I promised her I'd be home by dark," Gilbert told the sheriff. "That episode the other night really got to her."

"Well, can you meet me somewhere? The checkpoint? It won't take long, like I say, you know. This is very important." The sheriff was persistent.

"The checkpoint will work," Gilbert reluctantly agreed. He intentionally didn't tell the sheriff about his conversation with Jamil. He wanted to hear the sheriff's version first.

Gilbert parked behind two Border Patrol vehicles and the portable floodlight unit next to the checkpoint office. The setting sun was reflecting in the pickup's rearview mirrors, preventing Gilbert from seeing the unmarked Tahoe pull in behind him. He was lost in thought about all the events of the day, especially the busy afternoon, when the sheriff tapped on his window.

"You scared the shit out of me, Juan! I didn't hear you drive up," Gilbert blurted, a little embarrassed.

"You better stay in yellow." The sheriff chuckled. "Like I say, you stay in white, you know, you could get killed. You know the Boy Scouts' motto?" the sheriff asked him.

"Yes, I know the motto." *Come on,* Gilbert thought, *I'm not here for a history lesson on the Boy Scouts, it's getting dark.* "Be prepared," Gilbert said. "Be prepared."

The sheriff got into the passenger side of the truck and just sat there, staring out the front windshield.

"Like I say, your friend Jamil may be in a lot of trouble. He may have been involved in the dairy murders." The sheriff stopped, as if trying to organize his thoughts. "Like I say, you know, I will just get to the chase. Cut to the chase, or get to the point."

Gilbert knew what he meant.

"Your friend's white ford truck was seen parked near the levee at the time of the murders." The sheriff turned his head from looking out the windshield and looked Gilbert directly in the eyes. "There was a witness, a Border Patrol agent." The sheriff went on to explain about the traffic accident on 281 and that the agent didn't stop because of it, but he did get a partial plate matching Jamil's pickup.

At the time, he just thought it to be lovers taking advantage of the isolated road.

"All of the agents were told at muster to report anything out of the ordinary, you know, especially if it occurred on the night of the dairy murders," the sheriff continued. "The agent got a partial plate on the Ford pickup, it was SPI. He didn't write it down, like I say you know, he just remembered, South Padre Island, like the island."

Gilbert knew that Jamil's plates began with SPI.

"We ran the make and model, you know, through DMV, with the partial, and your friend Jamil's name came up as a possible. Like I say, it's not a perfect match, but it is very interesting. A very solid lead. The only lead." The sheriff explained, "He said he was with you at a quinceañera at the El Jardin." More of a question than a statement.

"Not a quinceañera," Gilbert said. "It was an engagement party for his son, yeah, I was there. We were together most of the time."

"Most of the time?" the sheriff asked with a little skepticism in his voice.

An agent walked up to Gilbert's truck and tapped on the hood. It was dark now, and the two men didn't see him approach. "Oh, it's you, Judge," the agent said. "I thought this vehicle looked familiar."

"Just a quick meeting with the sheriff, it's closer than going all the way to the ranch. We'll be out of here in a minute," Gilbert said.

"No hurry," the agent replied. "I didn't know who was here, you've gotta be aware of your surroundings these days, you know."

"Thanks," Gilbert said. "We'll be out of here in just a few minutes."

"What time did you last see him?" the sheriff asked.

"I'm not exactly sure," Gilbert replied impatiently. Something told him this was going to take a while. Just like the nitpicking commissioner on the teleconference this afternoon, the sheriff was going to want specific details. And Gilbert realized he was right. The sheriff had a job to do, and he couldn't leave any stones unturned.

"Look, Juan, I've known Jamil for a long time, and I can vouch for him. He couldn't have done it. He was with me most of the night, and besides, we both had too much to drink. I even spent the night at the hotel. He wasn't physically capable of doing anything complicated anyway."

Gilbert's phone rang—his wife. "I'm at the checkpoint with the sheriff," he told her. "I'm leaving now."

"Hurry," she said. "The dogs are riled up about something."

"I'm on my way." He folded his phone closed and told the sheriff he had to go.

"Okay," the sheriff said. "But come by my office first thing in the morning, and if you don't, then I will go by yours, you know. I think, you know, that it will be better if you visit me," the sheriff said, not as a friend, but as a lawman.

"I promise I'll be there. And thanks, Juan." Gilbert appreciated the courtesy the sheriff showed him by not making him come in tonight.

"Sheriff!" Gilbert yelled as he got out of the truck and started toward the sheriff's Tahoe.

"Sheriff, Jamil didn't do it. I remember now, he loaned his truck to his cousins. I saw him meet with them in the hallway of the hotel near the cantina. I saw him hand them something, I thought it was odd at the time, so when I saw him in the bar a little while later, I asked him about it. He told me that the cousins asked to borrow the truck because they needed a four-wheel drive vehicle to go down the beach past access 5. What I saw was him giving them the keys. He couldn't have done it." Gilbert spoke like he had just solved the case.

"I need you to come to the sheriff's office so you can give me a written statement, you know," the sheriff told him.

"Tonight!" Gilbert asked defiantly.

"Yes, right now, we need to know who had the pickup, you know, they could be the killers!" the sheriff barked back at him.

Gilbert knew the sheriff was right. This had to be solved. and it was an important development in the case. But he couldn't. His wife.

"Look, Sheriff, I can't go tonight. Marianna is waiting for me, the dogs are worked up about something, and she is very nervous." Gilbert was adamant about not going. His wife was alone at the ranch, it was dark, and something was alarming the dogs.

"Hey," he said, like a light bulb just went off in his head. "Why don't you come out to the ranch, and I can give you the statement there," Gilbert asked persuasively.

Sheriff Aguliar thought about it for a few seconds and then agreed. Time was of the essence. He hadn't taken a statement himself in quite a while, many years in fact, but the formula should still be the same. Get the facts in the sequence they occurred, the five Ws, and have Gilbert sign it. The clerk could review it in the morning and make sure everything was technically and legally correct. He could get the details and let his detectives follow the evidence.

*****

Johnny got out of bed before dawn. He hardly slept a wink all night. The dead man dominated his thoughts and invaded his dreams. The plans he made to himself about spending the morning in bed with his wife would have to wait. He was so consumed with finding out the identity of the dead man he didn't remember the drive to his office at the Mercado. He didn't even recall crossing the Gateway Port of Entry. He only remembered leaving the ranch, and the next thing he knew, he was parking his pickup in Mexico, nothing in between.

Johnny considered calling Julian, describing the floater again, see if he remembers anything different than he did yesterday. He quickly dismissed the idea. La Hormiga was up to something. He could sense it yesterday. The two bodyguards at Garcia's were his pistoleros, the dairy murders, something was off. Julian knew much more than he was letting on.

"Hola, amigo," Johnny said into the receiver. "Habla Johnny Williams."

The fat old cigar-smoking Mexican rasped a hardy laugh into the phone. "Juanito! How have you been, mi amigo?" the old man still fancied himself as a high roller. They reminisced about the old horse racing days at the dirt tracks in Matamoros, and how Julian and he would smuggle the horses across the rocks at the pump. They rehashed all the good times with the girls and tequila and how they bet on the fistfights as often as they did the horses. After what seemed like an eternity, listening to the fat bastard rasping into the phone, Johnny hinted at the floater in the newspaper.

"Si, yo lo conocises, I know who he is, or I guess you could say, who he was." The man laughed into the phone again. He explained to Johnny that the dead man always wore matching boots and belt. He wore a lot of gold around his neck and gold rings on his fingers. They were his status symbol. "He wanted everybody to think he was a macho rich plaza boss," the old man explained. "But he was just a peon."

Johnny's heart rate increased as he listened to the old man brag. *Come on…come on, tell me who he associated with.* Johnny was anxious. He didn't want to come right out and ask. He wanted the fat man to volunteer the name. "I think he was a lieutenant for your old friend, como se llama, your smuggling companiero, Julian, se llama La Hormiga yo creo."

Johnny couldn't even reply. His thoughts were racing through his brain a million miles an hour, but his mouth was stuck in idle.

"Are you sure, Patron?" Johnny was finally able to ask.

"Si, si, por seguro," he said. "I am sure, 100 percento. Por Que, why, did you know him?" the fat man asked.

"No, no," Johnny told the old man. He wasn't lying; he really didn't know the man.

"Just the tiempo loco we live in these days, you never know." Johnny was trying to pretend that it didn't matter to him one way or another.

Johnny used to enjoy hanging around with the fat Mexican. Even though he could be very obnoxious, he was always laughing, always having fun. Johnny got the information he wanted and was trying to cut the call off, then it occurred to him to ask him about Julian. See what the old man knew about him.

"Y me amigo, Patron? What is he up to these days?" Johnny tried to be nonchalant, like he really didn't care, like he was just making small talk. "No lo visto por mucho tiempo, I haven't seen him in a long time," Johnny added, prodding the old man for information.

"He runs his own business a hora," the fat man said, laughing. "But yo no sabe nada, you did not hear it from me."

"What kind of business, selling flowers on the puente?" Johnny joked.

Everyone in that circle knows what "running a business" means. The fat man was laughing so hard he started choking and gagging. Johnny thought he might have shit in his pants.

"Are you okay, amigo?" Johnny asked him. He needed a few more questions answered before the man died of a heart attack.

"Si, si, I am okay, you make a funny joke, Juanito," the man rasped into the phone, still out of breath, barely able to speak.

"I picture La Hormiga walking up to the carros on the puente, telling the touristas that if they don't buy his floras, he will shoot them in la Cabeza." The fat man started gagging and choking all over again. Johnny thought the old man was going to puke. Listening to the old fat bastard gag on his own mucus made Johnny feel like puking too.

"I hear he has hired some rancheros from the playa, but I know nothing, eh Juanito?"

"Rancheros?" Johnny asked him.

"Si rancheros," the man rasped into the phone, still a little out of breath. "He needs two kind of mulas, the ones with two legs, and the four-wheel-drive ones, burros." He chuckled a little, a raspy chuckle, but no gagging. "Mucho lodo on the flats, burros the only way to get through the mud."

"Why doesn't he wait until it is dry or go somewhere else?" Johnny asked him.

"Won't dry out 'till Junio, if no more rain comes. Y la migra no tiene four-wheel drive mulas. Only sure way for La Hormiga to deliver to 48 without getting caught. Esse vato is trying to clean his name. He promised tonight." Then he added, "No dijo nada, remember, I did not say anything."

"Perfect." Johnny got what he was looking for without coming out and asking for it. He let the old fart think he was just making small talk, and he got all the information he needed on the first call. "Perfect."

Johnny had to act fast. The flats of Boca Chica consisted of thousands of acres of bottomless black mud and shallow bays, dotted with low hills, not much more than sand dunes. Where would Julian cross? Where? That was the million-dollar question.

Johnny ran the river area through his mind. He once knew it like the back of his hand. At the mouth, Boca Chica? No, not at the mouth. Johnny was sure, if that were his selection, he wouldn't need the burros. Johnny calculated that it was about twenty highway miles from the outskirts of Brownsville to the mouth of the river, many more riverfront miles with all the twists and bends. Johnny revisited all the areas in his head, the ones he would use if it were him, on both sides, in the United States and in Mexico. Where? Where would La Hormiga cross his contraband? He needed the burros because of the mud and the vaqueros as handlers. He would likely choose the shortest route available.

Johnny pondered all the possibilities, from the Playa Baghdad Highway, across the tidal flats in Mexico, then across the river, then the mud flats on this side, all the way to the Brownsville ship channel. What would make the most sense, the route with the least resistance and the least likely to be discovered by the Federales in Mexico and Border Patrol here?

He had to narrow it down, and he had to do it quickly. If the drugs were to be smuggled tonight, he had to act fast. There was a lot of territory to consider, and he was alone, a one-man team. There was no room for error. If he was one mile off, he might as well be a hundred miles off. He needed to get into La Hormigas's head. They used to smuggle horses together, so he had some insight to his thought process. He must come to the same conclusion as Julian. But there was so much river and so little time. Julian's tactics and mindset may be very different from when the two were a team.

He needed to stay focused, but he was having difficulty, his mind was consumed by the reality of the coming confrontation.

His thoughts were dominated by the revenge he was going to inflict on his old friend. Julian was going to pay for what he put his family through. Letting that stinking pig put his paws all over his wife and terrify his babies! He was going to pay tonight! Finally! The score would be settled, the fine paid, the sentence carried out. Death! It would be painful, and Julian would know who was inflicting the pain! And why! A slow death! Johnny felt euphoric. The thought of revenge pumped adrenaline through his system like heroin into the veins of a junkie.

He had to concentrate. He couldn't let his mind wander. He had to conceive a plan. A perfect plan, one with no room for failure.

"Patron, habla Juanito again, I tried to call mi amigo, Julian, pero no contesto, he doesn't answer." Johnny knew he was taking a big chance and could ruin the opportunity to make his move, but he had no other options. Time was running out; the clock was ticking. If he scared the fat man, causing him to alert Julian that someone was asking too many questions, it could be over even before it began.

Just like everybody else, the fat man was out for himself. He had to secure his own future, his own existence in this new era, where a life could be taken on nothing more than a rumor.

"I would like to offer my assistance tonight," Johnny explained to the Mexican. "I have some time on my hands, and I could use some extra money. It would be like the old horse-smuggling days, me and Julian always worked well together." Johnny surprised himself at how convincing he was. He hoped the old man felt the same.

"Pos...no se." The old man was balking. "I don't know if La Hormiga would be too pleased if he knew I told anyone about his business." There was no humor in the old man's voice now. The rasping wasn't even noticeable. "I have told you too much already."

"Patron." Johnny didn't want to sound desperate, like he was pleading. "No one will know you told me anything, I will just show up, pretend I am scouting a crossing for myself. It would be a great coincidence...and you know he will be glad to see me, it would be like old times again."

Silence. "Patron?" Silence.

Johnny could hear his rasping now. He could hear that the old man was still on the line.

"Patron, not to worry, I miss the old days, the excitement. I am not getting any younger, it would be good for my heart, for my soul."

Still silence.

"Patron?" the old man still did not reply, but he didn't hang up either.

"Patron, are you still there?" Johnny knew he was. He was just prodding him, urging him before he had too much time to think it through thoroughly.

"Rancho Martinez," the voice said. The line went dead.

*****

It was almost midnight when the cousins crossed the Gateway POE, headed back to South Padre Island. They were content now, laughing as they exchanged the exaggerated tales of their sexual escapades, describing every minute detail to each other. And bragged about what a great friend Julian was. He was dependable, reliable, and produced the girls just like he promised. What a great friend.

The conversation turned serious again as they worked out a plan to pick up the ammunition. They would leave for Brownsville first thing in the morning and pick up the goods from a bar on Fourteenth Street. They pulled into the parking lot of the hotel, tired and spent, and ready for some well-deserved rest.

"Wait!" Moe said. "We will do the Martinez Ranch tomorrow, tomorrow night, as soon as it gets dark." Larry and Shep perked up, surprised at Moe's sudden revelation.

"The time is right," Moe said. "We will have all of the tools we need in the morning...we will avenge our honor tomorrow!"

"Yes," Larry said. "Tomorrow. This is our destiny, everything is right...tomorrow!"

"The dairy is being blamed on the cartel violence in Mexico," Moe declared "This will be carried out exactly the same. The ranchers will be castrated and marked with the hot iron, treated the same way they treat the cattle. The Mexican cartels will take the blame again. The timing is perfect!"

*****

Marianna met the two men at the end of the driveway. "I heard gunshots earlier, and the dogs have been going crazy ever since." She didn't even take the time to greet her husband or the sheriff. "They have been barking in the direction of the river, something has their undivided attention."

"Slow down, slow down," Gilbert told her. "I'm here now, and I have the sheriff with me," he said, in a half-joking manner.

"I'm sorry," she apologized, "I am probably just overreacting, I'm really glad you're home." She gave Gilbert a heartfelt hug then turned and hugged the sheriff. The sun had already set, and the dark night air was cool, almost cold.

"Let's go inside, and I'll fix you some coffee, or would you prefer something else?" Mrs. Martinez offered.

"I'd like to sit out here," Gilbert said. "I like this weather. It's cool but dry, nice not to have the humidity. And I want to watch the dogs, maybe we'll be able to see what is bothering them. It might be that bull again, he's tasted freedom and may have found another way out."

As they sat at the picnic table on the front porch, the dogs came over and laid at Gilbert's feet.

"I think I'll have a Jack, straight up, how about you, Sheriff?" Gilbert asked.

"No, just coffee for me, you know," the sheriff replied.

Marianna went inside to brew some coffee and pour two drinks, one for her. She rarely drank anything stronger than wine, but a dose of Jack on a cold night would calm her restless nerves.

"Like I say, you know," the sheriff picked up right where he left off at the checkpoint, "your friend Jamil may be in a lot of trouble."

"Like I told you earlier, Juan, he couldn't have done it, he was with me, and besides I witnessed him give his cousins the keys to the truck," Gilbert stated emphatically. "He could not be in two places at the same time, and besides, again, we both had way too much to drink."

"Well, you know, I need to take that statement, like I say, we need to move fast. These guys could be the killers." The sheriff thought for a moment. "Does your friend have his truck now, or do his uncles still have it?"

"I don't know," Gilbert replied. "His cousins, not his uncles, the men who borrowed his truck are his cousins," Gilbert corrected him. "But I will call him now and ask. I told him I would call him back anyway." He didn't wait for the sheriff to reply as he started to dial Jamil's number.

Jamil was still in a state of disbelief. "I tried to call my cousins all afternoon, but I can't seem to get in contact with them," Jamil said slowly, the trauma evident in his voice.

"No, no, do not contact them!" Gilbert told him "This is now a police matter. I have no idea where this is leading, but now it is police business. Do not contact them." Gilbert was speaking from instinct. He didn't have any official law enforcement training. "Right, Sheriff, he should not contact his cousins?" Gilbert was looking for reassurance. "I have the sheriff here with me," he explained to Jamil.

"No," the sheriff said, "we will contact them, like I say, we don't want to alert them, you know."

"I explained to the sheriff," Gilbert continued. "You were with me, and you loaned your truck out. That is what we need to know now, do you have the truck back? Have your cousins returned it?"

"Yes," Jamil told him, "they brought it back yesterday afternoon, washed and waxed."

"Yesterday? What time?" Gilbert asked him, not sure that it mattered. It just seemed like a logical question.

"I don't know," Jamil replied. "It was in my parking space yesterday afternoon. The same spot they took it from. They may have returned it in the morning, I guess, I really don't know. I can ask, if I ever get a hold of them."

"No, no! Remember, do not contact them," Gilbert reemphasized. "The sheriff department will take care of that."

"What is his license plate number?" the sheriff interjected. Gilbert repeated the question into the phone. "And the plate of his cousin's car," the sheriff added. "The make and model, you know, of the cousin's car."

Jamil gave Gilbert the information on his truck, but he had no idea on the cousin's vehicle. "It is a minivan," Jamil told Gilbert, "but I don't know what year, make, or model or anything. It's white, with Texas plates is all I know." Gilbert relayed the information to the sheriff. "Ask him for the owner name, you know, like I say, we can run the information through the Department of Motor Vehicles. It will take longer, but we can get the information from them."

Then the sheriff asked about any security cameras at the hotel. The El Jardin should have all the modern technical devices since the renovation. "Excellent idea," Gilbert said. "Jamil, can you check your cameras, all of that information should be on video."

"Yes," Jamil replied, his voice revealing some much-needed relief. He was very aware that he was possibly facing some very serious charges—murder. "I will check right now, I'll get right back to you, give me thirty minutes." He hung up without waiting for a reply.

Three dogs jumped up and barked in unison. Gilbert and the sheriff jumped up instinctively at the same time, a muscle memory reaction to the alarmed dogs. The dogs ran off the porch and stopped at an imaginary line at the end of the lawn, barking into the darkness toward the river.

The two men looked and listened, keenly tuning their senses to any sight or sound, like what triggered the dogs' alarmed reaction. The dogs quit barking but stood guard at the boundary between the porch light and the darkness beyond.

Gilbert called the dogs back. They reluctantly obeyed but were still preoccupied with whatever lay lurking in the darkness.

"Maybe wets," Gilbert told the sheriff. The dogs were all back on the porch, but their attention was still focused in the direction of the river. All three were emitting a guttural growl, little more audible than a loud purr of a cat. An instinctive reaction to a threat, real or perceived, and they were on standby to defend their territory.

"Something has their attention," Gilbert said to the sheriff again. "If it's not my bull, it could be some Mexico strays. I saw some sign in the same area a couple of weeks ago, tracks of a horse and a couple of donkeys. I'll call the checkpoint and ask if they can send a unit out. It's still pretty muddy in some places, so they may not be able to get in with a vehicle. I'll call the tick rider too, he can get back there on his horse. If it is a Mexico, then he can apprehend it."

Gilbert's cell phone rang.

"Good news," Jamil said. "Their van was parked right in front of the camera, white Astro van, Texas plates, USP-40C."

"Perfect," Gilbert replied. "We have the vans ID," Gilbert told the sheriff.

"What time did it leave?" the sheriff told him to ask his friend.

"I didn't check the time," Jamil said. "I didn't think about it. I'll check and get back to you."

"We don't need it right this minute," Gilbert told him. "But get it anyway, just in case."

Marianna came through the door with the steaming coffee and two glasses of Tennessee Whiskey. She had her glass in a koozie, and she was wearing a jacket and wearing roping gloves.

"Do you think it's going to snow tonight?" Gilbert joked. Before she could reply, the dogs' alarm sounded again. Startled, she almost dropped her glass. "Oh yeah," Gilbert said. "I need to call the checkpoint."

*****

Larry was driving the van. Moe was in the passenger seat, and Shep was sitting in the back seat behind him. As they pulled into the alleyway behind the Gato Prieto Lounge on 14th Street. They pulled over just enough in the narrow alley to allow room for a vehicle to squeeze by. Moe and Shep folded down the third seat in the rear of the van and half of the back seat, creating enough space to load the ammunition. Allowing enough room so the ammunition wouldn't need to be double stacked and could be easily concealed by covering the boxes with newspapers. Anyone peering into the van would think they were delivering the bargain book to the local business establishments.

Larry knocked on the back door of the bar then stepped back so he could be seen easily through the peephole concealed at the top of the door. He waited a few seconds for a response and rapped again, this time a little more aggressively. No reply. The plan was to knock and wait for someone inside to knock back, a simple but effective secret code used by schoolchildren all over the world.

They began to second-guess themselves and thought they may be at the wrong door. 14th Street was comprised of bar after bar, almost exact copies of each other, distinguished at night only by the shape and color of the neon lights. In the daylight, they looked like row houses, many sharing the same walls and foundations. When approached from the back, from the alleyway, those unfamiliar would never distinguish one from the other.

Moe was getting anxious, impatient. He didn't like and couldn't afford stupid mistakes. If they knock on the wrong door, a hundred years of planning could go down the sewer. As luck would have it, the Black Cat Lounge was right in the middle of the block, easy to get confused and disoriented.

Moe told Shep to walk around to the front, the street side, and count how many doors down they needed to be. They had already done this earlier, before they turned into the alley, but just to be on the safe side, Shep would count them again.

14th Street wasn't the safest place for a foreigner to go for a stroll down a back alley, even in the daylight. There had been many a dead body with slit throats and stab wounds discovered in these barrios.

Larry knocked on the door again. He banged on it with his closed fist, a lot harder than the first time. He wanted to make sure that he could be heard. This time, to the relief of the cousins, the knock was answered right away. They all could take a deep breath. They were at the right door.

They walked down the alley and cut over to the street and went down a couple of blocks to the White Owl Café. They decided to get something to eat and to kill some time while the van was being loaded. They drank more coffee than they could hold, stalling, not wanting to return to their vehicle before it was ready. It was only a five-minute walk back to the Gato Prieto, so they had plenty of time.

14th Street was coming back to life, and people were beginning to stir. Ladies were hanging their laundry out to dry on the front porches of the casitas that lined up across from the cantinas. Little kids, almost naked, were kicking soccer balls and running in and out of the light traffic on the one-way street.

As they rounded the corner into the alley, there were two young girls washing glasses behind one of the bars. They each had a white five-gallon bucket. One was washing the glasses, and the other was rinsing them and lining them up on cinder blocks to dry. The young girls were pretty and looked up and smiled at the cousins as they walked past. As the girls bent over to wash and rinse the glasses, their dresses would ride up the back of their legs, exposing their smooth bronze skin, all the way up to their naked rear ends.

The cousins couldn't help but to look, and the girls knew they were being watched, and they seemed to enjoy it as much as the men did.

They were startled by the deep voice of a man standing between them and their vehicle. "Que le pasa pendejos, ella es me esposa," the man stated, his right hand clenched in a fist, the other gripping a fillet knife with an eight-inch blade.

"Sorry, sorry," Moe said. "No Spanish." He did speak some, enough to know that the guy called them stupid for looking at his wife. He knew enough, that if he misspoke and was misinterpreted, especially in a circumstance like this, he could make things much worse. Better to say "No habla nada" than to tell him his mother was a whore!

The way Moe sized it up, the man was just looking for trouble. He probably didn't even know the girls in the alley.

"For why you look at my wife, estupido?" His voice was deep and mean. And he was big. And he was drunk. Not falling down drunk, but fighting drunk. Just a slight slur in his words gave him away.

The cousins sized the man up. "We can take him," Shep whispered.

"No look at wife," Moe told the man. Wife. They could have been his granddaughters. He just wanted trouble. If the girls weren't there, there would have been something else, another reason, anything else.

"Si, you look at my wife," the man said as he stepped toward the cousins with an evil grin on his face. Moe guessed the man just liked to fight, probably liked pain. The expression on his face revealed what was in his sadistic mind.

Somehow they must get past this idiot, this obstacle that stood between them and a hundred years of revenge. Shep was right, they could take him, but if one of them were to get injured or the police showed up and they were arrested, then what? Their van would surely be towed, and the cache of ammunition discovered. One thing would lead to another and eventually to the dairy. Moe was getting aggravated, he was pissed that this drunk baboon was putting them and the mission in jeopardy. Moe looked back to see what the girls were doing. They had vanished. There was no one in the alley, only the cousins and the madman. They were alone.

He motioned to Larry to move against the wall and draw the man's attention.

The man's grin turned into a smile, ear to ear. He was having an adrenaline rush. This was his form of entertainment, his play-off game. He extended his arm, knife in hand, and made a half lunge at Larry and, just as quickly, stepped back in place. He was beaming with joy. He was elated. This crazed beast loved every minute of it.

He may have been intoxicated, but he was quick and agile. His moves were smooth and calculated, perfected through trial and error in the street battles of the Brownsville barrios. He has fought this fight many times. He craved the fear and pain he inflicted on his adversaries. He could achieve his objective solely through intimidation, but his goal was inflicting fear and pain on his victims. His whole purpose for existence.

Moe motioned Shep to move up the other side of the alley. Now Larry and Shep were parallel with each other, Moe just a few paces behind them. The four of them formed a triangle, the three cousins on one side and the big man on the other, like the Clanton's and Earp's on the dusty street in Tombstone.

The ogre lunged to the right, toward Shep, and made a sweeping motion with his knife, seasoned enough to keep enough distance and to advance and retreat without exposing himself.

Yeah, Moe realized, the madman has done this a time or two.

"Sir, just let us go by, we don't want any trouble. I apologize for looking at your wife." Moe was still trying to find a nonviolent way to get out of this situation. The last thing he wanted was a physical confrontation.

"We can pay you, how much do you want to let us pass?" Moe asked the crazed man. It reminded him of a fable taught in school when he was a young child in India.

The man's smile broadened. "I will take your money from your pockets as you lay on the ground bleeding," he replied, with the confidence of someone who has done this many times.

Moe was hoping to buy his way out. Now that option was off the table. Diplomacy wasn't going to work. There was no compromise. Now he had to come to terms with the only option left. He spoke to his cousins in Hindi. He directed Larry and Shep to rush past the man, go around him fast enough that he wouldn't be able to react in time.

The man reached out and took a swipe at Larry, the blade catching him on his left shoulder, tearing his shirt sleeve, and slicing into the muscle just above his bicep. It appeared to be only a flesh wound, and he and Shep were able to break the barrier and push past the man. The madman instinctively turned to follow the two cousins. When he did, Moe rushed him from behind, drawing his knife from his pocket, stabbing the man in the nape of his neck, instantly demobilizing him.

The man fell backward, almost knocking Moe to the ground. The street warrior lay faceup on damp pavement in the alley, alive, but unable to speak. He could only watch, wide-eyed, as Moe bent over him and slit his throat, Moe wanted to stand there and watch the old man bleed out, but he felt the urgency to flee. "Go, go," he motioned to his cousins.

Moe glanced into the back of the van as he jumped in the passenger seat. Everything seemed to be in order. All he could see was the newspaper covering the boxes of ammunition. Ideally, he would have verified that all the goods had been loaded and counted, but that would have to wait, no time to waste. They must leave the alley in a hurry. Larry ran over the man's legs as he drove out of the alley. He had no choice; the dead man's huge body took up most of the easement. He drove deliberately but not fast enough to draw attention, and when he ran over the man's legs, it caused the newspapers to shift, exposing the boxes of ammunition.

"Slow down!" Moe yelled as Larry pulled out onto 14th Street and headed to the expressway. Larry turned onto the frontage road, pulled over to the curb, and stopped. "What are you doing?" Moe yelled at the cousin.

"I can't drive," Larry replied in agony, reaching over and grabbing his arm with his left hand. Shep and Larry traded places, and Moe stayed put in the passenger seat. He inspected the wound, deep but clean, only some muscle damage. He took some of the newspaper sections and told Larry to hold it tight against the cut and put pressure on it to stop the bleeding. Instead of entering the expressway, they stayed on the frontage road to Boca Chica Boulevard, drove east, and took Highway 48 back to the hotel on the island.

Moe inspected all the boxes, making sure that they were full of bullets and not substituted with dummy rounds. Naive people had been swindled before. Moe wasn't going to take the chance. Every bullet needed to be accounted for.

The three men went up to the suite and retrieved the empty duffel bags and returned to the parking lot. The bags were packed with only enough ammunition they could be carried without too much effort. With Larry sidelined, Moe and Shep had to make several trips back and forth from the room to the parking lot. Larry's wound wasn't serious, but it was problematic, and they all hoped that it wouldn't become an obstacle and hinder the operation.

They left a case of the 9 mm and 223 rounds in the van and stored the rest in a closet of the hotel suite. A case of each caliber will be much more than they will need to accomplish tonight's mission. Moe told them that it was better to have it and not need it than to need it and not have it.

They tried to relax for a while, even contemplated going down and lounging around the pool, but decided against it. There were still too many half-naked girls hanging around, and they didn't need the distraction. They had to stay focused.

Moe went out on the balcony and just stared out at the surf, his thoughts consumed with excitement, anticipation of what the night will bring. There was no room in his mind to allow Poseidon another opportunity to invade his imagination.

The other two stayed inside, lounging on the sofas, enjoying the cool sea breeze, and watching the top 10 best beach getalways on the travel channel.

It was three o'clock. Time to go. Moe roused the other two, and they started taking the rest of their gear down to the van.

Larry insisted on helping. He put three fishing poles under his good arm and tried to head out the door. His wound wasn't serious, but it was painful. He could not lift his arm enough to turn the doorknob. The pain shooting through his body was unbearable. He didn't complain. He didn't say a word to the others. He didn't want to appear that he couldn't pull his own weight. Moe was watching him. He could see that Larry was having difficulty, so he took the poles from him. He told him to just go down and wait in the van.

"I can do my part," Larry protested. "I will move a little slower, but I will still help."

"It's not your fault you got cut," Moe explained, uncharacteristically sympathetic. "You were in the wrong place at the wrong time. It could have been any of us, it could have been much worse."

Moe and Shep finished loading the other items in the van. They took a portable propane tank and burner, three wrought iron stakes with a ring welded to the end of each one, designed to hold fishing poles, three fishing poles, and three tackle boxes. Disguises needed in case someone questioned them at the checkpoint or a game warden approached them near the river.

The propane burner will be used to heat up the wrought iron rings to brand the ranchers. The tackle boxes and poles were just a guise in case anyone asked. They were just scouting for a place to fish.

*****

Twilight was turning into darkness as the caravan headed north toward the Rio Bravo. Julian led the group as they rode single file, pack burros in tow, following the brush line along the edge of the loma. The ground was firm, for the most part. If they stayed close to the hill, they were able to avoid the boggy quicksand traps that lay between them and the river. The riverbank in Mexico sloped down into a broad sandy beach, bordered by thick motts of catclaw and huisache. Across the river in the United States, a solid wall rose out of the water, forming a black clay cliff, broken by a small narrow tractor cut, used by farmers years ago to irrigate their crops. The cut was steep and overgrown with thorny vegetation and a small path created by wildlife that drank from the river.

Now the work would begin all over, the animals were unloaded, the cargo stacked on dry ground, as near the river as possible. One of the vaqueros rode his horse into the river, still saddled, slid from the steed's back, and swam beside him, guiding him by the reins from the water. Just before landfall, the vaquero remounted the horse and rode him up the cut and tied him to a mesquite tree.

He swam back across to Mexico and retrieved a coil of rope from a small wooden boat. The homemade craft had been stashed in the brush and used to smuggle contraband for years, everything from produce and people to marijuana and cocaine. He swam one of the other horses across to the US side, just like the first one, but this time he stretched the rope across behind him. One of the vaqueros in Mexico tied the rope to a burro, and the man in the US pulled him into the river and guided him to the tractor cut. When the burro arrived at the bank, he refused to leave the water and climb the steep path to the top of the cut. The vaquero pulled on the rope, but the donkey would not budge. Instead of gaining ground, each time the man pulled, the donkey would pull back and get farther away from the bank, out into the water. The vaquero was near exhaustion and not making any progress, and this was the first of the remuda to be crossed.

Frustrated, watching the problem unfold from the Mexico side, Julian reluctantly yelled at the vaquero to get one of the horses. The man looked back at the horses tied to the mesquite. They were both where he had left them and turned his attention back to the burro.

"Caballo!" Julian yelled again.

The vaquero looked at Julian bewildered. He didn't understand what La Hormiga was telling him. Both horses were still tied where he left them. He knew full well what the consequences were if Julian's expectations were not met.

Julian could hear the dogs barking on the US side. He did not want to yell to the vaquero again, realizing sound would carry a long way in the cool evening air.

The vaquero extended his arms out, gesturing to his boss. "Que...what?" he was asking in sign language.

Julian was furious. He was pacing up and down on the bank, stomping his feet and flailing his arms in animation and pointing at the horses.

Finally, the Mexican cowboy understood. When Julian put two fingers of one hand over one finger on the other, it dawned on him what La Hormiga was telling him.

"Ah...caballo," the cowboy said to himself, finally understanding the concept. Now it made sense to him.

The vaquero led one of the saddled horses down the cut to the river, wrapped the end of the rope around the saddle horn, and easily pulled the stubborn donkey out of the water and up the bank.

This was repeated successfully until the last burro was safely up the bank and secured to the trees with rest. Julian made up his mind that if he ever used this method again, it would be with horses only or human mules.

Now that the animals were safely across, the drugs had to be transported in the small wooden boat. One vaquero swam alongside the boat to keep the load stable, while the other pulled it across with the rope, just as he did the burros. Julian waited in Mexico until all the marijuana was across. If the load was busted on the bank, he would be safe in his home country. The vaqueros were replaceable. He wasn't.

Now all the animals were repacked and tethered to the saddle horses, ready to finish their journey across the salt flats to the

Brownsville ship channel. That would be the end of the line for the horses and burros. Once they were unloaded, they would be turned loose, set free to fend for themselves, and revert back to the wild, as nature intended.

The men could clearly hear the dogs barking in the near distance. Julian was sure they were from the ranch nearby and hopefully would be able to avoid them as they skirted their way around downriver.

The black clay was still wet from the recent rains, causing the horses to bog down, and the burros, normally able to traverse any terrain, were having a lot of difficulty. Handicapped by the two hundred pounds of dope, the small donkeys were sinking up to their knees in the mud, causing them to lunge and risking loosening the valuable cargo.

Julian was going to have to deviate from the original route. The ground was just too soft, wearing down the pack animals, and there were still several miles left on the journey. They wouldn't be able to hold up for that distance in these conditions, and if one became lame, his load would need to be transferred and distributed to the others. Too time-consuming and creating an unnecessary risk, one he wasn't willing to take.

Julian remembered that Palmitto Hill Road came close to the river, near where they were now. But it was a caliche-topped road, and the small pebbles of the caliche could be hard on the unshod hooves of the animals, another source of lameness. If the animals were out of commission, then the goods wouldn't be delivered. The whole purpose of this mission was to reestablish his creditability, his reputation. No, he couldn't take that chance. It cost him too much last time, when Johnny stole it from him. And because it was more navigatiable. It would be riskier. A lot riskier.

Julian had a major decision to make, and he didn't have much time to make it. He had to get the product to its destination before dawn or risk losing it.

He decided to take the Palmitto Hill Road route but stick to the shoulder. The caliche was much finer, limiting the risk of the rocks getting stuck in the animal's hooves. They would be able to see headlights approaching from the distance, allowing them enough time to escape into the darkness to avoid being detected. There was not a lot of brush on that stretch of the road, but they would be able to get out of the trajectory of the headlights if any vehicles were to come down the road. Once across Highway 4, they would be able to hug the lomas all the way to the ship channel. The edge of the small hills would be just high enough to keep them out of the mud.

Julian could hear the dogs barking again. He couldn't tell how many there were, but in the clear night air, it sounded like there were many. He decided to find a spot and hold up long enough to let the dogs settle down and review his new route in his mind, make sure he hadn't overlooked any obvious obstacles. His new path would take him closer to the ranch, so he would have to deal with the dogs at some point, he knew, but he would cross that bridge later.

He had enough time to take all the necessary precautions to ensure safe passage for himself and the animals, as long as he reached his destination before dawn. The pistoleros would be staged at the blue gates on Highway 48, waiting for his call. They realized that it might be close to sunup before the call came.

*****

Johnny had a lot of preparation to do before nightfall. He headed back home to his ranch to retrieve his AR-15. The long gun may be needed. It could come in handy tonight. He was always armed with his Glock, even carrying it back and forth across the border. If you were connected, knew the right people to pay, you had nothing to worry about. The strict Mexico gun laws were very effective against the targeted few.

Johnny kept many weapons at the firm in Matamoros, but trying to cross the port of entry back into the United States with a long gun was a risk not worth taking. He didn't have anyone on the payroll on the US side of the bridge.

Johnny was greeted by his new dogs, barking and chasing his truck all the way down the driveway, from the gate to the barn. He would need to break them of that habit before they got run over.

He went to the house first, before going to the bunker in the barn. It was well after noon, but the aroma of chorizo lingered. The maid was sorting pinto beans from the pebbles and dirt, ready to wash and prepare them for dinner. The familiar smell of home cooking filled the house, triggering his appetite and making his stomach grumble.

His wife appeared from the den, both kids hanging from her legs. "Well, what brings you home so early?" She had a big smile on her face. He could tell she was really glad he was there. He regretted not waking her up last night. He considered asking the maid to take the girls outside to play for a while. He was tempted, and she was inviting. Now both the kids were hanging on his legs, one on each side. They were glad to see him too. He couldn't run them off.

Tomorrow will be the start of a new era, an era where he will uphold the oath he made to himself and his sleeping little girls last night.

"I need to get some things from the barn," he explained. "I just wanted to come and see you first. I have a meeting this evening, it may run a little late, but I need some material from the barn first."

"Please be home early," she pleaded, still afraid to be alone after dark.

"Don't worry," he told her, "I'll be a little late, but you will be fine, I promise."

He made that promise with confidence. The leader of the invasion team was dead, and soon the man that gave him his orders will be dead too. No one was going to bother her tonight—that he knew for sure. Or ever again.

Johnny removed the bales of hay that concealed the bunker door. He went straight to the gun safe behind his desk. The safe contained an assortment of weapons, 3006, a 223, both used for hunting and target practice, a variety of military-style fully automatic machine gun–type long guns, different capacity magazines. Revolvers of all types and styles, Ruger, Smith and Wesson, a Colt .45 with a seven-inch barrel, even a snub nose Charter Arms five round .38, and two nickel-plated single-shot derringers.

He grabbed the AR and three thirty-round fully loaded magazines, put one in the weapon and the other two in his back pocket, and picked up the bowie knife and the bayonet for the AR.

The bowie knife was the only weapon he had definite plans for. The AR was for backup, just in case. He knew from the fat man, La Hormiga had some vaqueros with him. He didn't say how many, and maybe his pistoleros were accompanying him also, for added security.

The dogs were lying under his pickup, relaxing in the shade. Johnny was impressed by the aggressive appearance their cropped ears portrayed. His aspirations were diminished though when the dogs cowered and ran off whimpering, tails tucked, when he approached the truck. They looked mean, but they were afraid of their own shadows. Well, that was the point. They were there to intimidate. They were still new, and once they learned that this was their territory, their home, they should become more protective, hopefully more aggressive.

Johnny laid the rifle in the bed of the truck and covered it with a feed sack. He didn't want his wife to catch a glimpse of it, give her any hint of his intent, or cause her any reason to worry.

The dogs chased him down the driveway as he was leaving, reaching out and biting at the wheels of the truck, keeping perfect stride with the speed of the vehicle, not realizing that one wrong bump by his mate, or one misstep, tripping in a rut, and the dog would meet his fate. Johnny let them follow him all the way to the gate before he slammed the brakes, jumped out, and pelted the dogs with rocks. The dogs hightailed it back to the protection of the house, hopefully learning a valuable lesson, allowing them to live another day.

Johnny got the weapons from the truck bed and put the AR and magazines in the cargo hold under the back seat. He strapped the bowie on his belt. He wanted it close at hand. Knives were commonly carried overtly and didn't draw any undue attention. He waited for the gate to close behind him, latched the chain, then headed off toward Boca Chica, thirty minutes away.

He had plenty of time to survey the area before the sun went down. He knew that there would still be plenty of wet boggy areas on the flats from the recent weather. He remembered the Martinez ranch house was on elevated ground, built atop one of the small lomas, and it would stay high and dry in even the wettest seasons. That didn't hold true for the access roads. Johnny remembered that Palmitto Hill Road had some low spots that historically held water for a long time after the rains had stopped. He hadn't been out there for years, so he had to do some reconnaissance first. Ideally, he needed more time, there was a lot of area to consider, but unfortunately, he wasn't afforded that opportunity. Time was not on his side. He had to rely on his recollection of the area and hope that it had not changed much over the years.

He knew La Hormiga was crossing near the Martinez ranch, but he still had several routes available from the river to the ship channel. He knew his options may be limited, but he would like to engage him as close to the river as possible before he could choose another route that Johnny wouldn't be able to access. Palmitto Hill Road went south from the highway then hooked back to the north just past the Martinez headquarters gate and then came to a dead end. One way in, and one way out.

Johnny stayed on the Boca Chica highway, passing the turnoff to Palmito Hill Road, and turning onto a small black top lane riddled with potholes and ending just a short distance from the river.

The road was close to Mexico, and in drier times, this was where he would choose to cross contraband. Johnny knew that from here to the Baghdad Highway in Mexico, it was almost two difficult miles through deep wet mud. He drove further east, toward Boca Chica beach, looking for any other area that may be chosen by La Hormiga, but all the land was submerged in standing water, an extension of the Laguna Madre and influenced by the high tides from the channel and river.

Johnny made a U-turn and headed back to Palmitto Hill Road. It was in pretty good condition most of the way considering, but at the low spot near the first turn, the caliche turned into a pink slippery slush, but the base seemed solid. If he kept the vehicle to a crawl, he wouldn't have any trouble negotiating the turn.

Johnny drove past the ranch's main entrance. It had changed a lot since he had last seen it. It had a nice wide entrance with a wrought iron gate, landscaped on each side. It was framed by a tall pole structure, displaying the ranch's name and Circle M brand and flanked by antique wagon wheels.

Johnny was impressed by the detail. It must have been Gilbert's idea. Mr. Martinez wasn't the kind of man to waste his time on landscaping. He was strictly a cow man, a rancher, who worked hard from dawn to dusk every day. His idea of landscaping was to mow the hay field or shred mesquite and huisachi in the pastures.

Johnny stopped at the last bend in the road, just past the ranch gate, and just before the end of the road. From this vantage point, he could watch the road to the north, toward the dead end, and to the west, all the way to the bend, past the ranch gate. He backed the truck into the native brush for camouflage but left enough room to let him monitor the road without blocking his view.

The sun disappeared over the horizon, and it was beginning to get dark. Johnny rolled down the truck's windows. He wanted to listen for any sound of La Hormiga approaching. The evening was nice and cool, light jacket weather, and except for a few mosquitoes and gnats, the conditions were ideal. The bend in the road coincided with the bend in the river, so he would be able to see anything crossing the road in either direction, and he would hear anything going around behind him, between him and the river. The cadence of the chirping crickets and the chicharas low baritone alarm escalating to a deafening shrilling scream was the only sound in the night air. The mating calls of the cicadidae could create a problem, but they normally quieted down soon after sunset.

Johnny removed the AR from the cargo hold and snapped the bayonet onto the end of the barrel. He released the magazine and rechecked it to make sure it was topped off, replaced it, and chambered a round into the weapon. He stood the weapon stock down on the floor of the pickup and lay the barrel between the console and the passenger seat. He drew the bowie from the scabbard on his belt and wiped it back and forth against the denim of his pant leg. He held the knife out in front of him and caressed the stainless steel blade with his thumb, and he admired the custom grip he had made in Matamoros. The stainless steel contrasted nicely with the black ebony wood on the dorsal side of the handle, and the finger grips were so perfectly carved the knife felt like a natural extension of his arm.

Suddenly the night noises stopped. The crickets stopped singing, and the chicharas went deafeningly quiet. Not a sound could be heard in the calm evening air. Johnny could feel the pulsating of his heart through the carotid arteries on both sides of his neck. He didn't take a breath. He didn't move. He heard the ranch dogs start barking off in the distance. He opened the pickup door and grabbed the AR simultaneously, instinctively, in one smooth motion.

"That's him!" Johnny said to himself. Dogs' barks were very revealing. Sometimes they would bark to each other, bark in a rhythm. Sometimes they barked at a varmint, a high-pitched shrill as they closed in on their prey. They bark at the moon and even howl with the coyotes. These were warning barks, Johnny knew, high-pitched, half-scared, half-aggressive barks. "That him!" Johnny undid his belt and ran it through the slats in his leather holster. He stuffed two loaded magazines into the top pocket of his brush jacket. He released the magazine from the holstered 9 mm Glock, made sure it was filled to capacity, quietly slipped it back into the weapon, and tugged on it to make sure it was reseated firmly. He drew the pistol from the holster, pulled the slide back, and revealed the shiny brass of the chambered round.

He left the keys in the ignition and partially closed the door but didn't let it latch. He laid the loaded AR in the bed of the truck, up against the closed tail gate. He climbed into the bed, stepped up on the wheel wells, to the side of the bed, and up onto the tool box. He just stood there and watched and listened. He faced the rear of the truck, toward the ranch, listening intently for any sound. The bugs were still mute, and the dogs were silent. "It is him," Johnny said to himself again, confident he chose the right spot to stake out.

He went over the different scenarios in his mind. There was the loma directly behind him. It went all the way to the river. La Hormiga would have to go around the hill on the ranch side or go behind him on the downriver side. If that was him setting off the dogs, and Johnny was pretty sure it was, then he didn't have much time. He better be ready.

Suddenly the brush popped to his left, the passenger side of the truck. Johnny instinctively drew his pistol and spun around to face the threat. A huge shadow appeared from the thicket, stopped dead in its tracks in the middle of the road, then spun around and disappeared into the same spot it came out of. Johnny had dropped to one knee on the toolbox and was aimed in on the target, holding the pistol with one hand while bracing himself with the other. His heart was beating so fast and loud that he was sure anyone within a mile would hear it. Johnny guessed that it was either a white tail buck or a nilgai bull. He was amazed with himself for not firing a shot. Maybe the split second it took to brace himself, keeping him from falling off the toolbox, gave him enough time to access the threat. He realized if he fired a round, it would all be over. He would have revealed himself and given away his position, ruining any chance for a surprise attack. "Dumb luck," he realized.

"He's coming," Johnny said to himself again. Nilgai have very acute senses, much more than the white-tailed deer and most of the other wild hoof stock. Something startled it enough to force it to break through the thick brush. Whatever species it was, it was getting out of harm's way, its instincts warned of approaching danger. "He's coming." Johnny was sure of it.

Johnny needed to make his decision quickly. If La Hormiga was close enough that the wildlife sensed him, then he was close. Johnny had to act. Johnny ran all of La Hormiga's options through his head. He knew he had to go around the loma, one side or the other. He had a fifty-fifty chance of guessing correctly, but he knew he had a fifty-fifty chance of being wrong. He couldn't afford to guess. He had to be certain. He grabbed the AR from the bed of the pickup and headed south, toward the river, straight over the top of the hill to a place where he could monitor both routes.

The dogs were barking again. Johnny stopped and listened. He wasn't quite to the summit of the loma, so the direction of the sound was confusing, disorienting. He picked up his pace, careful not to step on any branches or cane that would pop and crack and echo down to the flats surrounding the hill. He arrived at the peak of the hill and listened for a few seconds then moved to where it started to slope down toward the river. The dark, still night was eerily quiet, the dogs stopped their barking, and the insects were gone. His eyes were adjusted to the dark, but there was no moon, and the starlit night sky didn't offer enough light to let him see beyond ten feet.

Wait. A familiar noise. It sounded like a horse snorting, clearing gnats or grass seeds from its nostrils. Johnny couldn't tell for sure, and he couldn't gauge the distance. He didn't know how far away the noise was. Sound is deceiving on the flats, especially at night. The noise seemed to be coming from the upriver side of the hill, but if that was Julian, the sound didn't give away his intended route.

Johnny decided to stay put, wait to get a better read on the situation. An owl screeched off to his left. To Johnny, that was a good omen. He knew from Indian lore that according to their mythology, a hooting owl meant that someone was going to die. This owl screeched, so Johnny took that as a good luck token.

He was tempted to move closer to the river, position himself to ambush his old friend. He could take him by surprise as he rode past on the trail. La Hormiga would never know what hit him. In the dark, in the brush, Julian would ride close enough that Johnny could hit him in the head with a stump if he chose to do so. But no, that was not what Johnny had planned for him. He would know when death was coming. Johnny would make sure he would know.

Instead he decided to move to the southwest side of the hill. This would give him plenty of flexibility, whichever way Julian decided to go. Johnny would have time to reposition himself.

*****

"Hello," the voice on the other end of the line said. Gilbert thought he dialed the wrong number. The phone rang several times, and just when he was going to hang up, the line was answered.

"Sorry," Gilbert said, "I was trying to call the checkpoint." As he pulled the phone away from his ear to hang up, he heard the voice say, "This is the checkpoint."

"Hey, this is Judge Martinez from out here at the Circle M Ranch. I was parked there earlier, meeting with the sheriff."

"Sorry, Judge," the agent replied, out of breath. "We usually ID ourselves when answering the phone. I just answered without thinking, we've been tied up outside, I don't even know how long it was ringing." The agent continued, "Yeah, I was the one who spoke to you in the parking lot."

Gilbert explained to the agent about the dogs alerting to something in the direction of the river. "My wife told me she heard gunshots coming from across earlier in the evening," Gilbert reported to the Border Patrol agent. "The dogs have been barking on and off for quite a while now. I think there's some wets crossing, it must be a big group, it's taking them a long time."

Gilbert realized he called them *wets*, not a good term for an aspiring politician to use. Wetback was once a common name used by everybody, then it was illegal aliens, and now its undocumented aliens. The Mexicans refer to themselves as *mojados*, wets in English. The agent didn't seem to take notice.

"Can you send some agents out here to check it out? It's still pretty muddy in some places though," Gilbert said.

"Sorry, Judge," the agent replied, "we just caught a load here at the end of the levee. It was only fifty pounds, but we apprehended all of the mules, sixteen juvies. All of our resources are going to be tied up at the station processing. Seems futile doing all of the paperwork, when we're gonna kick 'em loose anyway. DEA will talk to them first, then it's bye-bye, see ya next time. No rap sheet on a juvie, and we cut 'em loose, sorry, procedures." The agent didn't sound sorry. "There are only two of us here at the checkpoint," the agent continued, "and we need to have at least two agents at all times for officer safety. I'll call it out though, if they can spare some agents from the station, then someone will respond."

"So what do you do about other traffic?" the judge asked him. He never considered it. He just assumed there were enough agents on the line at all times to handle whatever comes up.

"We don't have a choice, Judge," the agent explained. "If we catch 'em, then we process 'em, that's the procedure. Your case, your file." The agent was unapologetic. "Last week, on the midnight shift, we had a sensor going off for two hours while we were all at the station busy processing. The whole shift was at the station. Well, except for the two at the checkpoint. Had to been dope, no telling how many pounds got by us that night."

"You must be kidding!" was all Gilbert could say, rhetorically, not expecting an answer. Good thing he didn't get one.

The judge relayed to the sheriff and Marianna what the agent told him.

"I'll call the chief in the morning," Gilbert said disgusted. "This is the most inefficient way of doing business I can think of. The Border Patrol should have agents on a shuttle crew on standby to transport the illegals to the station and office personnel there to process them." He didn't say *wets* this time, but he wasn't sure about calling them illegals either. "That way all of the agents could stay in the field and available to respond to any situation," Gilbert told them. "Don't you think the coyotes and mules know about this policy?" another rhetorical question. "I'm calling the chief first thing in the morning.

"Sheriff, can you check with your dispatch, maybe they can have a deputy in the area, just in case."

The dogs jumped up and began barking again. This time they were facing the road, toward the front gate. They didn't leave the porch this time. They just took a stance by the rail, poised like pointers, the hair standing up on the nape of their necks.

"Sheriff," Gilbert said. "You better call dispatch."

"Ten-four," The sheriff agreed. He went inside to use the house phone so that the barking dogs wouldn't interfere with the call.

"Marianna, can you grab the 410, put it behind the door in the bedroom, just so we have it handy," Gilbert told his wife. "Don't let the sheriff see you though. He probably wouldn't say anything, well, I know he wouldn't, but I don't want to put him in an awkward position."

She gave him a funny look. A serious look. She wanted her husband to reassure her, let her know that there wasn't anything to worry about. She wanted to hear that she was overreacting. She nervously set her glass down on the picnic table and disappeared into the house without saying a word.

Gilbert stood there on the porch, alone, just watching the dogs. The cool air was quiet again. The dogs were silent, but they were focused on the darkness, at whatever was out there looming beyond the porch light. One of the dogs jumped off the porch and cautiously walked out to the middle of the lawn. The other two quickly followed, going around the railing, using the steps, and joining the other one in the yard. All three stood in the damp grass, heads up, and their noses raised appraising the night air.

The sheriff came out of the house and joined Gilbert watching the dogs, looking for some subtle clue to the object of their distress.

"There will be a unit in the area later, you know," the sheriff said. "The dogs are looking to the north now."

"Yeah," Gilbert said, "I guess whatever, or I should say, whoever it was, went around us, probably wets, headed north, to the channel."

"Aliens," the sheriff said. A gentle reminder to be politically correct. "I better go, you know," the sheriff told Gilbert. "You can come by in the morning and give the detectives a statement, yes?" With all the commotion, they decided it would be best to have the statement taken at the Sheriff Department, by the detectives. That way no vital information would be missed.

The dogs ran back to the other side of the yard, barking excitedly and howling in the direction of the river. They stopped at an imaginary line where the porch light met the darkness and stood their ground, daring to be challenged.

"What the hell is going on!" Gilbert said to the sheriff.

"I don't know, like I say, you know, maybe some wets went around, and more are coming. Maybe you know, they know the Border Patrol are busy, maybe the ones at the levee are decoys to keep them busy, you know, so they can cross here."

The sheriff called them wets, Gilbert noted.

The dogs ran back to the north side again.

"Where is your gun, Sheriff?" Gilbert asked him, looking down at the sheriff's empty holster.

"In the Tahoe," the sheriff replied. "Let me get it. I have been leaving it in the SUV so that I don't forget and go to a meeting or a classroom armed. I am trying to lead by example, you know," the sheriff continued, trying to justify his complacency. "These new laws are very serious, you know, I don't want to intimidate anyone, like I say, lead by example." He was thumbing the strap of his empty holster while he lamely tried to explain his empathy. "I have carried a gun for so long, you know, it was very strange not to have it with me. Now, like I say, I forget that I forgot it."

"I'm going to challenge this gun legislation when I run for office again," Gilbert told the sheriff, realizing Jamil was completely right about the law. "When law enforcement feels uncomfortable carrying a weapon, there is a problem."

"Our new policy, you know, the new law, allows us to only carry two six-round magazines, that is all," the sheriff told him.

"Two plus the one in your weapon," Gilbert said.

"No, two magazines," the sheriff replied. "Everybody knows that the deputies carry seven rounds, six in the magazine, and one in the chamber, but it is not allowed, you know, like I say, it's against the law." The sheriff continued, "The armor is supposed to keep very strict records of all of the bullets, you know, but the deputies find ways to sneak extras from the range during training."

Gilbert noticed, and was pleased, the sheriff didn't say they stole the bullets. They snuck off with them.

The vehicles were parked just out of the span of the porch lights. When the sheriff stepped off the porch, the dogs almost knocked him down, running to his side, growling and barking as they escorted him to his Tahoe. Gilbert grabbed a flashlight from a shelf on the porch and lit up a path for the sheriff to follow, providing a little exposure from the darkness. He scanned the light toward the road, the direction the dogs were focused on, and then back toward the river. It took the sheriff a few minutes to retrieve his gun from the locked safe behind the console. He fumbled around in the dark trying to find the correct key.

It was a good thing it wasn't an emergency, Gilbert thought, as the sheriff headed back to the porch. He would have been dead five times over.

The dogs ran to the corner of the yard again, raising and lowering their heads, sampling the air and quietly standing guard on the imaginary boundary line.

Gilbert aimed the flashlight back in that direction. He was hoping to see the light reflect back from the eyes of a stray cow or a nilgai. Something else was getting the dogs' attention, Gilbert knew. They never reacted this way to livestock or wildlife, not to this extent. He scanned the light back and forth, looking for illuminated eyes or a silhouette or any hint of what was provoking the dogs.

Wait! What was that! Something reflected in the light. He scanned back and forth again, trying to catch a glimpse of the source of the reflection, but nothing. He scanned closer and farther away and widened the search area, but still nothing. He shut the flashlight off. He thought maybe it was a firefly. The lightning bugs emitted light, not reflect it, so if that was the source of the reflection, then it would reveal itself. Nothing.

The dogs were quiet but still focused toward the road, still on guard, ready to defend their territory.

"Are these perritos always like this?" the sheriff just rejoined Gilbert on the porch, weapon safely secured in the holster.

"I have never seen them behave like this before," Gilbert said. "That is why Marianna is so concerned, that and the gunshots she heard earlier. She is still edgy about the incident the other night.

"Something is going on here, Sheriff, is there any way you can stay until your deputy gets closer or the Border Patrol show up?" Gilbert hated to ask. He didn't want the sheriff to think he was scared. "Something is going on, and the only defense I have is my old 410, and I'm not even sure if it shoots." He hated to put the sheriff in an awkward position by revealing that he had an illegal weapon in his possession, but he didn't have a choice. "The shotgun is a family heirloom, and I wasn't going to surrender it to be destroyed like all of the other guns," Gilbert explained to the sheriff. "We can deal with it tomorrow if you choose, but tonight I've got to have it with me, and I hope it works. If I need it." Gilbert looked for some hint in the sheriff's eyes. "This is what I am going to fight for," Gilbert continued his defense. "Responsible citizens like us, we should be allowed to have weapons, especially to defend ourselves and our property."

"Look," Sheriff Aguliar said, "I agree with you, you know, I keep a 12 gauge in my casita too. I think most of us weigh the risk of life or death. Like I say, you know, with a shotgun, you don't have to be a marksman, you just point and shoot, you will hit something." The sheriff continued, "We know the risk, you know, even we could go to jail, me and you, you know, a judge and a sheriff, like I say, they would make an example of us."

Gilbert was surprised. He would never have guessed the sheriff felt this way. He was absolutely surprised to hear the sheriff had a weapon of his own at home. "They, I mean we, you know, are not searching people's homes looking for weapons, at least not yet."

"If you and I feel this way," Gilbert said, "then probably a lot of us feel this way, how the hell did this law get passed?" Gilbert asked the sheriff emphatically.

"It is politics, you know," the sheriff replied. "We all, like I say, you know, want to get elected, puro politics.

"I will stay around for a little while longer, a deputy should be here soon," the sheriff agreed. "Do you have any Rolaids? I ate too much pico de gallo at lunch."

"No," Mrs. Martinez said. "I have some Topo Chico, that will help, it will make you burp."

"Ten-four," the sheriff said. "Then make it like Gilberto's."

*****

It was already dark when the cousins passed the checkpoint. Highway 4 was the only road from Brownsville to Boca Chica beach, so only the returning traffic had to go through inspection. One road in, and one road out. They only saw one vehicle at the checkpoint and only two agents, and they were busy inspecting a pickup coming from the beach.

"Where are all of the police?" Larry asked. He referred to all law enforcement as police, regardless of their agency.

"I don't know," Moe answered. "Maybe they are patrolling. Not by the ranch, I hope."

Moe slowed the van down but didn't turn onto Palmito Hill Road. "Look for car lights," Moe told the cousins. "We will drive down a few miles and see if the Border Patrol are around the area." Moe drove past the old Palmitto Hill water plant, passed Massey way, and turned into the entrance of Port Isabel pump. The lights from South Padre Island illuminated the eastern horizon, appearing like a mirage, like an apparition of a town out in the middle of the Gulf of Mexico, like Atlantis. They didn't see any vehicles on the highway and no headlights along the river, so Moe turned the van around, almost getting stuck in a pothole on the well-traveled easement and headed back toward town.

He turned off the headlights before leaving the highway. He put the vans transmission in neutral and let it coast to a stop in the middle of the road, then rolled the windows down and turned the motor off. The river valley and the Martinez ranch lay below them. They had a clear view of the whole area and watched and listened for any activity. They didn't see any vehicles, and the only lights were those barely visible from the ranch, and only the faint sound of barking dogs could be heard in the distance.

Moe stepped on the brake pedal to start the engine, and the whole sky lit up like a red fireball crashing through the atmosphere. He quickly shifted the vehicle into gear and started down the caliche road. Conscious of the brake lights, Moe shifted the transmission into neutral and allowed the van to coast to a stop at the bend in the road. They were close to the main gate of the ranch. It was just out of sight, only a few hundred feet around the corner. Shep opened the passenger door, triggering the dome light and automatic alarm. Startled, he quickly jumped out and slammed the door shut behind him. He was on autopilot and forgot about the lights and alarm, something they planned for, a major mistake that could have been very costly. They tried to disable the automatic system by pulling several fuses, but to no avail. They even considered cutting the wires at the doorjamb but decided against it, not knowing what other systems would be affected.

The ranch dogs' barking sounded close, like they were out in front of the vehicle, just beyond the brush line. Moe motioned Shep over to the window. "Do not open the door!" he scolded the cousin. "We knew that would happen! Use the windows, we will climb out the windows like we planned."

Shep cut the ranch fence, pulled the wire back, and tied it to the fence post so it wouldn't recoil back into the gap. Moe climbed out of the driver's window, and Larry gingerly maneuvered himself from the back into the driver's seat. Moe reached through the window and helped him steer the van through the cut in the fence, into the pasture, then he went to the rear and helped Shep push the vehicle. "Do not step on the brake," Moe sternly reminded him. "Leave it in neutral, and let it coast to a stop."

Larry's arm was throbbing, and he could barely lift it above his waist without the sharp pain shooting all the way up to his neck. It took both of the other two cousins just to get him through the window and out of the van.

Shep pulled the wire back in place and attempted to wipe away the tire tracks, an impossible task in the black muddy clay. He climbed back through the window and inside the van and handed Moe the wrought irons and the propane tank. He retrieved a blanket he brought from the condo as an afterthought, to cover the hood of the van, hopefully to prevent any reflection from the metallic hood of the vehicle.

The three cousins huddled together in the clearing next to the van. They bowed their heads, and Moe put his hand on the shoulders of Larry and Shep. He whispered a prayer to the Hindu god Brahma, one of their most powerful deities, creator of the universe with superhuman strength and the lord of sacrifices. He understood their plight, and the cousins believed Brahma was responsible for the special circumstances that were allowing them to follow their destiny, in a time in history when the stars were aligned specially for them. He protected them at the dairy, watching over them with his divine power, providing them the opportunity to perform the sacrifices, an honor denied to all the others. They felt especially blessed to be the ones chosen to fulfill his prophesy.

Moe handed Larry the irons to carry. They were small and light enough he could grip them with his good arm without too much difficulty. Moe grabbed his 9 mm pistol and stuffed it into Larry's waistband. "No holster," he whispered to Larry. "You can shoot with your good hand if you need to." Then he looked his cousin in the eyes. "You won't need to." He gently reminded him that only the knives would be needed for this mission, then he slid a small satchel over Larry's head.

Moe and Shep each slung an AK over their shoulders. They both picked up the propane tank, one on either side. The firearms were for insurance purposes only. The blades of their pocketknives were honed to perfection, the only weapon they would need.

They quietly maneuvered their way along the brushline near the fence, stopping just short of the clearing, affording them a clear view of the ranch house. The outside lights were on, and they could make out the silhouette of a man standing on the front porch. When Moe moved closer to the edge of the brush to get a better view of the house, he tripped over the stump of a dead huisachi tree, echoing the sound of the cracking branches off into the night. He froze in place as the ranch dogs bolted toward him, barking and growling and miraculously stopping at the boundary of the yard. The person on the porch aimed a light at the vehicles parked in front of the house, and to the surprise of the cousins, there was another man there, walking toward the house. The beam from the light swept across in front of Moe, stopping just short of his exposed position in front of the brush line. The light scanned back to the other direction, away from the cousins, to the opposite side of the house, and lit up the tree line, going back and forth, systematically searching the darkness. Then the light turned back toward the cousins, lighting up the grass just in front of Moe, giving him just enough time to conceal himself back behind the brushline as it illuminated the spot he just abandoned.

"Give me the bait," Moe told his injured cousin. Shep helped him carefully lift the satchel over his head, trying not to move the injured arm and cause him to involuntarily let out a cry of pain.

The dogs were already cued to their position, and he didn't want to antagonize them further. Maybe next time they wouldn't stop their advance. They didn't need any unfortunate distractions, not at this stage. Shep removed a large storage bag from the satchel and handed it to Moe. "Call the dogs," Moe told him.

Larry made a high-pitched smooching with his lips to attract the dogs, mimicking a wounded rabbit, and was just high enough that the men on the porch couldn't hear it. Moe removed three huge bone-in pork chops from the baggie and threw them as far as he could in the direction of the dogs. The stench of the rotting meat was nauseating, almost causing Moe to throw up. He had to quietly clear his throat and spit several times in an attempt to get the lingering taste of the decaying flesh out of his mouth. The chops landed just far enough apart so the dogs wouldn't need to compete over the timik-laced meat, their prey drive not allowing them to ignore the imitated call of a distressed rabbit. Moe watched the three dogs disappear from the protection of the lit yard and disappear into the darkness in the direction of the foul-smelling bait. He knew he would not have to wait long; the fast-acting poison would kill them quickly.

With the threat of the dogs gone, the cousins headed off toward the ranch house. They didn't count on the Martinezes having company, and with Larry injured, Moe and Shep would have to secure everyone themselves. A third person could create a problem. Mr. Martinez and his wife would be easy to subdue, but a second man on the scene would definitely complicate the mission. The firearms may come into play after all. Moe had to reassess the plan on the fly. It was too late to stop their momentum now.

They stopped just out of reach of the porch lights to watch the house, to assess the activity inside, and adjust their formulated plan. They decided to enter the house from the back and take everyone by surprise instead of barging in through the front door. The back offered more cover and was not lit up by the porch light like the front and sides of the house were.

All the blinds on the windows were open, and they could see all three people inside. One of the men was sitting on a stool at the breakfast bar, and a man and a woman were standing, facing him, seemingly deep in conversation.

Moe whispered to Larry to go to the front porch, stay out of sight, and be ready to block the front door so that no one could escape when the action began.

Moe and Shep snuck around to the back of the house, concealing themselves in the darkness, careful not to step on any obstacles that would give them away. Moe went to the back door and tried the knob. It was unlocked. He turned the handle as far as it would turn and held it tightly, slowly pushing the door into itself to minimize any squeaking from the hinges, then easily swung the door open. He and Shep slipped into the house, quietly closing the door behind them. They found themselves in the laundry room at the rear of the house, waited for a few seconds to orient themselves, then proceeded down the hallway in the direction of the muffled voices. They passed a large bedroom with the door open on one side of the hall, then an office and a bathroom on the other side, at the end of the hallway before it opened up to the dining room. They could hear someone coming toward them, so they ducked into the office and stood silently behind the partially opened door. They both drew their pocketknives and unfolded the blades. With their backs against the wall, they were ready to silence whoever would enter the room. They saw the light come on in the room next door and heard the exhaust fan. Luckily the person went into the bathroom instead of the office. Moe and Shep breathed a sigh of relief, not ready to begin the killing just yet. Protocol had to be followed. A quick kill would be meaningless. It would be murder. They were not murderers. They were crusaders!

"Patience," Moe whispered to his cousin. "Patience."

The toilet flushed, and the light went out, and the fan stopped. Now they could clearly hear the voices in the other room. "You need to check the septic line tomorrow," Marianna told her husband. "There is a foul smell coming from down the hallway. It must be coming in through the back door."

"I better get going," the sheriff said as he rose from his stool. "I need to get some Rolaids, you know, that pico is eating my pansa."

"Have another Topo," Marianna told the sheriff. "Without the Jack, it will make you burp some more, get rid of the gas."

"Sheriff!" Moe whispered to Shep. "The other man is a sheriff! That means he has a gun!"

"I didn't plan on any guns. Just ours," Moe told him.

"Have another Topo," Gilbert reiterated. "The dogs haven't barked in a while, let's give them a little longer to make sure that whatever was bothering them is gone." The judge didn't want him to leave. "You have time for one more to help get rid of your heartburn."

Larry could hear the conversation from his hiding place on the front porch. He also thought about the gun when he heard Mrs. Martinez refer to the man as Sheriff. He reached under his shirt to feel the butt of the pistol in his waistband to reassure himself that it was still there.

Larry could hear some faint noises coming from behind him, somewhere in the darkness. He wasn't clear on what he was hearing. Something, maybe some ranch cattle, he thought. He saw the dead dogs with his own eyes, so he knew it wasn't them.

The sounds seemed to be growing louder. He didn't like night noises, especially ones he could not identify.

*****

Johnny clearly heard a horse snort this time. *I knew it was him!* he excitedly thought to himself. He moved further down the loma and positioned himself at the point where the trail split. He could hear the hoof beats of the horses clearly now, but the sound was still deceiving, and he couldn't judge how close they were. It sounded to Johnny like a lot of horses.

They were starting to come into view, and he could almost make out their silhouettes. Four men in the rear, spread out evenly, each with an indistinct number of pack animals.

No wonder it sounded like a lot of horses...it is a lot of horses! Johnny thought to himself. He knew he wouldn't be able to take them all at once, unless he opened fire with the AR and sprayed them with gunfire. If he did though, he realized there would be a chance that Julian could escape. That was not an option he was willing to consider. As they grew closer, he could distinguish the different riders. He knew the man in the lead, out in front of the rest, had to be Julian. He was much larger than the other three.

Julian! La Hormiga! The Fire Ant! Mi amigo! You pince culerro! You ordered the raid on my familia! You are mine tonight! Johnny excitedly thought to himself. He could feel the adrenaline pouring through his veins.

From his new vantage point, Johnny could see that the trail between the loma and the river has been washed out. The recent rains have eroded the black clay and cut a deep ravine into the trail, making it impossible to cross. This made it easier for Johnny. The caravan didn't have an option. They had to take the trail on the ranch side of the hill.

He hurriedly moved toward the trail, careful not to step on any dead branches or cane that would alert his prey. He stopped and listened. They were still moving in his direction and getting closer. He picked up his pace, carefully navigating the brush-covered hill, anxious to make it to the trail before they did. He adjusted his plan as he moved into position. He had to improvise due to the unexpected size of the entourage. He wondered if he should take out the man in the rear first then work his way up to La Hormiga, or take him first and deal with the mules second. Lost in thought, he found himself trapped in a thicket of catclaw. He didn't have time to look for an alternate route, so he pushed through, the thorns scraping loudly as they scrapped across the canvas of his brush jacket. The last branch snapped back and slapped Johnny across the side of his face. The hooked thorns of the catclaw opened a gash under his bad eye and cut all the way to his earlobe. He could feel the warmth of the blood dripping down his cheek and coagulating under his collar. He tried to wipe it off on the sleeve of his jacket, but the waterproof canvas material just smeared it across the side of his face, painting him like an Apache brave.

He moved into position at the bottom of the hill and stopped at the edge of the trail. They were close, almost upon him. Close enough that he didn't have time to think. Johnny jumped out in front of the caravan, right in front of La Hormiga, and attempted to rechamber a round in the AR, ejecting the loaded round from the weapon. His intent was to cause everyone to freeze in place at the unmistakable sound of racking a round in the rifle. Like the sound of an alarmed rattlesnake, it is a sound you will always recognize and never forget. He expected everyone to instinctively stop in their tracks and heed the unspoken warning.

The impromptu plan didn't go as Johnny had hoped. The bullet didn't clearly enter the chamber, causing the weapon to jam. Johnny instinctively worked the action on the AR, attempting to clear the weapon and replace the round, but to no avail. He dropped the weapon at his feet and drew his pistol from the holster and raised it to cover his target.

La Hormiga's horse reared up on his haunches, almost throwing him to the ground. A natural reaction from the horse, one that Johnny hadn't calculated into his plan when he decided to use a surprise attack strategy.

La Hormiga lost his dally on the snubbed donkeys, causing a chain reaction like dominos falling through the mule train. One of the vaqueros was bucked off, and his horse ran off into the darkness still tied to the donkeys. The other bailed out of the saddle voluntarily, deciding to control his fate and take his chances on the ground. His remuda headed toward the loma. The other vaquero, thinking they had just been attacked by the Chupacabra, hightailed it back to the river, scared to death.

La Hormiga regained control of his horse, looked behind him, and realized he was alone. All the vaqueros and all the donkeys loaded with the dope had disappeared into the darkness.

"Hola, mi amigo," Johnny said out loud, still standing in the middle of the trail. He bent down and picked up the AR. He didn't care that it wouldn't fire. He wanted the bayonet. He had his 9mm. That was all he needed anyway.

Julian stared at Johnny's silhouette, his nervous horse dancing around in circles, instinctively wanting to bolt and join the rest of the herd. He was still trying to grasp the situation, trying to figure out what just happened. All his escorts had disappeared, along with all the drugs. Disappeared somewhere out into the darkness, somewhere out of his control.

He knew that voice. He stared at Johnny's silhouette for just another second then took off at a run toward the river. He could only see one person, but he was sure there were more, probably a group of border bandits intending on robbing wets, with no idea who they were confronting. No one in their right mind would try to steal a load from him. Not alone for sure. He would find out and teach them a lesson. River Etiquette 101.

That voice. He knew that voice.

He slowed his horse to a lope and then to a trot and then to a prance. He wanted his horse to walk, but he was still too jacked up from the ambush. He wanted his horse to conserve his energy because he still had a lot of work to do. He still had to find and gather the burros and somehow get them and the goods to the ship channel. And now he had to do it all by himself. All the cowards he hired had fled or were hiding somewhere in the dark.

Johnny could have shot him. He was in his sights. He could have shot him in the front or in the back. It wouldn't have mattered to him. And he may have, if he hadn't by chance seen one of the horses run into the thicket he had been tangled in earlier.

La Hormiga wasn't going to die from a gunshot. He was going to die slowly and painfully. And he would know why. He would die tonight. Johnny was on a high, the adrenaline pushing him excitedly, just like after a jump. Destiny! Finally!

Johnny cautiously approached the tangled horse, cutting the snub rope with his bowie, freeing the horse from the burros. He swung up into the saddle with one arm, holding the AR in the other, and loped off toward the river. Toward La Hormiga.

The donkeys were still stuck in the catclaw. Just like quicksand, the more they struggled, the more they became entangled. *Good,* Johnny thought. *A bonus.*

La Hormiga could hear the screeching, the stretching of wire. A string of the burros had blindly run through the ranch fence, still loaded with their valuable cargo. Two of the donkeys had their hooves tangled in the fence, trapping them, while the other two were pulling on them, trying to continue their flight. Julian dismounted and attempted to untangle the still-spooked animals so that he could tie them to a tree and retrieve them later when he caught the others.

Julian heard a horse approaching, hoping it may be one of his vaqueros coming to help, then he remembered they were both afoot. He hurriedly remounted his horse, realizing it may be the banditos. He headed to the ranch pasture, his horse nervously side passing from left to right, back and forth.

The burros spooked as Johnny approached the broken fence. The tangled donkeys broke free and headed toward the ranch, heads and tails up in the air, still tied together, bouncing on all four legs like pogo stick cartoon characters.

La Hormiga's horse reared up and spun around, facing the sound of the approaching stampeding donkeys. He managed to stay in the saddle again and started after the burros. He wasn't intentionally chasing them; he was just trying to keep up with the leery animals, intending to catch them as soon as the opportunity presented itself. This was why he hired the vaqueros. Situations like this, this was their expertise, not his.

Julian could see the light of a house in the distance. He hoped this would not present a problem for him. He didn't need another one to contend with tonight.

*****

Moe grabbed a horseshoe paper weight from the desk in the office and threw it down the hallway, landing against the back door.

"What the hell was that?" Gilbert blurted out. "It sounded like a bird flew into the back door, but all the birds are roosting for the night." They all three stood in the gap between the kitchen and the dining room, looking toward the hallway.

"The dogs did not bark, you know," the sheriff said.

"Yeah," Marianna replied. "If something was there, they would let us know, especially with all of the racket they've been making tonight. I'll go check."

"No, no, I'll go," Gilbert said. "You finish getting the sheriff his Topo Chico."

They dismissed it as nothing serious, and Marianna handed the sheriff his soda. The sheriff drank half the glass, then stood up, arched his back, and tried to burp.

"I don't mean to be rude," the sheriff apologized. "I can't seem to get this bubble out of my chest."

"Don't worry, sheriff, we're out on a ranch, not in church," she said. "Gilbert's not back?"

"Gilbert!" she called down the hallway from the kitchen. No reply. "Gilbert!" she called down the hall again. She gave the sheriff a bewildered look, and they both headed down the hallway. Gilbert was nowhere to be seen.

The door was closed, and the welded horse shoes were lying on the floor. They stopped and looked at each other. The sheriff gripped his pistol and unsnapped the thumb break.

"Maybe he went outside," Marianna said as they both headed toward the back door, the sheriff leading the way.

Marianna's body slammed against the wall, bounced back, and fell to the floor behind the sheriff. The sheriff spun around, weapon drawn, and fired two rounds at the stranger on the hallway. His years of training and experience, his muscle memory reflexes took over as his fight-or-flight reactions kicked in. He opened fire on the threat instinctively, with no time to process the developing scenario, but both shots missed their target. One bullet hit the floor and ricocheted into the wall of the master bedroom, and the other lodged in the ceiling.

Shep retreated back into the office, inspecting himself for bullet holes. He couldn't believe that he wasn't hit. The sheriff was less than three feet away from him when he fired the shots.

Larry came bursting through the front door at the sound of the gunfire, weapon drawn, holding it with his left hand as he rounded the dining room and into the view of the sheriff.

"Stay down!" the sheriff yelled to Marianna as he fired three shots at the intruder. This was nothing like being at the firing range or real-life active shooter trainings. He never looked at his sights. He kept all of his focus on the gunman and just pointed and fired. Larry spun around and disappeared into the kitchen.

"I hit him!" the sheriff said as he headed toward the gunman. The sheriff had tunnel vision. All his attention was on the armed intruder. He didn't look left or right. He had no peripheral vision at all. His total concentration was on the activity out in front of him.

As the sheriff moved past the office door, Shep reached out and attempted to grab him. Startled, and caught completely off guard, the sheriff made a half turn and fired a round into the bathroom wall. Before he completed his turn, the sheriff fell to the floor and fired another bullet into the ceiling. He dropped his gun, grabbed his chest with both hands, and fell over backward onto the dining room floor.

Shep rushed out of the office in the hallway, picked up the sheriff's gun from the floor, and aimed it at the still-stunned Marianna. She froze in place, still lying down on the floor of the hallway, and curled her body up in anticipation of being executed.

Shep turned his attention back to the sheriff. He walked over to the man's motionless body on the floor and kicked him in his side. There was no reaction, so he rolled him over with his foot and stood back, out of reach in case the sheriff was playing possum. There was still no reaction, no movement, no twitching, no sound, and no sign of breathing.

The sheriff was dead.

Shep jammed the sheriff's semiautomatic pistol into his waistband. He looked back at Marianna. She was still curled up in a ball on the floor, and except for the rise and fall of her chest, she could have easily passed for a dead person.

Moe stepped out from the office and into the hallway holding Gilbert by a fistful of hair. He guided him into the dining room while holding a knife to his throat with his other hand.

"Gilbert!" Marianna screamed her husband's name as she staggered to her knees.

"Go check on cousin," Moe told Shep.

Larry was stooped over the kitchen counter, holding his injured arm, blood completely covering his support hand. He was still standing and winced in pain when Shep pulled his hand back to look at the wound. "You are very lucky, cousin," Shep told him. "The bullet hit you in the same spot that the knife did." Shep grabbed some hand towels that were hanging from the oven door and pressed them on Larry's wound. "Hold these in place," he told Larry then hurried back to the hallway to help Moe.

"Bring the woman," Moe told Shep.

Larry came into the dining room, holding the towels to his wounded arm, leaving a solid trail of blood behind him. Moe glanced over at him and told him to bring the duct tape from the satchel. Larry gave his cousin a look like, "How?"

Moe looked back, and Larry hadn't moved. "Tape! Now!" Moe yelled to him. He made excuses for him earlier in the day, but his sympathy had long faded. He was disappointed that his cousin allowed himself to be critically injured, not once, but three times. His lip was still slightly swollen from the dairy and his arm completely useless. Just the sight of him aggravated Moe. He was beginning to get a bad feeling about cousin Larry. He was bringing bad karma to the crusade. Shep hurried over to help his cousin pull the satchel over his head and slide it down his lame arm. Shep could feel the tension building and tried to keep Larry from antagonizing Moe any further.

He returned back to the dining room and helped Moe tie Gilbert to one of the dining-room chairs. "Where is the woman?" Moe asked as they both looked down the hallway. Shep headed down the hall to the back door when Marianna stepped out from the master bedroom in front of him, cutting him off. Without saying a word, Marianna pressed the trigger of the 410, and she flinched in anticipation of the noise and recoil. Nothing happened. She pressed the trigger again. Still nothing.

Shep looked at her in disbelief, amazed he was still alive. He then rushed her and grabbed the barrel of the shotgun just as it exploded. He deflected the shotgun at the exact moment Marianna pulled the trigger for the third time. In a life-or-death involuntary reaction, Shep punched her with his closed fist, knocking her unconscious to the floor of the bedroom.

"Stop!" Moe yelled. "Do not kill her!"

Shep looked at the baseball-sized hole in the wall and realized that could have been his head.

"Marianna! Marianna!" Gilbert yelled to his wife, trying to stand and pulling the chair with him as he struggled.

"Drag her over here and tie her to the table across from him," Moe said. He went to help Shep drag the unconscious woman to the table and tape her to the armed dining-room chair.

"Where is your gun?" Shep asked his wounded cousin. Larry nodded in the direction of the kitchen. Shep found it lying on the floor next to the range, the grip lying in a puddle of blood from Larry's wound. He picked the weapon up by the barrel and laid it on the counter next to Larry, then he drew the sheriff's gun from his waistband and laid it next to it. "Keep watch on these," Shep told his cousin.

Moe and Shep disappeared out the back door and returned quickly with the propane tank and the iron rods.

"Please!" Gilbert begged the cousins. "Please don't burn the house down!" A logical conclusion from Gilbert, watching as the men enter the house with the fuel.

Marianna was regaining consciousness. She was mumbling and trying to raise her head. She pulled against the duct tape securing her to the chair and started screaming. She was disoriented and was beginning to panic at the sight of these strangers in her house.

"Tape her mouth," Moe said, looking at Larry. Shep reached for the roll of tape and tore a piece off with his mouth. He knew Larry wasn't up to the task, and he was unsure of how Moe would react if his cousin wasn't able to complete this simple task. He would cover for his cousin as long as he could.

"I'll stop!' Marianna pleaded, her memory of the strangers in the hallway returning.

"Tape her," Moe ordered. He showed no emotion, just a matter-of-fact demeanor. He was running on automatic pilot. He knew what had to be done and was resigned to the fact that it would be done.

"What do you want?" Gilbert asked. "Tell me what you want, and I will give it to you." Gilbert was trying to keep his composure in front of his wife. He was ready to bargain. They picked this ranch for a reason; they knew what they came for.

"I have money, how much do you want? I have fine cattle, you can have your choice." Gilbert was drawing on his refined negotiation skills, learned from his many years of political experience.

"Oh, you will give me what I want," Moe said through gritted teeth. The reference to his cattle reinforced their reason for being there, justified the whole crusade. This man was willing to sacrifice the sacred cattle to save himself. *Infidel!* Moe thought.

"Tape his mouth too," Moe told Larry. Again, Shep rushed to his cousin's rescue.

Gilbert was thrashing his head back and forth with such force that his chair almost toppled over backward.

Gilbert and Marianna stared at each other from across the table, looking for reassurance in each other's eyes, for any sign of communication.

Their eyes widened, and Marianna started sobbing when Moe and Shep unfolded their pocketknives and passed a small steel back and forth between themselves. Moe ran his knife over the steel several times, stopping to test the sharpness of the blade by rubbing his thumb over the edge. As he honed the blade, he stared off blindly toward the back door and recited all the sins committed against the sacred Hindi gods by Gilbert and his relatives.

He recited the history, step-by-step, beginning with the theft of the sacred cattle by Gilbert's great-grandfather, Gustavo Martinez. Tricking the local Indians and recruiting some to aid them with their blasphemous ambitions. He described the penalties suffered by those accomplices left behind. He described in detail how the men's children were sacrificed like goats in front of them, forcing them to listen to their family's screams and watch them beg while suffering a slow and painful death. He described how the sacred cattle had been abused by the Americans, how they mocked the Indian culture. He told Gilbert and his wife what they had witnessed firsthand at the Williams dairy. He told the couple that they had been sent to avenge the atrocities committed by his ancestors. Moe graphically described how the punishment would be administered. The penalty was an eye for an eye, and they would pay just like the men at the dairy.

Moe showed no emotion as he recited their manifesto from memory. He explained that the Martinez ranch was the redemption. The original destination of the sacred idols from the homeland. After the Martinez ranch, others like the Williams dairy would follow, all part of the greater plan, the greater prophecy.

The pear burner popped and spit sparks all over the room as it ignited into a flame thrower, emitting thick black smoke that rose and followed the ceiling to the corners of the room, hovering above them like a cumulonimbus thunderhead. Moe took one of the fishing rods with the ring and heated it under the flame of the burner until it glowed bright red.

He ordered Shep to remove Gilbert's shirt. The obedient cousin drew his knife again and slit the rancher's shirt on the sides from the tail to the collar. He grabbed the shirt from behind, pulling from the collar, stripping it from Gilbert's body and sending buttons flying across the dining room table.

Gilbert squirmed in the chair, trying to stand and pulling on the restraints that were binding his arms. He looked across the table at his wife. Her eyes were glued to Moe, and the expression on her face revealed the terror in her heart.

As Moe heated the rod, he continued to describe how they witnessed the torture of the cattle at the dairy.

"Remove her shirt too," he told Larry.

Gilbert was beside himself at the thought of any harm coming to his wife. He'd read reports of women being raped while their husbands were restrained and forced to watch. He thought what a terrifying, helpless feeling that must be. How sadistic humans could be. And now, he was about to experience his worst nightmare.

Larry gingerly pulled her chair away from the table, careful not to bump his arm. He began unbuttoning her blouse, leaving his uncoagulated blood on her bra, transferred from rubbing the back of his hand across her breasts. His pain was replaced by lust. He fumbled through the process of undoing her blouse with the anticipation of seeing and groping her bare breasts.

"Hurry!" Moe yelled at Larry. He could see that the injured cousin was distracted by the woman's smooth soft white skin. He sympathized with Larry when he was cut in the alley. It could have been any of them, and it could have been much worse. But the second injury could have been avoided. He should have been aware of his surroundings. He should have anticipated what happened to him before it did. This was one of the scenarios they trained for, and he failed. Now he was becoming distracted at the sight of a half-naked woman, fumbling through a simple task. Shep could see that Moe was approaching his breaking point. He could sense the disappointment and anger at Larry. Shep could tell that Moe was in a frenzy, fueled by the unfolding developing destiny he had long anticipated. He was afraid Moe may harm their cousin. He was a different person tonight, his personality had transformed, and Shep had never seen him like this in all the years he had known him.

Larry clumsily attempted to retrieve his knife, painfully trying to manipulate his injured arm to reach into his pocket. Shep intervened again on the behalf of his wounded cousin and slit the side of Marianna's blouse, moved around behind her, and jerked the garment from her body just as he had to her husband.

He covered for Larry again. He knew that Moe, in his present state of mind, may turn on him too if he kept coming to Larry's defense.

Marianna sat in the chair, half naked in her bloodstained bra, sobbing through her gagged mouth, fully aware of the pain about to be inflicted on her and Gilbert. She anticipated being raped in front of her husband first, to further humiliate them both and satisfy the sadistic, twisted minds of the men that had invaded their home.

Gilbert tried to yell through his duct-taped mouth. His screams were barely audible, mere muffled grunts, and tears of anger were streaming from his raging blue eyes. He was bouncing his chair so violently his knees were hitting the underside of the table.

Their eyes locked on each other again. Marianna was sitting motionless, tears flowing down her pink cheeks, deflected to either side of her mouth by the tape. She seemed resigned to accept the torture that was about to be bestowed on her as vividly described by the Indian heating up the iron.

She too now realized that these were the men who tortured the ranch hands at the dairy. If she was right, she knew what was in store for her and Gilbert.

*****

The burros headed straight toward the ranch house, with Julian following closely behind. The donkeys followed the fence, designed to guide the ranch cattle into smaller paddocks during roundups. The smaller trap was a holding area for the cattle, a place for them to loiter, clam down, drink water, before being moved into the working pens.

The burros followed the square wire fence around to the closed gates of the corrals then continued around to the other side of the trap, making a full circle, following the fence back to the gate they entered through. Julian could hear them approach, so he dismounted and closed the gate to the gap. The burros ran right up to the closed gate and slid to an abrupt stop, causing La Hormiga's horse to jerk away from him and bolt toward the corrals, the donkeys following in pursuit. He could hear the remuda making the round, following the fence again, and heading back to the gate. They stopped in the corner of the closed gap, pushing against the gate in a desperate attempt to escape the confines of the trap. Julian was agitated. He wasn't a horseman. He needed his vaqueros to tend to this kind of unforeseen circumstance. He was close to losing his temper. It seemed that everything was going wrong tonight. The only problem he expected to encounter was the condition of the trails he had planned to use to deliver the goods. Now he was performing unnatural tasks, and he was doing it in the dark. At least the animals were contained and not running loose back to Brownsville loaded with hundreds of thousands of dollars' worth of marijuana.

Julian walked up behind his horse, his left hand slowly moving up from the horse's hip, along his flank, and across the saddle. He squeezed his body between the wire fence and the horse, slowly, calmly inching his hand up the horse's neck, soothingly talking to the horse in Spanish. Just as he slipped his fingers under the headstall, the horse pivoted on his hind legs, pushing La Hormiga into the smooth square wire fence, pelting him with mud as he ran off again, escorting the burros on another lap around the trap.

His patience was wearing out fast. He reached for his pistol and started to draw the weapon, planning on stopping his horse with a bullet. He walked up the opposite side of the trap, intending on heading the remuda off as they came from the corrals and back to the gate. The few minutes it took for the horses to round the entrapment gave him enough time to realize that discharging his weapon would not be a very good idea. If he missed, it would just make catching the animals that much more difficult. If his aim was true, then he would be on foot for the rest of the trip. It was a long walk to the ship channel, even worse when it was muddy.

He could hear the wire stretching at the far side of the pen. He could hear the animals struggling in the wire, hoping his horse was hung up enough that he would be able to catch him. He slowed his pace down, not wanting to run up on the animals and spook them further. He was disappointed to see the fence lying on the ground, and he could hear the hoof beats of the horse and burros running off into the night.

"Damn!" he said to himself, rethinking his plan to shoot the horse.

He could hear the herd running back toward him, returning to the hole in the fence just as they did to the gate at the trap. Instinct was bringing them back to the escape route they knew. Their determination to survive was driving them to flee to familiar territory.

Julian stepped out in front of the stampeding pack, knowing that if they got past him, they could break through the fence on the other side and be gone for good.

The horse was still in the lead and slowed to a trot as he got close to Julian. His hopes returned as the horse cautiously walked toward him. Almost within Julian's reach, the horse slowly turned and walked back through his harem of donkeys. They followed the fence line to the ranch house and entered the lit yard through the open gate.

Julian shadowed the calmed remuda to the ranch house and closed the gate behind them. He was relieved, confident he would be able to catch the horse and secure the donkeys in the confinement of the fenced yard.

His brief exuberance was quickly broken when he realized he still needed to find and recapture the other burros. But at least he would have his horse. Things were looking up, but ever so slightly.

The lights from inside the house partially lit up the side yard. He could plainly see the horses and donkeys grazing on the green Saint Augustine grass, lush from the recent wet weather and thriving in the cool temperatures.

Julian heard a familiar noise coming from the direction of the paddock. It sounded like horses coming, following the same route he used. The banditos! They were coming!

La Hormiga eased up to the grazing livestock, slowly pushed past the donkeys, and again made a failed attempt to grab his horse. He must sense the tension and anxiety in Julian, allowing him to get so close, then bolting just out of reach to stop and graze again. As if the horse were playing a game of tag with him.

He decided to take cover in the house. He could hear voices coming from inside. He had no choice, either face the people in the house, or encounter the banditos by himself outside.

He would make up a story when he gets to the door, flat tire, out of gas, something. *Hurry! Hurry!*

When Johnny got to the gate to the trap, he could see La Hormiga in the yard of the ranch house. Johnny stood motionless and watched as Julian stopped and seemed to look right at him.

He must have seen me, Johnny thought to himself.

There was another gate that led from the trap to the road outside the pasture. The front yard was well lit, so Johnny rode wide enough around, staying in the shadows, hoping he wouldn't be seen. When he rode around to the north side of the house, he could see Julian stepping up onto the front porch. He wondered what La Hormiga was up to. He was sure that he didn't know the judge or his family.

And he knew the judge well enough to know that he wouldn't let a stranger into his house or even onto his property, especially at night.

Where were the dogs? Johnny wondered. He definitely heard dogs barking from the ranch earlier in the evening.

Where were the dogs?

"Hold him tight," Moe told Shep.

He raised the makeshift branding iron up to inspect the bright-red ring at the end of the rod. He wanted to make sure it was hot enough to penetrate deep into the flesh of the rancher's body.

"You will be marked the same way you mark and torture the sacred cattle," Moe calmly explained the process as he closed the distance between the burner and Gilbert.

"Hold him tight," Moe told the cousin again.

Gilbert rocked his chair so violently. He managed to flip it over backward, knocking the iron out of Moe's hand and landing on the rancher's forearm.

The front door of the ranch house burst open, catching the cousins off guard, as they dove for cover behind the breakfast bar. The weapons and ammo were in the satchel, unreachable without exposing themselves, and the other two handguns were on the kitchen counter just within Larry's reach.

"Que Paso!" La Hormiga bellowed with a grin on his face. His gun drawn as he stepped through the threshold of the house. He immediately recognized the two Indians hiding behind the bar.

"What are—"

He never had a chance to finish his sentence. The gunshot echoed through the house, and Julian fell to the floor. He never saw cousin Larry in the kitchen.

"Why did you shoot our friend!" Moe yelled at Larry in his native Hindi language.

Another black mark against the wounded cousin. Moe was beside himself as he berated Larry in his native tongue.

"He is our ally! We will need him again!" Moe removed the pistol from Larry's grip and put the barrel up to his temple. Moe had had enough of the bad luck his cursed cousin has brought to the crusade.

"No!" Shep yelled. "He is our blood! You cannot harm him!" No one had ever questioned Moe before. He had always been the self-proclaimed leader.

Shep realized that he had crossed the line. He had never stood up to his cousin before, and by doing so, he had challenged him. Now it was like a pack of dogs with two alpha males. There was only room for one leader of the pack.

"It was an honest mistake," Larry pleaded. "I shot him before I knew who he was. I thought I was protecting you."

Moe lowered the gun without answering either man. He looked at Shep through piercing eyes. The challenge has been made, and accepted, but now was not the time. But the time was near.

The sheriff department vehicle turned the corner onto Palmitto Hill Road and slowly drove down the pothole-filled caliche road. The deputy was just meandering around, killing time, and being available like the sheriff had requested.

"Shots fired! Shots fired!" the deputy yelled into the microphone of his two-way radio.

"Martinez Ranch. Palmitto Hill Road!" he yelled into the radio, racing toward the ranch with his red-and-blues lighting up the night sky and his siren blaring. "Judge Martinez Ranch!"

A Border Patrol agent was at the intersection of Highway 4 and Palmitto Hill Road when the call came in. He managed to escape the tedious processing detail at the station and was in the area to investigate the report of illegal activity. He wasn't far behind the deputy, and he could see his lit-up unit well before he turned off the highway.

"Cameron...Papa 144," the agent called over the common channel.

"Cameron!" the deputy yelled, replying into the mike.

"En route, be there in two. Have you in sight," the agent replied. He lit up his Tahoe and sped toward the ranch house with his siren screaming into the night air.

Johnny just arrived on the north side of the ranch house when he heard the gunfire. He tied his horse to a scrub mesquite bush and headed to the house.

He stopped his advance when he heard the sirens and saw the lights of the approaching vehicles.

The tan SUV, emergency lights on and siren blaring, sped past him and slid to a stop on the wet caliche, coming to rest behind the sheriff's vehicle.

Gunshots from inside the house were immediately fired at the arriving deputy.

"Shots fired! Shots fired!" the deputy again yelled into the mike.

The green-and-white Border Patrol unit slid up next to the deputy's vehicle, and more gunfire erupted from inside the house.

The deputy cracked open the driver's door of his vehicle and turned his front wheels all the way to the left, as far as they would go. He wedged himself between the body of the vehicle and the door, giving himself as much cover and protection as he could.

Pop-pop-pop! Three rounds fired from the house lodged into the roof of the vehicle, just above the windshield, sending sparks flying across the deputy's face.

The deputy answered with three shots of his own.

The agent slid over to the passenger side of his vehicle and took cover using the SUV for protection.

Gunfire from the house again, so many rounds neither of the men could count how many shots were fired. The windshield of the sheriff's vehicle was completely shot out, and the tires of the deputies' SUV were flattened. Both men returned fire, aiming at the muzzle flashes coming from the window to the left of the front door.

"Keep them pinned down!" Moe yelled to his cousins. He grabbed three magazines from the satchel then threw the bag to Shep.

"You take the kitchen window," he told Shep as he moved to the opposite side of the house and took cover next to the window by the fireplace. Larry had his pistol in his left hand and was crouched down by the front door. His injuries limited him to handguns.

"Let's get this over with!" Moe yelled to both of them. "Before more police come. We will finish our obligation later. We will take them with us!" With that, Moe emptied his magazine on both of the vehicles in the parking lot.

"Larry, you go out the back door and move around the side of the house and start shooting at them," Moe told him. "They will think they are surrounded."

Larry was already injured and was becoming a problem, so if he was sacrificed, so be it. They had been chosen by the holy deities to carry out the crusade, chosen at this perfect opportune time in history to successfully instill revenge on those that betrayed the homeland and mocked the Hindi gods. If Larry was sacrificed as part of the crusade, then it must be his destiny. Moe could not succeed by himself. He must protect Shep until the mission was complete. They would settle their differences when the time came.

"Get more ammunition first," Moe told Larry. "Just keep shooting, don't stop. They will not be able to return fire because they will be hiding from your bullets." Moe could see that his cousin was apprehensive, and he wanted to assure him he would be safe. "Shep will go to the other side and do the same," Moe lied.

Bullets were now penetrating completely through the sheriff's vehicle and hitting the deputy's vehicle. The deputy wedged himself lower into his cover. He emptied his magazine, dumped it, and quickly reloaded.

"Partner!" he yelled to the agent. "Do you have any ammo?"

"Two rounds in the gun, and one magazine, eight rounds!" the Border Patrol agent answered back.

"Better make 'em count!" the agent yelled.

The gunfire from the house was constant, nonstop. The Border Patrol Tahoe was parked at an angle, and all the bullets were hitting the driver's side of the vehicle.

Then, all of a sudden, the deputy was receiving gunfire from the darkness from his left. The only cover he had available now was the door of the vehicle. He lay down and rolled under the door and crawled between his vehicle and the sheriff's. Bullets slamming into the door and fender where he had just been, and one round went into the Border Patrol Tahoe directly behind him. The deputy fired three rounds blindly into the darkness as he raced around the Border Patrol vehicle to join the agent on the other side.

"Shit, I've only got three rounds left!" the deputy yelled to the agent standing right beside him. More gunfire coming from the house, three round bursts, and rapid fire from the darkness.

"Hold your fire," the agent told the deputy. "You're almost out, you gotta make 'em count."

More gunfire from the darkness. This time it was further to the east.

The agent fired at the muzzle flashes from the darkness. "Either he is moving around behind us, or there is more than one of them out there!" the agent yelled to the deputy.

La Hormiga must have his pistoleros waiting for him in the house. Johnny couldn't think of any other scenario for all that was happening. Somehow the judge must have gotten word out to the sheriff department.

Johnny went back to get the AR from the scabbard on his saddle. He reached up to make sure the magazines were still in his jacket pocket. With all the commotion, he was afraid they may have fallen out. They were still there. Lucky, he thought.

He retrieved the loaded AR and tried to figure out what his next move should be.

This was his golden opportunity to get even with La Hormiga, but with no cover between him and the house, he could easily be caught in the cross fire. Besides, the cops would shoot him thinking he was one of the bad guys, and La Hormiga and his pistoleros would shoot him thinking he was one of the good guys. A no-win situation.

He decided his best bet would be to ride back to his pickup before any more police showed up. They would surely think he was involved in whatever was going down at the ranch house. At the very least, he would spend a long time in prison for firearms violations. He knew the back roads along the river and could avoid the check-point easily. *Better go now,* he thought, *before it's too late. La Hormiga will get his later.*

He slung the AR back over the saddle horn and was getting ready to mount up when he got a whiff of a terrible smell. He looked round and saw what appeared to be a body lying on the ground. The smell was nauseating, gagging him as he approached the body.

Dogs! Dead dogs! But they were fresh; they hadn't been dead long. They weren't bloated or stiff. So where was the smell coming from? he wondered. These must be the ranch dogs he heard earlier in the evening. He found the source of the smell, chunks of rotted, foul-smelling meat of some kind. A piece of the bait was partially eaten and lying next to the head of one of the dogs. Someone poisoned the dogs.

What was going on down there? Johnny couldn't believe his old smuggling buddy La Hormiga would go to such extremes to smuggle a load of marijuana across the river. He knew him well enough to know he would avoid conflict at any cost.

He mounted his horse and headed to his truck.

More gunfire from the dark, but this time it was directly behind the two law enforcement agents.

The deputy instinctively returned fire. Emptying the last of his magazine. He was out of ammo.

"You hit him," the agent told the deputy. "I saw him shoot at the ground."

More gunfire from the house, now coming from two different directions.

"Look," the agent said, "I'm going to empty my weapon on them, then we are going to have to make a run for it!" The deputy was standing right next to him, but he was yelling. "I don't have enough ammo to stay in the fight, our only chance is to make a run for it. We can't do anything until backup arrives except die."

"Ten-four!" the deputy yelled back to him.

More gunfire from the house. No more shots from behind, so the agent must be right. The deputy killed him.

The Tahoe's windshield was completely shot out, and both front tires were flat.

"I am going to return fire. When I'm empty, we both make a run for the shadows, and then to the gate. Ready?" the agent yelled.

"Ready," the deputy replied.

Another volley of gunfire from the house. The agent stood and emptied his magazine.

"Go!" the agent yelled. "I'm empty!"

They tried to leave, but every time they attempted to step out from their cover, they were barraged with more gunfire. To expose themselves now would be certain death.

They were trapped. They were pinned down.

Johnny just settled in the saddle when he heard the man yell, "Go, I'm empty!"

He sat and listened for a second. He noticed there wasn't any return fire from the vehicles.

How could the cops be out of ammunition? They will die for sure, Johnny thought.

He listened for the sound of sirens coming from Brownsville. Nothing. If backup was on the way, it would be a while before they arrived. In the night air, sirens from as far away as Brownsville and South Padre Island could easily be heard.

He ran around the parking lot in the darkness, grabbed the AR from the saddle, and let the horse go. He could see the body of the cousin lying in the dark, out in the open, his pistol still in his hand.

Johnny picked up the gun from the dead man and ran to join the two law enforcement officers behind what was left of their vehicles.

Johnny took the two officers by surprise; they had no idea he was behind them. They raised their hands over their heads, believing they were surrendering to the gunman that had been shooting at them from the dark. He must have only been stunned by the deputy, and realizing the lawmen were out of ammo, he was confident enough he could just walk up and take them without firing a shot. He just waited them out, and now he was either going to take them prisoner or kill them.

"Get down!" Johnny yelled at them. Another barrage of bullets embedded into the grill of the Tahoe.

"I'm on your side!" Johnny yelled. He handed the agent the gun he took from the dead man in the field and gave the deputy his 9mm pistol. The two lawmen looked at each other and then looked back suspiciously at Johnny.

"I'm on your side! If I wasn't, you'd be dead," Johnny told the two men, not wasting any valuable time to elaborate. "You're out of ammo?" Johnny asked them in disbelief.

"What!" the agent yelled.

Johnny put his finger up to his lips and whispered to the men not to yell.

"What!" this time it was the deputy that yelled.

Johnny put his finger up to his mouth again, gesturing to the men to be quiet. He made a zipper motion across his mouth to emphasize the point. He realized that their hearing must be impaired, ringing from all the gunfire.

The agent had Johnny's pistol and a full fifteen-round magazine with one bullet in the chamber.

Johnny loaded the weapon for the deputy and handed it back to him. He took a full magazine from his jacket and stuck it in the deputy's back pocket.

Johnny took cover behind the door of the Tahoe and sprayed the front of the house with bullets.

There was no response for a few seconds, and then the house erupted in return gunfire.

Johnny couldn't ask the men if they had any military training. He would have to raise his voice loud enough it would be heard in the house.

He tapped the agent on the shoulder and signaled him to go around the river side of the house. He tapped the deputy on the chest of his body armor and signaled him to go around to the other side, toward the road. He put his hand up in the air, telling them to wait until he started shooting before they made their move.

Johnny shot three rounds at each window, alternating back and forth between the two, as the men ran to the house. Johnny finished his magazine, shooting rapid fire, putting enough pressure on the shooters in the house so that the deputy and agent could safely run across the clearing without getting shot. There was no return fire for a few seconds, and then a burst of bullets came from the right-side window. Nothing from the other side.

Johnny wished he could have communicated better with the two men. He didn't want them to kill Julian La Hormiga. That was for him to do.

Gilbert was lying backward on the floor, still prisoner to his chair, unable to loosen the straps enough to free his arms. All he could see was the wall and the dining room ceiling. He had no idea where his wife was. He wiggled and kicked as much as he could, eventually manipulating the chair and turning it enough he could see his wife's feet from under the table. His arm felt like it was on fire. The branding iron only glanced him, but it only took a fraction of a second to burn a circle into his flesh.

The person that burst through the door saved his life. Whoever he was, Gilbert was pretty sure he was dead. He had no idea who would be at the ranch this time of night. He obviously wasn't part of the team invading his home.

Moe picked the iron up from the tile floor and went back to the burner to reheat it. He was glaring at the judge, his eyes glazed over like a zombie from one of the late-night horror movies. He was back to finish his task. The other man was out of Gilbert's sight, but he could hear him walking in from the kitchen, not saying a word. They all must be high on something, putting them in a trance, was all Gilbert could imagine.

All of a sudden, sirens could be heard. They were loud, like they were in the front yard of the house. Gilbert thought maybe someone triggered the alarm in the sheriff's SUV, but the sound was clearly sirens, more than one.

Moe threw the iron back on the floor, grabbed the satchel, and ran to the front door, out of Gilbert's sight.

He could see Marianna's feet tapping the floor, but he couldn't reach her. He was relieved to see her, and as far as he could tell, she was still okay. Hopefully, she could hear him thrashing around on the floor, giving her a little glimmer of hope. He felt relieved hearing the sirens. The cavalry was here.

The gun battle began. The reports of the gunfire echoing through the house was deafening, and the smell of the gunpowder and gun smoke was overwhelming.

It sounded like a war was going on, constant, never-ending gunfire like Gilbert had never experienced.

Larry ran into the dining room, stopped, and aimed his gun at Gilbert's head. He mouthed "Bang, bang" and then ran out the back door. Gilbert thought he was dead. He closed his eyes, anticipating the impact of the bullet, and as if in slow motion, he wondered what it would feel like. He wondered if his soul would look down on the scene as it left his body. He felt bad for Marianna, forced to watch him be murdered.

The firefight seemed never-ending. Gilbert was worried about her getting caught in the cross fire, and there was nothing he could do to help her. She was going through this terrible ordeal by herself, and there was nothing he could do for her. He felt helpless. He was helpless. If he could only make eye contact, she would see that he was still alive and relatively unharmed. It would at least give her some hope. Maybe the sirens outside would lift her spirits like they did his, just knowing help was just outside the front door. He worried about the cross fire again. She was in a vulnerable position, sitting at the table, strapped to her chair, nothing to protect her from stray bullets soon to be flying around the house. He thrashed his chair again, this time with a new purpose. If he could get close enough, he may be able to topple her chair and take her out of the line of fire.

Gilbert could hear the bullets hitting the front of the house now. He could hear glass shatter and the bullets lodging in the walls of the kitchen and living room. He squirmed harder, faster, trying to cover the ground between himself and Marianna's chair. Help was coming, and coming fast. He couldn't bear the thought of her being shot, especially if she was shot by friendly fire. He was almost there.

Marianna watched wide-eyed as the window of the den slowly slid open. She thought it was just her imagination, spurred by her desperate hope of being rescued. A man appeared in the window, signaling for her not to acknowledge him. She realized it wasn't her imagination when she saw the CCSO logo on the man's cap. He raised his fingers and made a circular motion. She discretely nodded no. He raised two fingers. Again, she nodded no. Three fingers. Before she could reply, the house erupted in gunfire again. She blinked three times, afraid she might be discovered sending signals by nodding. The deputy pointed to the front of the house, toward the living room where the gunfire was. She tilted her head to the left and then to the right. The deputy looked confused. She then blinked twice and tilted her head to the front of the house, then she blinked once and nodded to the rear, to the back of the house.

The Border Patrol agent met up with the deputy at the window on the side of the house. The deputy told him there were at least two hostages in the dining room, a lady tied to a chair, alive and communicating with him. And a man on the floor, tied to a chair, not sure if he was dead or alive.

The woman indicated, the best he could understand, that there were two gunmen in the front room of the house, and another at the rear. The agent told the deputy that the back door was wide open. The third man must be outside. Maybe he was the one shooting at them from the dark.

The deputy signaled to Marianna that they were coming in. He raised his hand, holding his finger and thumb slightly apart, telling her it would be just a few minutes, be ready.

The men entered the house through the open back door. The agent entered first, cleared the way, and took cover in the laundry room and covered the hall. The deputy leapfrogged around him and ducked into the office, covering the hallway. He waited for the agent to join him. Together they had a clear view of the dining room. Marianna watched anxiously as the men took their position in the office, analyzing the situation, sizing up the mission and waiting for a sign from the new man on their team.

When Shep reached for a new magazine from the kitchen counter, he caught a glimpse of a shadow in the hallway. He carefully peeked over the breakfast bar and saw that the judge and his wife were still there. Marianna was still secured to her chair, and the judge was still on the floor, but now he was halfway under the table. Shep could only see his legs and part of the chair.

"Cousin, cousin," he called down the hall, thinking that Larry had returned. Maybe he needed more ammunition. There was no response. He saw the shadow move again. If it was Larry, he would have responded when called. If it was him, he would have announced himself. He wouldn't be holding up in the hallway. Shep saw the shadow move again and opened fire.

"Someone is inside the house!" he yelled to Moe and fired another round down the hall.

"They're in!" This was Johnny's cue. He opened fire as he raced across the front yard and rushed the house. The return fire was aimed at the vehicles. Obviously the shooter hadn't realized he left his cover and didn't see him approaching the house.

Johnny threw himself through the front door, landing on his side. He opened fire on Moe, sending him flying backward into the fireplace. As he fell, Moe's dying finger shot a volley of bullets that embedded in the breakfast bar just above Johnny's head.

Johnny rolled over and came face-to-face with La Hormiga. His eyes wide open, pink saliva oozing from his mouth, Julian La Hormiga tried to speak, uttering something in Spanish that Johnny couldn't understand.

Shep was in the kitchen, just across the bar, trading gunfire with the two law enforcement officers down the hallway. He heard him enter the house shooting, and he saw Moe fall, but he didn't see where Johnny landed. He turned his attention to Johnny, reaching over the breakfast bar and shooting blindly, his bullets shattering the floor tiles, sending shards of ceramic flying across the room.

Johnny rolled over his old friend and wedged himself against the bar, "You're not dying yet, you son of a bitch!" he whispered into Julian's ear.

The two men in the hallway saw Johnny enter the house and kept shooting at the Indian, providing cover for their new friend and ally. Johnny crawled around the breakfast bar and snuck up behind Shep. He rose to his knees and buried the bayonet deep into the middle of the man's back.

"I've got him!" Johnny yelled to the men down the hall.

"Clear?" one of the men yelled back to him.

"One down, but alive in the front room!" Johnny yelled back, still holding the Indian, impaled on the bayonet at the end of the AR. "Leave him for me!"

Johnny rose to his feet and forcefully pressed the cousin's torso onto the kitchen counter, holding him there until he was sure the man was dead. The blade of the bayonet was difficult to remove and made a sucking sound as Johnny pulled it from the man's body. Shep's limp corpse slid from the counter and fell hard to the floor, smearing a puddle of deep red blood across the countertop where his mouth had been.

Johnny walked over to Julian. His body was pathetically lying motionless on the cold tile floor. He knelt down beside his old friend and grabbed a handful of his hair, and lifting his head from the floor, he stuck the point of his bowie knife under Julian's jaw. The hot-tempered La Hormiga was now reduced to a vague shadow of himself, oozing life on the cold ranch house floor.

"I am going to start here and cut you all the way down to your balls, you piece of shit, one layer of skin at a time. It will be slow and painful," Johnny whispered to La Hormiga. "You will never cross me again, you greedy bastard."

Julian looked him in the eyes and grinned, spitting a mouthful of pink slobber that only managed to roll down his chin and onto the blade of the bowie.

"Is it clear?" one of the lawmen yelled, still standing by in the hallway. "Clear?" he yelled again.

Johnny didn't answer. He wished they weren't here. But they were, and he would have to deal with it. They didn't know anything about him. They didn't even know his name. So when this was done. He can escape without leaving a trace of who he was. He planned to carry out a slow and painful death sentence. It had consumed him since the invasion on his family. It was like a song you heard and couldn't get it out of your head. He had rehearsed it over and over in his mind. He knew exactly how the sentence would be carried out. A trickle of dark red blood from La Hormiga's neck was dripping down the blade of the bowie and mixing with the doomed man's saliva. Johnny knew that it may not go as planned. If the lawmen came in, he would just slit Julian's throat and watch as the life drained from his body. The only consolation, La Hormiga would know who killed him. And why.

"Clear!" the agent yelled, leaving the cover of the office and moving down the hallway. He headed straight toward the front door, pistol drawn, gripped with both hands, and aimed at the floor, ready to shoot from any position as he hurried across the dining room. The deputy followed, his weapon drawn and held in the same tactical manner as the agent. He rushed over to the sheriff, his body lying on the dining room floor at the threshold to the hallway. He knelt down and felt the sheriff's neck for any sign of a heartbeat. No pulse or breathing. The deputy realized the sheriff was dead. He quickly checked him for bullet wounds and found it odd that there were none.

The deputy hurried over to Gilbert, expecting to find him dead. His chair was toppled over onto its side, and Gilbert was facing the wall. When the deputy knelt down to feel his pulse, Gilbert lifted his head and turned to face him. The lawman fell over backward, breaking his fall with his elbows, reacting like he had just been attacked by a ghost.

The deputy pulled the tape from Gilbert's mouth, and the judge immediately yelled for his wife. He called her name over and over as the deputy cut his arms free. He scrambled to his feet and saw the deputy checking her vitals as she lay slumped over in the dining-room chair, a small stream of blood painted in the corner of her mouth. The deputy could see a small wound in her chest. He moved around behind her to inspect for an exit wound when he saw her move. He checked her pulse again. "She's alive!" he yelled, surprised.

The deputy grabbed Gilbert by his arms. "She is alive, if you try to move her, you could kill her." He knew the deputy was right. He just knelt by her chair and held her leg.

The sirens were coming down the road, lots of them. They were close.

The report of the gunshot was defining. Louder than all the gunshots throughout the night.

Johnny instinctively released his grip on La Hormiga. He fell onto his back and aimed his bowie at the agent. Stunned and ears ringing from the gunshot, Johnny was surprised by the agent, still aimed in on the body on the floor. Johnny turned his attention back to the body on the floor next to him, La Hormiga was trashing and convulsing on the hard tile. He was bleeding profusely from the gaping bullet wound in his rib cage.

"What the hell!" Johnny yelled to the agent. "I had him! You could have shot me!"

Johnny felt robbed. Julian's dead body lay motionless on the floor. Dead. A quick and deadly shot by the agent killed him instantly. He didn't suffer the slow death that fate had planned for him. And it didn't happen at Johnny's hand.

"He was just about to shoot you," the agent calmly answered him. "He is still gripping the gun."

Johnny got to his feet and stood over La Hormiga's corpse, relieved the saga was over. It didn't go as planned, but it was finished. Now he could honor the pledge he made to himself. He could start his life over, dedicating his time to his family.

But now he must get out of here. He started to the front door and almost had his hand on the knob when the judge called him.

"Juanito," Gilbert said softly, almost inaudible. "Johnny Williams," Gilbert said again, more to himself than to Johnny, like he was digging deep into his memory to recall the name.

"Who are you!" the agent asked him.

"Johnny Williams," Gilbert told the deputy. "His family owned the Williams dairy for years."

"Who!" the deputy asked this time, unaware he was yelling. "If you hadn't shown up, we would all be dead!" The deputy realized how close he had come to death. "We were helpless! We were just sitting ducks, pinned down and ready to be slaughtered!"

"You better cuff me," Johnny told the deputy. "I don't want to be mistaken for one of these guys when your backup arrives, you will know all about me soon enough, I'm afraid."

The house was full of law enforcement officers from every agency, city, state, county, and federal.

They all gathered around the sheriff, watching the coroner inspect the dead man for an apparent cause of death.

Johnny was arrested by ATF agents and whisked away from the scene. He was charged with felony gun possession. A crime that would come with a harsh punishment in this new era.

The judge and Marianna were medivaced by helicopter to Brownsville Medical Center. Marianna was on life support, but her vitals were good, with a minimal loss of blood. She was expected to make a full recovery. Gilbert was taken in for observation, and wouldn't allow anyone to separate him from his wife.

The sheriff's funeral was held in the large auditorium at the Texas State College Ft. Brown campus. The eulogy was delivered by the US Attorney General and the Secretary of Homeland Security. Representatives from every law enforcement agency in Texas and surrounding states filled the building, along with state and federal politicians from across the country. The funeral procession to the Santa Rosalia Cemetery near the river was miles long. All the law enforcement vehicles had their emergency red-and-blue light on. Even the undercover vehicles activated their wig wags, vehicles that would never be suspected as law enforcement—minivans, pickup trucks, and even a Volkswagen beetle. The citizens of Brownsville and Cameron County lined the procession route as Secret Service helicopters loomed overhead.

*****

Washington Park was lined with protesters toting SOCSOF signs and shouting, "SAVE OUR CHILDREN, SAVE OUR FUTURE!"

Gilbert's magnificent blue eyes shined brightly as he spoke, revealing the optimism he felt in his heart, conveying to the large crowd of supporters the bright future the Valley could look forward to under his administration.

"I want to thank all of you who have supported me through these trying times. I pledge to prove to all of you, to all of my constituents, that I will do all in my power to protect you and your families and the United States of America and the great state of Texas to the very best of my ability!" the governor-elect promised the large crowd of supporters and curious onlookers. "Special thanks go out to

Johnny Williams, who, without his heroic actions, my beloved wife and I would not be here today!"

Johnny sat stoic in the front row, wearing dark sunglasses and flanked by his wife and daughters. A gold medal of freedom supported by red, white, and blue ribbons hung around his neck.

Marianna sat in her wheelchair at the end of the row, wearing a white gown, tears streaming down her cheeks. Tears of joy. Tears of gratitude.

Jamil and his wife sat behind Marianna. He reached up and, with both hands, squeezed her shoulders, a sign of his never-ending support and to signify his devout friendship and loyalty.

THE END

ABOUT THE AUTHOR

WJ Spellane has competed in rodeo events most of his life, bull riding, team roping, and calf roping. He has spent many years riding the Rio Grande River horseback for the Fever Tick Eradication Program. He has been protecting the livestock industry from fever ticks and foreign animal diseases. He is a firearms instructor for the USDA and trained at the Federal Law Enforcement Training Centers. Bill has used his experiences in life and his many hours riding the river to write this book.

CPSIA information can be obtained
at www.ICGtesting.com
Printed in the USA
BVHW081604170220
572579BV00006B/529